Catherine Robertson hails from Hawke's Bay (New Zealand wine country). She is the proud co-owner of a bookstore in Wellington, and is the author of romantic comedies and contemporary fiction, many of which have been #1 bestsellers for Penguin Random House NZ.

www.catherinejrobertson.com

instagram.com/catherinerobertson11

facebook.com/catherinejrobertson.author

Also by Catherine Robertson

You're So Vine

For my guys, David, Callum and Finn

Playlist

You Are In Love - Taylor Swift ♥
Austin - Dasha ♥
Kiss Me - Sixpence None The Richer ♥
Lover - Taylor Swift ♥
supernatural - Ariana Grande ♥
Skin - Sabrina Carpenter ♥
Unwritten - Natasha Bedingfield ♥
TEXAS HOLD 'EM - Beyoncé ♥
I Know Places - Taylor Swift ♥
Blue Jeans - Lana Del Rey ♥
Not Like I'm In Love With You - Lauren ♥
Mess It Up - Gracie Abrams ♥
Reckless - Madison Beer ♥
The Wave - Colouring ♥
What A Time - Julia Michaels, Niall Horan ♥
Little Bit Louder - Mimi Webb ♥
Everywhere, Everything - Noah Kahan ♥
Softly - Clairo ♥
When I Look At You - Miley Cyrus ♥
Love On - Selena Gomez ♥
Good To Be - Mark Ambor ♥
Wildfire - Cautious Clay ♥
Heaven - Niall Horan ♥

CORKSCREW YOU

Flora Valley

CATHERINE ROBERTSON

One More Chapter
a division of HarperCollins*Publishers* Ltd
1 London Bridge Street
London SE1 9GF
www.harpercollins.co.uk
HarperCollins*Publishers*
Macken House, 39/40 Mayor Street Upper,
Dublin 1, D01 C9W8, Ireland

This paperback edition 2024
1
First published in Great Britain in ebook format
by HarperCollins*Publishers* 2024
Copyright © Catherine Robertson 2024
Catherine Robertson asserts the moral right to be identified
as the author of this work

A catalogue record of this book is available from the British Library

ISBN: 978-0-00-865791-8

This novel is entirely a work of fiction. The names, characters and
incidents portrayed in it are the work of the author's imagination. Any
resemblance to actual persons, living or dead, events or localities is
entirely coincidental.

Printed and bound in the UK using 100% Renewable Electricity
by CPI Group (UK) Ltd

All rights reserved. No part of this publication may be reproduced, stored
in a retrieval system, or transmitted, in any form or by any means,
electronic, mechanical, photocopying, recording or otherwise, without the
prior permission of the publishers.

Chapter One

SHELBY

There's a Porsche in my parking space. OK, so it's not actually my parking space, it belongs to McRae Capital, but it's the one JP said I should use when he asked me to meet with him today. I'm not even late. Cutting it fine, sure – but the space was promised to me, not some rude interloper with terrible taste in cars.

I mean it's black, for one thing, and a basic spec. Why buy a Porsche that's boring and sedate? If you're going to show the world your thingy extension, then don't be shy! Go for orange or lime green, with racing stripes and bling wheels and all the other trappings of inadequacy. Get a bumper sticker that says *My Real One is Teensy* while you're at it.

Sure, the owner could be a woman, but you just know it's not, don't you? You know it's a guy with slicked-back hair, a custom-made suit that's too shiny, and a tie that may as well have "rich douche" emblazoned all over it. No doubt that's the chip on my currently flat-broke shoulder talking, but come on – the only fan of a man like that is the reflection that stares back at him in the mirror every morning.

Fig. No free spaces at all, and now I *am* late. JP's great and he likes me, but this meeting's too important to screw up. I need to *slay* it. I even dressed up. Put on my best boots and everything.

Too bad. I'm blocking Porsche guy in. Doubt he'll rage around the office building looking for me – the Flora Valley Wines Dodge pick-up looks straight out of *Sons of Anarchy*. He won't find out it's being driven by a five-foot-four strawberry blonde until I hop back in the cab. And even then, who's to say I don't have a hulking, tattooed gang-brother riding shotgun?

Oops. Keep forgetting the Dodge has a big tow hitch. I set the brake, and jump down to check the damage to the Porsche's hood. Hmm. It *might* buff out. Any case, Tiny Johnson will no doubt have full-cover insurance. I don't bother locking the Dodge. I *don't* have insurance, but no one round here'll steal the late Billy Armstrong's ride. They know my dad's ghost would rise up and kick their butts into next week.

On the way up to JP's office, I practice my spiel. I've edited out the part where I fall at his feet and kiss his shoes while grovelling my thanks for saying yes to buying Flora Valley Wines. JP's firm was the last I pitched to because I'd heard he was a renowned hard man, with a reputation for biting off heads and spitting them out again half-chewed, like olive pits. But after being turned down by every venture capital firm in the entire universe, I was desperate. And not staunch desperate, either, but hyperventilating ugly-cry in the Dodge and occasionally in the elevator going down desperate.

Short story: when Dad died, Flora Valley Wines went to Mom, and she didn't want it. Turned out, she hadn't loved every minute of working fourteen-hour days for no pay, raising four kids, and living hand to mouth in the lean years. She loved *Dad* with all her heart and would have done anything to help him achieve his dream, but now he was dead, and Mom wanted out. She wanted time to paint, which she'd never properly had before, in a small studio by the coast, with enough money to be comfortable in her golden years.

Not unreasonable, huh? You'd have to be a real Grinch to begrudge her. And, oh yes, I *was* that Grinch. You see, Dad had told me that Flora Valley Wines was to be mine. Only he didn't get around to putting that down in actual writing, and so with no will, by default everything he owned went to his wife, Lee, and not me, his daughter, Shelby.

My sisters and brothers were happy for Mom to sell up, which was fine for them because they all had jobs that paid real money, and besides, none of them enjoyed working in the vineyard, either. They won't even buy grape jelly now. I was—I *am*—the only one who truly cares about my dad's business, his passion, his dream. He taught me how to make wine, and I'm *good* at it. For the five years before his death,

Dad managed the business and I made the wine. We were a team. A somewhat chaotic, seat-of-the-pants team, I admit, but we were *getting* there. We were *so* close to turning it around.

That's why I begged Mom and my grape-hating siblings to let me find an investor. Someone who'd keep the business going and let me stay on as manager and winemaker, to build it up, expand. They gave me six months, because they're not actually horrible people and might even love me. They definitely feel sorry for me. They know I've given everything I have to the winery, *all* my time and energy, to the point where my social life consists of an occasional drink with my two besties, and my bedmates have all been cats. It suits me fine. Cats are great. They're natural-born foot-warmers.

And when they agreed, my siblings knew that either way, Mom would get her money. The only person set to lose out was me, but they all assured me I was young enough to bounce back. I didn't argue because I don't like conflict, plus I'm a natural optimist. Some might say unrealistic dreamer. Potato. Potahto.

And I didn't argue because honestly, back then six months seemed an age. I'd nail this easily! Flora Valley Wines is a *great* business! All natural, biodynamic wines, made right here the old-fashioned way – hand-picked, and pressed by human feet, not a cold, soulless machine. What's not to love?

After five months, one week and four days of hearing "No" (which took a while because they were usually laughing so hard that they couldn't speak), the end was racing toward me like the cliff in my mom's favourite movie, *Thelma and Louise*. Only I did *not* want to plummet to my death, taking the 2009 Pinot Noir with me. (Yes, I have a save-in-a-house-fire favourite vintage. Doesn't everyone?)

So I approached McRae Capital and its hard-man CEO, JP McRae. He said yes. Then he had to say it again, because I was convinced that I hadn't heard right. He said he'd been a long-time admirer of my dad and loved the Flora Valley ethos. He said he was nearing retirement and was ready to speculate on a worthwhile, if risky, investment. He said some other stuff, too, but I'd stopped listening owing to the fact that sheer relief was making my heart pound in my ears, and I possibly might have been chanting "Thankyouthankyouthankyou" under my breath.

That was last week, and today I'm meeting with him to go over the contract, work out the details. Assure him that I'm the right person to manage the business. That I *do* know how to take Flora Valley Wines into the future, or whatever it is they say in corporate-speak. Better learn all that jargon if I'm to add "Manager" to my business cards.

Better get some business cards, too.

OK, here's JP's door. Deep breath. Aannnnnd – knock!

"Shelby."

There he is – JP McRae. Lean and Arctic foxy. Holding his hand out, smiling at me in such a warm, grandfatherly way that I almost fling my arms around his neck and hug him.

Good thing I have *some* self-control. For one, hugging is

deeply unprofessional, unless you're in the Mafia, and two, seems we're not alone. There's a guy with his back to us, staring out the office window. Youngish by the looks, tall, dark, broad-shouldered, in a fitted black shirt. Being extremely rude at the moment by ignoring us, even if the view *is* pretty appealing. JP's local office is in Martinburg and overlooks the town plaza with its cute pond and gazebo thingy. His main office is in San Francisco, but he's only there a couple of days a week now. For which I give thanks. The Dodge is on its last legs. Regular trips to San Francisco could break it and force me to put a bullet through its grill.

Focus. JP is talking.

"Shelby, I'd like you to meet Nathan Durant. Nate, this is Shelby Armstrong, daughter of the famous Billy."

Rude guy turns. Oh poop. He's gorgeous. Blue eyes with long, dark lashes; why *is* that so sexy? Cheekbones! Holy knife edges, Batman, look at them! And that *mouth*...

Focus, Shelby! He can see you gawking and that puts *him* on the front foot. Not that you have a clue yet why he's here, but still. Professional is your word of the day. Managerial is your vibe.

"Good to meet you, Nathan."

I stick out my hand because shaking hands is what managerial-type professionals do. Though if I'm to be *strictly* honest, my real aim is to see him surprised. Years of grape pruning have given me a grip of iron. I've brought tears to the eyes of war veterans with forearms like silverback gorillas, and while it's a petty wish, I know, I'd quite like to hear a small whimper escape rude-guy Nathan's delicious mouth.

My wish is denied. He clasps my hand for a nanosecond and then drops it. Instead of replying, "Good to meet you, too," all he does is nod. Once. Like he's taken a vow of silence in some monastery for jerks.

"Shelby—"

JP again.

"You know I say it straight."

I do know this. He's like Dr Phil with hair; he doesn't sugar coat.

"You don't have the skills to manage Flora Valley Wines," he says. "You make excellent wine, but you lack commercial experience and—forgive me for being blunt—so did your father. Billy Armstrong was a visionary, but he was a winemaker first and foremost, not a businessman. He scraped by because people loved him and wanted him to succeed. Flora Valley needs to be run properly from now on. By a business manager."

Damn it, I feel tears welling up. First gawking, now crying. And not all of it's grief for Dad. There's a goodly load of humiliation and frustration in there, too. I didn't convince JP I could do it, and now he's going to bring someone in over and above me. All I can hope is that it's someone who *gets* us – who shares the same ideals and wants to achieve the same vision. Dad will haunt me if I let a stranger mess with his life's work.

"You and your father have built a great brand."

JP dips the knife in salt and jabs it in my heart again.

"And with you making wine, and Nate here managing the commercial side, Flora Valley will be guaranteed a great future."

Wait *what*? No!

"Nate has an MBA from Harvard."

So? I have a Player of the Day certificate for peewee soccer. Takes more than a piece of paper to make you an expert on wine.

"And over the last four years, he's managed to turn around a failing French winery and make it a global success."

Don't care. I don't like him. Well, OK, I don't know him, but I know his *type*. Harvard business folks are all about the money, profit before people, and they don't hesitate to, as they so charmingly put it, "cull the dead wood." Flora Valley Wines is a *family* business, and we treat each other well. We pull together, through hard times as well as good. We *always* have each other's backs.

I notice a flicker of something cross Nathan Durant's face. Gone too quickly for me to register the emotion. If I were in a charitable mood, I might call it sympathy. But because I'm furious and humiliated, I'll choose to see it as gloating amusement. He's enjoying seeing me brought low. He's looking forward to destroying all that Dad and I have created, and replacing every Flora worker with a robot. I'm so angry, I'm making stuff up, but I know in my heart that he's wrong for our business. I can't – I *won't* work with him.

"Nathan's appointment is a non-negotiable part of our contract, Shelby."

Guess what? I'm working with him.

JP smiles at both of us in turn, like we're the oldest grandkids he's trusting to mind all the younger ones, so he and Grandma can leave the house and go line dancing.

And then *he* smiles, and damn it, my nervous system lights up in a traitorous response.

But only for a second, because that's how long the smile lasts.

"Let's talk," he says.

Nathan Durant, my new boss. Breaking his jerk vow of silence.

"I'll run through the changes I intend to make."

Chapter Two

NATE

I should cut her some slack. Guy she's never met—doesn't know, doesn't trust—taking over from her late father, shaking the place up. I saw her face back there in JP's office. Fear as well as hurt. And I know how willing to cooperate I'd be if I were in her shoes.

But after a solid half hour of her stonewalling any discussion on my business plan—a plan that JP has already one hundred percent approved, I might add—I'm looking around for something to brain her with. We're in a restaurant within walking distance of JP's office that doubles as an upmarket kitchen shop, selling status gadgets like oyster-shucking sets and vinegar crocks. I spy a cast iron spice grinder. That'd do it. I wonder if I can reach it from here.

"You don't *know* Flora Valley," she says for the forty-millionth time. "So how can you expect to impose a one-size-fits-all plan on us and have it work?"

"I don't need to know it," I reply, yet again. "A winery is a winery. Like an apple orchard is an apple orchard. The only variables are the climate, the soil, and the skill of the workers. The former I *do* know, and workers can be managed and trained." And I add, because she's pissing me off, "Or fired."

She screws up her mouth. No lipstick. No makeup at all that I can see. Shelby Armstrong goes for the *au naturel* look, which in this place makes her stand out like a drunken gatecrasher at a wedding. I grew up just outside this town, and I've watched it move up the social scale. Right now, we're surrounded by the kind of wealthy women who consider Natural-ville a hellhole to which they never intend to return. I've seen more than a couple of polished taut-faced specimens glance our way, take in Shelby's Daisy Duke outfit – cowboy boots, denim shorts, and a shirt that looks like she snatched it off the floor of her bedroom.

Even if they don't think much of her taste in clothes, I bet the taut women would give their next implant for that mass of coppery-blonde hair and those blue-green eyes. Sure, she has freckles on every piece of exposed skin, including her makeup-free lips, but I've always had a thing for freckles. Blame it on my teen crush on Penélope Cruz.

I also didn't expect her to be so petite. That said, she does have the hand strength common to everyone who works in agriculture, male or female. Modern technology only helps so much when you need to hoist a cow or change a wheel on a tractor. And, yes, despite its romanticized reputation, wine *is* an agricultural crop, no different from apples or corn or beets.

Not that Shelby Armstrong would agree. Mind you, I could say two plus two equals four and she'd argue tooth and nail against it. She may not be as stubborn as it sounds like her old man was, but on the mule scale, I'd place her at a solid 8/10. Something we have in common. Except that I top the dial at 11.

"Why are you doing this?" she says. "If you don't give a flying fig about the winery, then why take this job in the first place? I mean, the money can't be *that* good."

"Who says I don't give a fig? And who under ninety says 'fig' anyway?"

"I do. And *you* said, 'A winery's a winery.' Like it's nothing special."

"It isn't. *No* business is special just because it happens to be yours, or your family's."

I'm trying to be patient here, but this is Commerce 101.

"The basic requirement to remain solvent applies even if the business was founded by Great Grandfather Lemuel in 1700-and-whatever," I tell her. "And to stay solvent, you need more than a familiar name over the door. You need income that exceeds expenditure, and you need cash flow, so you're not running on empty. Flora Valley Wines' last statement of position looks like a kid's moneybox that's filled with Pokémon cards, three pennies and a gummy bear. How the hell did you survive this long? Did you make meth on the side?"

"No, I sold my body," she says, and immediately blushes like the aforementioned beets.

I could be an asshole and remark on the blushing, make a sarcastic comment. But while she might be a royal pain in the butt, she doesn't deserve to be humiliated. More importantly, I don't want to give any impression that I might have noticed her body. That is *not* the way to start a professional arrangement.

It's also, inconveniently, a lie. She's biting on her lower lip now, right where a freckle is, and part of my brain is trying to convince me that *I'd* like to bite on that lower lip. Luckily, the smarter part of my brain reminds me that (a) I don't want to be reminded about my last relationship, and (b) the bottom lip belongs to someone who, as they say in France, *ça me fait chier*. Translated and adjusted for local idiom: gives me the shits.

Yep, forget the Louvre and the stinky cheese. The greatest thing about France is how inventively they trash talk. The worst thing about France is how badly I was humiliated there. But that was then. Now, I'm back home. With a plan that I need to get back on track.

"Flora Valley would be bankrupt without JP," I remind her. "But all he's done is taken it off life support. *I* can make it profitable. But *you* need to follow my lead."

"And if I don't, you'll what? Fire me?"

In that instant, she reminds me of my sister, Ava. A human incendiary device from day one. When Ava's eyes flashed like that, everyone but Dad would duck for cover.

Dad would laugh and call her Little Miss, which, naturally, riled her even more.

The thing with Ava, though, is she gets shit done. She's goal-oriented, pragmatic – all us Durants are. When JP first described Little Miss Shelby here, he called her "a fine young woman, with an optimistic spirit and her father's same magic touch with wine." The words he failed to include were, "hidebound and next-level naïve." Neither quality is of any use to me, and I'd be doing neither of us a favour to pretend otherwise.

"Frankly," I tell her, "if you're going to be more hindrance than asset then I won't hesitate to cut you loose. I know plenty of skilled contract winemakers. JP might not like it, but he's given me free rein. And, ultimately, it's the success of his investment that JP cares about."

I expect a salty retort, possibly some name-calling. Small risk of a glass of water thrown in my face. But there's no flash in her eyes now. I've made her sad, not angry. Wow. Don't *I* feel like a figging asshole?

"We were doing fine," she says, "until Dad got sick. I'm sure you don't think cancer is an excuse for non-performance – you'd probably have fired him, too. But we *were* making a profit up till then. It was just that he—"

Her voice cracks and she swallows, trying to keep it together. I can't let her see that I'm affected. *I* don't want to admit I am.

"The winery was so important to him," she goes on, "that he felt compelled to control everything. He did it in such a way that no one complained. They *wanted* to be part of it. We all did. But when he got sick, he didn't have the energy to do all the stuff he'd done before, and things kind of got away from him…"

"And let me guess," I say, without thinking. "He denied there was a problem and refused all offers of help."

Her eyes widen with surprise and then become curious.

"You've had something similar with *your* dad?"

Fortunately, one of the superpowers of a Durant upbringing is a perfect poker face. Ava insists I have a tell – a slight hitch of my left eyebrow. It's her usual wind-up. I know I give nothing away.

But why not? Where's the harm in telling Shelby that, yes, I *have* had the same experience. That the whole reason I'm sitting across from her is because my dad would sooner die than admit how sick he is. He wouldn't admit the irony of that, either.

I could tell her that all five Durant siblings freaked out when we discovered our father wasn't immortal. We might not leave cookies for Santa anymore but we still secretly believed that Mitchell Durant was indestructible. When news of his heart condition reached us, we raced back to our hometown from all corners of the world to help out Mom, to spend time with our father, and to figure out what the hell to do from now on. We made a plan, swiftly and decisively, and now we're in the process of executing it. The Durants are a tight team, even if we fight more like MMA opponents who persist in ignoring the "no biting" rule.

My part in the plan is to take this job. I don't particularly want it. Vineyards bring up unwelcome memories, mainly about my own behaviour. I put work before my relationship and that ended as you'd expect, with my ass being dumped. Dad's illness gave me the excuse to slink back home, and his stubborn refusal to get proper medical help means my family have been mercifully focused on him and not me.

Now, ironically, I'm in a position where work *has* to come first. If I'm to have any hope of reviving this dead duck winery, Shelby Armstrong needs to step right back. She might be a decent winemaker, but she's got the acumen of a moth in a candle factory. She needs to follow my instructions, to the letter, no debate, I need her to see me as her boss, and keep a professional distance. Which is why I won't tell her anything about my dad. And I *certainly* won't mention my ass-dumping.

But, being pragmatic, it would pay to make a small concession. It's going to be hard enough work turning this business around without having Shelby Armstrong up in my face every minute. Besides, I do know what it's like to feel you have something to prove. And if she works with me, not against me, we can both get what we want.

"How about this?" I say. "This first week is all about you showing me how the winery works. If there's any evidence that I need to amend the business plan, I'll take it on board."

She doesn't reply. She's trying to work out whether I'm sincere. I am, but time is ticking on, and every second we delay, Flora Valley Wines haemorrhages more money.

I stand up and extract my wallet from my jacket pocket.

"JP's treat," I tell her.

Then I pull out my car keys and she jumps to her feet like she's been electrified.

"Great, yes, great," she says in a rush. "Great plan. Really. Great."

I have no idea what's got into her.

"So... see you 9am Monday?" I say.

"Great! OK! See you Monday!"

And she hightails it like a jackrabbit.

I decide to buy the cast iron spice grinder for Mom. She loves that kind of thing. And I can always borrow it and clock Shelby Armstrong over the head if she gives me trouble.

When I get back to the car, some *caca boudin ostréipyge*, that's "shit sausage buttock oyster", has put a huge dent in the hood. How, I have no idea, and I'm too pissed off to try to imagine.

On the way back to *chez* Durant, I should be focusing on how to get Dad to see sense, and the most practical next steps for the winery, and any number of other useful, constructive thoughts. But the dumb part of my brain keeps chiming in with images of the freckles on Shelby Armstrong's lower lip, and speculation about where else she might have freckles, and how goddamn cute it is that she says "fig", and at one point, I genuinely consider pulling over and smacking my *own* head with the spice grinder to reboot my sanity.

Fig almighty. Next week is going to be *long*.

Chapter Three

SHELBY

"So he's a human-shaped sack of dick cheese, but hot?"

Jordan, one of my two best friends of all time forever and ever, is on her second beer.

"With terrible taste in cars," I add.

"Which he might have to send to the wreckers now," Jordan says with a grin.

"No! It was just a scratch!"

I can't afford spirits and I don't like beer, so I'm drinking the house white, which is one step up from polecat spray but fourteen percent alcohol. Brendan, owner and manager of the Silver Saddle, won't stock Flora Valley wine because he says it's too fancy. He won't let me bring my own wine bottle either, even though I offered to pay a corkage fee. So in a way, it's his fault that I have to sit on this one glass for the whole evening. Fortunately, I drink with people whose jobs pay them real money, so Brendan doesn't get *too* shirty.

"How hot?" says Chiara, my other best friend of all time forever and ever. "On the Skarsgård scale?"

Alexander, not Stellan, of course. We don't have daddy issues. Not that sort, anyhow.

"Hard to gauge," I say. "He was fully clothed."

"And he starts Monday?" says Jordan.

"Yep. Team briefed and warned."

"You *do* need help though, don't you."

Chiara's best friend of all time status is on shaky ground.

"I need *money*," I insist. "*Investment.* Not some interfering Harvard automaton who gets a woody from a spreadsheet."

"Oo... you said 'woody.'"

Jordan definitely does *not* need a third beer. But it's an old joke. My inability to properly curse has been a long-standing source of amusement for pretty much the whole population of Verity, and a fair proportion of the wider Sonoma County.

And no, I don't know why I have such trouble with cussing. Dad swore like a sailor who'd hit his thumb with a hammer, and even Mom occasionally said the eff word. Perhaps I'm channelling some Puritan ancestor? I mean, I'm not uptight about anything else, like, you know – *that* stuff.

Not that I've had time for any of that stuff. I admit I do miss sharing my bed with a warm body that isn't entirely covered in fur, but the truth is I'm afraid that if I get distracted, something vital will break. Running Flora Valley Wines feels like juggling three hand grenades, two chainsaws and a pineapple, and if I drop a single one the business will be obliterated in a sticky mess. I couldn't face confessing to the ghost of my dad that I destroyed his dream because I didn't have what it takes to hold it together. Because I wasn't him.

That's why I have such mixed feelings about Nathan Durant taking over. Juggling for so long has made me *so* tired, and it could feel *so* good to have some of the load lifted from me, especially that stupid pineapple. But if I can't do it all by myself, does that mean I'm already a failure? Does that mean I *am* an unrealistic dreamer like all the potahto-people in my past have declared? I want so badly to prove them wrong, and I want so badly to have just *one* day free of grumbling anxiety that not even my natural optimism can muffle. And to be absolutely embarrassingly honest, I'd like the chance to get to know boy wonder on a less professional level. I mean, cats *are* great but it's also true that I haven't had time to meet anyone I'd be prepared to shove them off the quilt for. Nathan Durant is the first hot guy to enter my orbit since forever, and he's so hot that I just mentally blushed at the word 'enter'. He is *ridiculously* handsome. I could see all those Martinburg ladies eyeing him up at lunch. They were so excited, their foreheads almost creased.

But – and it's a huge one with a capital B – he's made it clear he's here to pummel the winery into shape, and if that shape isn't to my liking, then stiff cheese. (I mentally blushed again.) He might be hot, but he's a Harvard-bot (ooh, rhyme!), and I am *not* looking forward to next week.

"Harvard," says Chiara, thankfully only reading part of my mind. "Must come from money."

My two best friends of all time forever and ever are gorgeous, in completely different ways. Jordan's all honey blonde and tanned, with boobs I'd die for but would probably make me topple over all the time. She works for the local outdoor pursuits centre, doing terrifying things like rock climbing and whitewater rafting and minding large groups of teenagers.

Chiara's mother came from St Kitts in the Caribbean, and her father is Italian, and though her parents are both kind of dumpy and short, they managed to produce a tall, slender exquisite vision who regularly causes traffic incidents on Verity's main street. Her parents are also super sweet and huggy, whereas Chiara has more of a Bond villain vibe, like one wrong move and she'd take your eye out with a stiletto heel.

Chiara works morning reception at Bartons, the boutique hotel that used to be the roughest bar in Verity until its last customer's liver finally exploded. It still has a bar, but with gold velvet chairs and cocktails containing mulberry leaf root cider and barrel-rested bergamot tea. We gave it six months, but three years later it's still going strong because Ted, the owner, comes from some British noble family and knows every rich person on the planet.

Locals drink at the Silver Saddle. It has a jukebox and beer.

Chiara is also frighteningly ambitious. Which would

explain why she's drinking a Manhattan (the only cocktail Brendan will make), and her interest in personal wealth.

"He can't be *that* rich," I protest. "Or he wouldn't need this job."

"Might be a scholarship boy?" suggests Jordan.

"Makes no difference. He went to *Harvard*," says Chiara, explaining it to us simpletons. "Once you're in, you're *in*. With the *in* crowd."

Jordan swigs on her beer. "You could make your own money, Kiki. Instead of becoming a real housewife of – wherever he lives. Where does he live?" she asks me.

"In a coffin? Don't know, don't care."

"I *intend* to make my own money," says Chiara. "But connections never hurt a girl."

She gives me her trademark 'offer you can't refuse' look. "How about I come around on Monday and you introduce us?"

More mixed feelings churn in my stomach.

"Do you want to check him out as a person – or as a potential date?" I ask.

"Both, of course," says Chiara. "But I certainly won't hit on him, if you want first dibs, because that is the kind of friend I am."

"I can't hit on him. That would be too complicated and I hate complicated."

Jordan pokes me in the upper arm.

"But you'll be working right alongside him, close quarters and all, for weeks or months or *ages*. Do you really want him yapping on all that time about Chiara?"

"I'm *totally* worth yapping on about," Chiara objects. "I know how to do that thing."

"I have no clue what that thing is," I say. "Please don't ever tell me."

"OK, no, you're right..." Jordan has been doing some beer-thinking. "Complicated is bad. Much easier if he yaps on about Chiara, because with you working together at close quarters, it could get pretty uncomfortable if he dumped you, couldn't it?"

That's a fair point, but it fails to un-mix my feelings. I stare down into my almost but not quite empty glass in the hopes that the old saying about finding truth in wine is ... well, true.

"You done with that?"

Brendan's meaty hand gestures to my wine glass.

I pull it to me and glare. "No. There's a drop left."

He rolls his eyes, but leaves me be.

Jordan watches him walk back to the bar. "Brendan's so hot," she sighs.

"Did you pre-load?" I demand. "Brendan's like ... a big blond gorilla!"

"With a great butt."

I swivel to check. "OK, yes, pretty tight, but—"

"Tattoos. Muscles. General bad boy vibe."

"And old enough to be your much older brother."

Jordan waves her hand. "Details, schmetails."

It's too much for me. I tip my glass up to drain the last drop. It refuses to drip. I can't help thinking this is a bad omen.

"So I'll see you Monday at one."

Chiara makes it sound like a threat. She suspects I might go back on my word. And I might because what if she *does* decide to set her cap at Nathan Durant? How mixed would my mixed feelings be then?

I can hear his voice as clear as if he were here, all low and sexy: "Who outside the Victorian era says 'set her cap'?" I can see that delicious mouth almost flick into a smile – a sign there might be a real human inside that business-bot shell.

But Jordan's right. I *am* going to be working right alongside him for the foreseeable, and if I want to prove I'm capable, I'll need to focus, focus, focus. And being a natural optimist, I can see an upside to the super fun role of being third wheel if he and Chiara start dating. Which is – that thing she knows how to do *might* make him less uptight.

OK. Focus and optimism. Bring it on.

"Sure," I say. "Monday at one."

Chapter Four

NATE

I've never had a migraine but I think I'm having one now. This place is a shambles.

The surroundings are stunning. You look up from the vines to rolling hills and untouched woodland. There's a creek that probably won't give you giardia, and the whole place will turn to gold in the fall. Nope, can't fault the location.

But the operation's a *mess*. The equipment would have been scoffed at by Noah while he chipped away at his ark with a stone adze. There are no documented systems for production or logistics, which will mean chaos when we grow – and I *do* intend to grow this business. There's a *shoebox* in the office with receipts in it. And how many domestic animals can one vineyard support? I've counted three dogs, five cats and two pigs, and one really pissy goose that looked ready for a fight. It's a petting zoo, and to be frank, we might make more money if that's what we turned it into.

The last straw was the grape bins. OK, JP did tell me they stomp the grapes, but I assumed it had to be an add-on, a gimmick, something visitors could do for a souvenir photo. I thought the *real* pressing would be mechanical, like any normal winery. By the time I left France, we'd installed state-of-the-art pneumatic presses. Flora Valley has big wooden bins. And, I don't know, probably a resident Sasquatch to do the stomping.

Seriously, I need to lie down in a darkened room.

"Beautiful, isn't it?"

Shelby's completely sincere. Her face is aglow with love for this place, which in all other situations I'd find incredibly appealing. But she is *completely* out of whack with reality. I can't even ... I don't know what to say to her. Where to start?

"That goose is a hazard."

"Dylan?"

"Who calls a goose *Dylan*?" I ask.

"My mom."

The glow vanishes and her mouth goes all soft and vulnerable with sadness. Fortunately, the pounding pain in my temples suppresses any dumb urge I might have to kiss it better.

"You don't get on with her?" I ask.

"No! I adore her!" Shelby says. "But I miss her. This place used to be full of Armstrongs, and then there was Dad, Mom and me, and then just me and Mom, and now...'

26

JP told me about Shelby's mom buying the artist studio with her payout. He'd met Lee Armstrong and liked her a lot. Whereas I couldn't help feeling a little resentful that she'd left Shelby to cope with this all on her own.

"Your mom's happy on the coast, right?"

"As a clam. A happy, hippy clam."

Hippy, huh. That could explain a lot. Like the wagon wheel with flowers in it, the wind chimes, and the whale poster in the office. Along with the lack of systems, processes, and the slightest amount of financial prudence.

"Do you want some coffee?" she asks.

"*Oh* yeah." And if it can be administered intravenously all the better.

I follow her to the main house, which is built in a folksy style, all exposed timber and shaker tiles. It's a big place, shabby but comfortable, with traces of the Armstrong family all over it, as if they'll be back any moment. I know how weird it was coming back to my family home after four years away, that pang of seeing all the old familiar things, yet feeling like you no longer really belong, that you've grown up and moved on.

Whereas in Shelby's case, it's everyone *else* who's moved on, one way or another, leaving her all alone. I'm hit suddenly by the reality of how hard that must be for her, and how courageous she's had to be, to keep going here. Would *I* be strong enough to push on like she has? Or would my Durant pragmatism win over, and make me sell up and get out rather than risk failure?

It occurs to me that I'm undergoing that exact same test

in another arena: my family. All five of us Durant siblings think we're being super practical, combining our efforts to make sure Dad gets the best care, Mom isn't overworked, and the family finances are protected. That's what we talk about – the practical stuff.

What we *don't* talk about is how we'll feel if Dad dies. When we won't have his presence in our lives, keeping us grounded, focused. Or what will happen to Mom, how she'll cope, and how we'll look after her. How we'll go back to our own lives, knowing she's all alone. We're not talking about any of that because that would mean admitting that we took for granted that our parents, especially our hard-assed dad, would hang in there for a good long while...

Guess Shelby did, too.

She's making coffee with a percolator that looks like it served duty in the Civil War. She's wearing denim shorts again, and an old surf-brand T-shirt that's gotten a little transparent with age. No cowboy boots today. Blue sneakers. With a hole in one toe. She's the same age as me, twenty-eight, and she looks about twelve.

I'm overcome with an unexpected and deeply inconvenient urge to protect her. My sisters would give me crap for being a chauvinist pig. Is Shelby a helpless damsel, they'd accuse? Clearly not, or she'd have given up long since. So why should *you* feel the need to be the white knight, riding in to save the day?

I don't know, sisters dear. If us Durants had any inclination to undergo psychotherapy, I'd probably hazard a guess that I'm trying to make up for past wrongs. Last time,

I was responsible for someone's well-being, I did everything *but* look after it. And though I'm not quite ready to say I deserved such a publicly brutal dumping, I can at least see what I did to drive her away. I chose to focus all my attention on work, thinking that by turning around her family's business, I'd be making her life better. But it was the wrong choice, and she didn't give me any time to put it right.

So, is this my second chance? Could my obsession with work now actually make a positive difference to someone's life? If I rescue *this* winery, then Shelby Armstrong will be financially secure for the rest of her life.

Part of my brain knows this is a blatant justification. My motives might sound pure but it's my way of raising the middle finger to my ex. See? If you'd had the patience to wait until the winery was profitable again, you could have had me *and* a lifestyle *très heureux*. But no, you decided to run off with that hairy Scandi dickhead.

Let it go, Nate. Regroup and focus. Your first priority is to save Flora Valley Wines. If that helps Shelby, then wonderful, hooray. But sentimentality can't override pragmatic business sense. Winning here will require some hard decisions. It'll require change, radical change. And change can be cruel before it's kind.

Then again, there's no reason why my two inner guys can't co-exist. If Mr Pragmatist does the job, Sir Sentimental can take the glory. Flora Valley Wines is saved, and Shelby's secure. Everyone wins. And I look good. For once.

I feel strengthened with a new resolve. So what if the

bookkeeping relies on a shoebox, and there's a pissy goose? Bring it on.

Shelby places a mug in front of me. It appears to be filled with tar.

"Uh, it's quite strong," she says, unnecessarily. "There's cream and sugar if you want?"

"No, thanks."

This morning, I need my caffeine neat.

She perches on the edge of the chair opposite, elbows on the table, mug between both hands. Unlike me, all her emotions show on her face. I see anxiety vying with defiance. She loves this place and intends to defend it. But she knows it's in a bad way, and she's bracing herself, like you do before you rip off a Band-Aid. You know it'll hurt but maybe it won't hurt *that* much.

"I have questions," I tell her. I won't mention how many.

"OK…?"

"Where do you source your vineyard crews?"

She tilts her head as if I'm trying to trick her.

"Javi organizes all that."

"Harvey? Like the invisible rabbit?"

"No, with a J. As in Javier."

"Right. And Javi is … where?"

"At Bartons," she says. "He's the concierge."

I resist the urge to pinch the bridge of my nose.

"OK, so here's the thing." I say it slowly and distinctly. "All the information I've had to date is your accounts, and what JP has told me. Which was a basic overview of the vineyard's size and capacity, but mainly about how great a winemaker your dad was, and the potential he saw in you."

Her cheeks pinken with pleasure. "JP is *such* a great guy. How do you know him again?"

She has all the focus of a dog on a squirrel farm.

"Old friend of my father's." Moving right along. "So today, what I need to do is fill the gaps in my knowledge."

Shelby nods, with an earnestness that's both cute and exasperating.

"What I need from *you*,"—I have to spell this out—"are answers filled with details. Specific details. The kind you'd give someone who knows absolutely nothing about Flora Valley Wines. Or Verity, or Sonoma, or even Planet Earth. Do you get me?"

She screws up her face. "Kind of."

Seriously? Is she messing with me?

"Let me give you an example. When you say Javi is the concierge at Bartons, the details I need are: what and where is Bartons, and why is a concierge also organizing vineyard workers?"

"Oh, *right*. Because Ted lets him. Ted's very big on putting back into the community. And he has a lot of friends who want to come over and do seasonal work. They're all from posh British families, so you wouldn't expect them to be of any use, but they've been great. Only downside is they can sound like a pack of donkeys when they all get together."

She's definitely winding me up. She *has* to be.

Sure enough, she bursts out in a surprisingly rich laugh. I imagine giving her a dead arm, the Durant sibling revenge of choice.

"Sorry, couldn't resist," she says, grinning like an evil fairy.

"Funny. Do Ted and Javi actually exist?"

"Ted is the owner of Bartons, the hotel in Verity." She's all business now, the minx. "He *is* some British noble and actually *does* have a seemingly endless supply of young people who want to come and work here. Javi has connections all over this part of the world. He's been contracted to Flora Valley for, oh, must be five years now. Total godsend. He's coming over later this afternoon, so I'll introduce you."

"OK. Great. Next questio—"

"Of course, when we were kids, we were all forced to work on the vineyard."

Now she's started spilling the beans, I can't stop her.

"I was the only one who enjoyed it. Mostly. But we got that it saved on overheads. When my brothers and sisters left home, Dad had to bite the bullet. He knew they couldn't be roped back in, not even with emotional bribery. So he asked Javi to up the quota of workers he recruited."

She makes a face. "Took a bit of a financial hit that year."

No need to say, *and every year since*. We both know it. I'll move on.

"Who does your maintenance work for your equipment and so forth?"

32

"Cam."

She grins, and quickly elaborates before I can brain her.

"Cam Hollander. Ex-army. He's our cooper, too. Makes incredible oak barrels for us, and for other wineries round here. You won't meet him today, though. Cam doesn't really do people contact."

"Does he work under the cover of night?"

"He's fine as long as you don't try to make small talk with him," she says. "Or set him up on a date."

"You know this from experience?"

"Mom tried to set him up with an artist friend. Luckily, Cam adores Mom, so he's still speaking to her. In his own non-speaking way."

This place is full of lunatics. Simple as that.

"And Toothless Doug does the mowing and weed control, and Iris from the Cracker Café helps out with food for the crews. For the pigs, too – they make great garbage disposals. I get off-cuts for the dogs and cats from Ron, the butcher, and Toothless Doug also looks after the vegetable garden, plus he gives me produce from his own garden, which must rival California State as an agricultural economy."

She pauses. "He gives me a *lot* of corn."

"Because he has trouble with it, owing to the whole toothless thing?"

"Oh, no, Doug has a full set of teeth."

She stands up and says, brightly, "More coffee?"

"Please."

I feel instead like I'm asking for mercy.

"Hello-o?"

A voice in the kitchen doorway. Followed by a body. A truly sensational one, dressed in what looks like the kind of costume a man with a secretary fetish would ask his dominatrix to wear. As she nears, I see there's a little logo embroidered on the skin-tight suit jacket's lapel. *Bartons.* I *have* to meet this guy, Ted.

"Hi—"

She's coming straight at me, holding out her hand. I stand up, because I'm a gentleman, and besides, she's about six feet nine in those stiletto pumps.

"I'm Chiara."

She pronounces it the Italian way: Key-AH-ra. Rude to comment on someone's cultural makeup, but I'd guess that's not the only ethnicity in there. She's got a kind of Rihanna look with her hazel eyes, but her hair's a halo of blond-brown curls, which is cute as fuck.

I'm swearing. This does not bode well. Time to double down on the poker face.

I shake her hand. "Nathan."

"Hi, Kiki."

Shelby's leaning against the kitchen counter, arms folded. Her expression's unusually hard to read, wryly amused with a hint of … something?

"Oh, hey, Shel, didn't see you there."

Chiara is all breeze and no innocence. But Shelby's smile widens. She's genuinely glad to see her friend.

"I'm making coffee," she says. "Want some?"

"The Black Death? Hell yes."

Chiara takes a seat with more ease than I'd expect from anyone wearing a skirt like that.

"I didn't see your Porsche outside," is her opening gambit.

Shelby drops a spoon in the sink.

"Why do you think I own a Porsche?" I have to ask.

Chiara shrugs one shoulder. "Vicious rumour?"

"I *was* driving my brother's 911 last week," I say. "He needed my truck."

"*Ohhh...*" Chiara stares over at Shelby. "Your *brother's* Porsche."

Shelby keeps her back to us, pretending to be busy with the coffee pot. I get what's going on here. This morning, when I parked my pickup next to the Flora Valley Wines Dodge, I observed the trailer hitch protruding at precisely Porsche hood height. Shelby's reaction at lunch last week now makes perfect sense.

"Danny's a mechanic," I say. "Sports cars are his speciality."

I don't mention how shitty he was about the dent. We all make mistakes.

Shelby turns around, catches my eye and we have a little moment of understanding that in a sudden flash becomes a little moment of something else. I give thanks that my poker face is still switched on to maximum. Parts of me are tingling. Shelby has turned her back, so I can't see if she's blushing or not. Maybe I was mistaken?

I remind myself sternly that it's irrelevant what her

reaction is, and that coffee this strong would make anyone's parts tingle. Back to normal. Thank fig.

But then Chiara, who clearly misses nothing, smiles like a cat plotting to take over the world.

"So, Nathan," she says. "What do you do for fun?"

Chapter Five

SHELBY

Not that I really had any choice in the matter, but introducing Chiara to Nathan actually seemed to be a good idea. She only stayed for coffee, but during that time he lightened up, and the afternoon was *way* less painful than the morning. He met Javi, who reassured with his usual efficiency. All three of us took a tour of the vineyard, and by the time we returned to the house, Nathan didn't have any more questions.

I couldn't help feeling a little miffed that it was Javi who put Nathan's mind at ease about the operations and not me, but I'll take the wins where I can get them.

Wish it were reciprocal, though. Gaps in Nathan's knowledge might be filled, but I'm still in the dark about what he intends to do next. He pumped Javi about the neighbouring vineyards, what they were doing, and what changes they'd made over the years Javi had been in the industry, and I got the feeling he was double-checking that his plans for Flora Valley were viable.

Despite my resistance to Nathan taking over, I *know* we have to adapt. The limited runs of pinot noir we've always made still sell out, but they haven't sustained us for several years. Operating costs have risen every year but we can only bump up the prices so much or our customers' loyalty would be stretched too far. Which means our profit margins have become so small any cost overruns destroy them.

Dad knew our operating budgets were unrealistic, but every year he vowed we'd keep costs under control. There was no year we actually managed to do this.

Added to that is the risk of ... well, me. Our customers were loyal to Dad. To his skill and, let's face it, his personality. Big Billy Armstrong, enthusiast and entrepreneur. He made you feel like you were part of a select crew, handpicked to join his personal adventure. Customers *loved* Dad. When they bought a Flora Valley pinot noir, they took a piece of Billy home.

Our customers have known me for years and like me well enough, but I'm not my father. Last vintage released was the final one made by Billy Armstrong. My first wine, made with Dad's sick-bed guidance, is due to be bottled next month, August. Pre-orders are slow, understandably, I guess. And as for the customers who *have* ordered, I won't know what they think of my wine until they try it.

We'll harvest this coming crop not long after, during September, and it will age in barrels for eleven months, which is short by industry standards but works for us –

enough time for it to develop depth, but not so long that it loses freshness for those who want to age it further. If our customers don't like my wine, this coming harvest may never happen and the grapes will rot on the vine. And that'll be the end of Flora Valley Wines.

Nathan's readying to go. He looks a lot more relaxed than he did this morning. I'd like to say the same for myself, but that would be a lie.

"So I'll see you in a couple of hours," he says.

He ... what?

"Uh, did I miss something?"

Nathan gives me a steady look. He's good at those.

"Drinks. With Chiara. This evening at Bartons."

Yup, that completely passed me by. What was I doing when this was discussed? Oh, that's right. I was letting my mind be overwhelmed with anxiety about the future.

Besides, I figured the whole conversation was Chiara flirting, which she'd given me fair warning might happen. No need for me to listen in.

"Did Chiara invite me as well?" I have to clarify.

"*I* invited you," he says.

"Oh."

"And you said 'Sure.'"

"I *sort* of remember that."

"What did you think you were saying 'sure' to?" He certainly has a knack for the pertinent question.

"No idea," I admit. "I was ... distracted."

And now I'm confused. *He* invited *me* to go to drinks. He didn't want to go alone with Chiara, my impossibly

39

gorgeous best friend, who can make grown men drop to their knees with a single glance. If I was tech-savvy in any way, I'd say this does not compute.

But then there was that – look. Which I thought, for just a second, made the air between us go all fizzy and electric. It was probably the coffee. It's been known to jump-start motors.

Nathan jangles his car keys in his hand. Ford pick-up. Silver. Not at all flashy.

"Do you want to come or not?"

He sounds impatient, which is less confusing. Small problem, though—

"I have nothing to wear to Bartons," I confess.

He frowns for the eighty-fifth time today. "Who cares what you wear?"

"Ted does! He has a dress code!"

"In *Verity*?"

"No, only in the rarefied bubble of Bartons," I say. "It's a whole other world in there."

Nathan looks me up and down.

"What are you – five three, five four?" he says.

"Five four."

"I'll bring you a dress," he says. "I'll come by here with it around seven."

I'm too stunned to even say goodbye. This is *not* what I had planned for the evening. OK, so my plan was the same as every other evening – feed the animals, make my own dinner with the least possible ingredients and effort, crash on the couch and pretend to watch some TV, drag myself upstairs to brush my teeth, squeeze into the three percent of bed space not occupied by cats, and sleep like the dead until the alarm defibrillates me back into consciousness.

Seems I'll have to pass on all that excitement because *this* evening I'm going on a drinks date with ridiculously handsome Nathan Durant!

Oh, yup, that's right. And Chiara.

So it can't be a date, can it? Not a *date* date.

And why would I even think that? He's made it clear that he's all about the business and he's also made it crystal clear that he's not thrilled about how I have run it thus far. No, this is a recce, that's what it is. When I wasn't listening, Chiara no doubt suggested Nathan check out Bartons and meet Ted, and I'm coming because I'm 'officially' part of the Flora Valley team. It makes sense. It's a business date.

Typical Shelby. Head always in the pink fluffy clouds.

I can hear my mom: "You find it hard to keep your feet on the earth, don't you?"

She wasn't criticizing, just observing. She's a cloud head herself. Creative types usually are. You need to be creative to make good wine.

But I need to be a businessperson, too. I need to be an equal to Nathan Durant. A peer that he respects. Otherwise, even if we adapt and our profits lift, this winery will slip away from me like wine down a drain.

Fig. He'll be back here in ninety minutes, and I have animals to feed and chores to do. Better find time to shave my legs, too. They look like I walked through thistledown.

And I bet Ted's dress code will have something to say about *that.*

"Shelby, darling."

Ted kisses me on both cheeks. Like they do in England, I gather. He is his usual floppy blond-haired, immaculately dressed, handsome self. He also smells divine, but there's no point in asking what of. Any cologne Ted wears will be off-the-charts expensive. Probably distilled from some plant that only grows in an inaccessible valley and flowers once every thousand years.

"Gosh." Ted takes in my dress, which is short, dark gold and sheer. Nathan said it's his sister's. He didn't say if she minded him borrowing it. "You look…"

"Suitable?" I ask.

"I was going to say 'luscious'," Ted replies. "But, yes, eminently suitable."

"Ahem," says Chiara, in a warning tone.

Ted is unabashed. "You always look luscious, my dear. It's your default setting."

I wish I could be more like Ted. Nothing fazes him. Not even the presence of Nathan Durant, who I can *feel* squaring up behind us. It's an effect Ted has on most American males, who know a threat when they see one. Not a threat in the physical sense, but the kind who could whisk your woman away to a private Caribbean island and ply her with

Beluga caviar and Krug Clos d'Ambonnay '95 at four grand a bottle.

But as it happens, Ted is able to subdue even the most bristling alpha male. It's because he genuinely likes everyone, and if a person persists in behaving badly, he'll simply ignore it until they give in and shape up.

"And you must be Nathan," Ted smiles. "Chiara's told me all about you."

He extends a hand, which is gripped, at a guess, overly firmly. Ted does not flinch. Rumour is he was a British SAS officer, but Ted will neither confirm nor deny.

"Welcome. And *thank* you for what you're doing for Flora Valley Wines."

His sincerity is real and disarming. Nathan's shoulders relax a little.

"My pleasure," he says.

It doesn't sound quite right coming out of Nathan's mouth, but then Ted-isms are catching.

Assuming his gracious host role, Ted ushers us before him to the prized corner booth, where you can see and be seen. That would be Chiara's doing. For good reason. My bestie is well worth observing in a lipstick pink number that hugs her outrageously great figure like a coat of paint. And every guy in the bar duly observes her. I can almost hear the cartoon "ah-oo-ga" horn sound as their eyes bug out.

We settle into the gold velvet seats, and one of Ted's Europe-trained waitpersons appears like magic to take our drinks orders. If we were in the Silver Saddle, we'd be obliged to stand at the bar for several minutes, even if we were the only customers. Brendan likes people to know who's in charge.

"Now, enjoy," says Ted.

He won't be joining us. He spends just enough time with his customers to earn their undying worship, and then disappears. "Always leave them wanting more Ted" is Ted's motto. If he ever had anything as common as a motto, that is.

The waitperson waits silently while we peruse the cocktail menu. (You can only peruse in Bartons.) I glance up to find Nathan looking at me. He grins, shakes his head.

"What the hell is Anatolian menengic?"

"Coffee," says Chiara. "Made from wild pistachios."

"Yeah, you've got to watch those feral nuts," says Nathan. "Have your arm off."

Then he spots another gem. "Clarified *octopus* milk? You are shitting me."

"I thought you were a Harvard sophisticate?" I tease.

"Nobody at Harvard drinks octopus milk," he says. "Not even during hazing."

Chiara is done perusing and is now ready for alcohol.

"I'll have the Eastern Old Fashioned," she says.

"Does it contain mollusk milk?" Nathan asks the waitperson.

"Fifteen-year-old whisky, sir," is the reply. "And ruby port."

"Sounds safe," says Nathan. "Make that two."

"Along with an infusion of—"

Nathan holds up his palm to forestall further explanation.

"Very good, sir." Ted trains his staff well. "And for madame?"

"That's you," Chiara nudges my arm. "Hurry up."

"OK, I'll have whatever is closest to a tequila slammer," I say.

"With the eggfruit chicha?"

"I'll take your word for it."

The waitperson gathers our menus and glides away.

Nathan looks around, taking in the gold velvet, the arty flower arrangements made with dried lotus bulbs, and the food item on a neighbouring table that's puffing dry ice. I notice he ignores all the men who are still ogling Chiara.

"I'm impressed," he says. "I also feel like I'm being filmed by David Lynch."

"The Log Lady only does weekends."

Chiara picks an olive out of a bowl that's probably antique French crystal and places it slowly between her glossy lips, causing a roomful of guys to release a low moan.

Nathan, however, is looking at me. Again.

I don't know what to make of it. I mean, if anyone were asked to pick the odd person out at the table tonight, they'd take a nanosecond to point in my direction.

Nathan is wearing a sharp suit and a classy tie, and the low light emphasizes the amazing planes of his face. For every man here having desperate fantasies about Chiara, there's a woman storing those cheekbones in her memory banks for retrieval when she's next in bed alone.

Chiara is the one who matches him, not me. But even though she's currently committing a minor sex crime with an olive, she's not the one capturing Nathan's attention.

I can only imagine he feels sorry for me, being the dress-deprived little hick I am. Or he's seen what a dumpster fire my life is, and wants to keep a close eye on me, in case I do something foolish. My body might be feeling warm where his gaze lands, but that's just head-in-cloud talk. Focus, Shelby. This is business, business, business.

Our drinks arrive. I'm glad for the distraction. And I guess I'll soon find out whether I'm allergic to eggfruit.

"Holy swizzle stick, that's good," I announce.

Nathan casts a bemused look at Chiara. "Was it a head injury? Or has she never had the ability to swear?"

"The world's science community remains puzzled," Chiara replies.

She raises her Eastern Old Fashioned, which looks a weird colour to me but whatever.

"Bottoms up, as they almost certainly don't say in Britain."

We clink glasses, and the rest of the evening passes by in a bit of a blur.

Nathan drives me home, which is lucky as otherwise I'd have to walk. Dylan the goose has a lot to say about our arrival. Better than any guard dog.

"OK if I don't get out?" Nathan asks. "There are several parts of my body I'd like to keep."

"No problemo."

I reach to open the pickup door but then remember what I'm wearing.

"I should give this dress back to you."

I clasp the edge of the skirt. A gesture that, to be fair, *could* give the impression I'm about to take it off. Right here. In the cab of his pickup.

Which explains why Nathan says, "Whoa there!" and laughs. "Tomorrow is fine."

My expression makes him laugh more. "Are you drunk, Shelby?"

"No sirree," I deny. "I can *definitely* hold my liquor – or whatever that stuff was."

I look him right in the eye to show that mine are clear, as opposed to crossed. And I maybe tilt a *leetle* too far forward because all of a sudden, my mouth brushes his and my lips feel all hot and buzzy, like they've been stung. Maybe I *am* allergic to eggfruit…?

"OK—"

His voice snaps me back to now. His hands are holding the steering wheel tight like he wishes he could be driving away right now. He won't look at me. But I can see his face is all tense and hard. Angry.

I've made a *big* figging boo-boo. Oh boy.

"Sorry," is all I can say.

"Do you want me to walk you down the path?" His tone is one of flat, rote courtesy.

"I can manage."

I can open the pickup door by myself, too, and I do. I hop down, and amazingly do not rip the dress.

But then I do the worst, most feeble thing. I hold the door open and hover.

"Sorry," I say again.

He lifts both hands off the wheel in an impatient gesture, and finally turns my way.

"It's nothing," he says. "Go home. Sleep it off." I summon my last shred of dignity and shut the door. The second I've walked a safe distance from the pickup, Nathan floors it. I'm left standing all alone in a borrowed dress, feeling like a nincompoop, a word I learned from Ted.

I could blame Ted for this. Him and his cocktails. Or I could admit that I'm not used to drinking and that three of those eggfruit slammer things was two too many, even if Nathan was paying.

What I *cannot* do is linger on how it felt to brush my lips up against his. The electric buzz, the fleeting sense that his lips moved to meet mine, firm and soft at the same time. That's the eggfruit talking, and it and I are no longer friends.

I let myself into the dark house and am greeted by dogs, who will never care if you've been an idiot. I make my way upstairs, leave my teeth unbrushed, and slip out of the dress. The cats have occupied ninety-eight percent of the bed tonight, but I find a small sliver of space. Mercifully, I fall asleep before I can worry about whether or not I'll have a job in the morning.

Chapter Six

NATE

B *ordel de merde.* What in the fig just happened? Or what *didn't* happen? I didn't kiss Shelby Armstrong, which is a *good* thing, right? My brain's saying absolutely, my guy, stellar self-control. And the rest of me from the eyebrows down is calling me an *imbécile.*

And I am, but not for the reasons my dumb-fig body is giving. I know she didn't mean to kiss me, and I shouldn't have been so short with her. I should have laughed it off, helped her out of the car, risked a goose attack and made sure she got safely inside her front door. Instead, I practically broke the sound barrier in my haste to get away. What a *crétin.* What a *poltron.* What a total *loser.*

And now I'm halfway to the family homestead, and Shelby, I hope, is asleep, and not sitting up worrying. I know I'll spend my night trying to shut out even the merest thought of her lips on mine. For one, Mom has totally redecorated my childhood bedroom, and any furtive hand action would feel *very* wrong. I'll apologize to Shelby in the morning, reassure her that it was nothing. By which I mean that I'll reassure myself.

It's well past midnight when I pull up the driveway of our home, but immediately I spy a glow on the far side of the trees. It's the fire pit we Durants built eleven years back, a small act of rebellion initiated by my sister, Ava, when she turned sweet sixteen and decided *she* would host the party. Dad lectured us all about under-age drinking, and the evils of alcohol in general, but he let us do it because he knew nothing short of a bullet stops Ava when she's determined.

To be fair, she ensured Danny and the twins stayed teetotal until she considered they were old enough, and she never let anyone get into danger. But today, after many more parties, I still associate fires with the smell of cheap alcohol and, occasionally, singed clothing. I may also have lost my virginity at one of those early parties but I don't recall much about it. Another time where I let my balls override my brain.

As I walk from the parked pick-up, I can hear voices. It's the twins, the youngest Durants, Isabel – Izzy – and Max. Twenty-two and both still in college, back home only until term starts in September. Izzy's a scientist, studying nanotechnology or some such at MIT. Max is the only artistic one in the family, though he approaches it with the same Durant pragmatism. He's at Juilliard, training to be a concert pianist. I know nothing about music but if Max tells me he's next-level good, I believe him. Both twins have a healthy, and grounded, self-esteem. I've often envied them.

"Hey, bro."

Danny, too. And Ava. All four of my siblings are sitting around the pit, sharing a bottle of Jack Daniels. For a second, I hesitate on the edge of the firelight. I'm the oldest, and sometimes I think the others formed such a tight bond because I was the one Dad expected to be responsible. I was the wrangler, the keeper of order, the stand-in disciplinarian. That meant I got left out of a few things. Maybe more than a few, who knows? I don't blame them. Much.

But then Ava grins and holds out a plastic tumbler. "Shot?"

I take my place around the fire.

"Line 'em up," I tell her.

"Rough first day, huh?" asks Danny.

Danny is the number three Durant sibling, twenty-five, and the only one of us who refused to go to college. He apprenticed instead as a motor mechanic, and now he not only fixes high-end sports cars for the rich and famous in LA, he also buys them on their behalf. His wealthy customers pay all his travel costs and a frankly eye-watering commission. He makes a shitload more money than I do, the Harvard business grad. But then I haven't always made smart choices.

"How's the lady winemaker?" he asks. "Crazy as you feared?"

Inwardly, I cringe. The family got my account of the first meeting between Shelby and me, in which I relayed my impression of her as untethered from reality and possibly clinically delusional. Unfair and unkind. Seems I'm making a habit of being a jerk.

I take a slug of neat spirit and feel the burn like a reproach.

"We've got a big job ahead of us," is all I'll say.

Then I change the subject. "How was *your* day?"

Ava and Danny exchange a look.

"I'd rate it as a firm eight on the denial scale," says Danny.

"Eight?" I say. "Why so low?"

"Doc Wilson paid a visit and laid out the hard facts," says Ava. "And Mom burst into tears. Triggered a rare moment of introspection on Dad's part. Won't last."

"He was googling Peruvian altitude cures when I forced him to hit the hay," added Danny. "He'll be back up to a ten tomorrow."

In the Durant family plan, Ava and Danny volunteered as temporary in-home care. Danny has a crew back in LA who can work on the cars in his absence, and if he tag teams with Ava, he can travel for his clients if they need him to.

Ava's into horsepower of a different kind. Little and strong, she's an exercise rider for a racehorse stable in Kentucky. It's not that easy for her to take time off, but she's taken it. My guess is she's too valuable for her boss to play hardball with her.

The twins, of course, have to make college their priority. They'll pull their weight while they're at home, but come late August, they're out of here. Ava and Danny won't be far behind them.

That's where I come in. I've volunteered to donate half my salary to pay for whatever support is required when my siblings have to head back to their own homes, and their own lives. Made sense for me to stay because I don't *have* a life, and this is the only real home I've known. Only a few short weeks ago, I thought I was about to make a new one. I was wrong.

"He asked me if there were any bio-nanotech advances that would come on stream in the next couple of years," says Izzy. "I said I'd look into it."

"Really, Iz?" Max says. "Do you *have* to fuel the insanity?"

"Don't start blaming me!" Izzy slops bourbon from her tumbler as she waves both arms in protest. "If I'd said 'There's no chance you'll get organic nano-bots to fix your heart, Pops,' he'd have only heard the opposite anyway!"

Max nods. "True. And, to be fair, if some guy can breed flowers that glow bright enough in the dark to read by, then why not?"

Dan knocks back the last of his bourbon and gets reluctantly to his feet. "OK, team, I'm hitting the sack." He drops his hand onto Ava's shoulder. "Sis here is on monitoring duty, so I intend to sleep like a baby."

"And the babies will join you." Max gets up, pulls Izzy to her feet. "We have to be sharp tomorrow. We're taking Mom out for lunch."

"She agreed to that?" I ask, surprised.

Mom hasn't wanted to leave Dad's side for a moment, even when he behaves like a first-class heel and uses her as a verbal target for his anger and frustration. When we suggested she shouldn't have to put up with that bullshit, she told us she knows he doesn't mean it. She's healthy and he isn't, Mom said, so she can afford to be kind. Above all that, she loves him. She's loved Dad, and only Dad, for thirty-five years.

"She agreed just to shut us up," says Izzy. "Which means she'll find an excuse to back out at the last minute."

"But there are two of us against one," adds Max. "If necessary, we can carry her."

The twins jog to catch up with Danny, and link arms with him, one on either side. Danny is their favourite. He's *everyone's* favourite. He has an easy charm and our Mom's all-American blue-eyed blond good looks. Max and Izzy triggered some ancestral gene that gave them auburn hair and hazel eyes. Ava and I are the only ones with Dad's dark hair, and eyes in his particular shade of blue, way colder than Mom's and Danny's.

We've also inherited Dad's overbearing personality and his propensity for emotional constipation. While the other three, and Mom, share openly, Ava and I prefer to keep our feelings in check.

"You OK?"

Even in low light and with my poker face still intact, Ava can read me. Takes one to know one, I guess.

I appreciate her concern. But I'm not about to break the no-sharing habit tonight.

"Getting there," is all I'm prepared to offer. "What exactly did Doc Wilson say?"

"He said reducing stress is mandatory, as is limiting hard physical activity. He said Dad will need to be on drugs forever and will probably also need a defibrillator device implanted."

"Surgery."

"Yep," Ava says. "All of the above went down *super* well, as you can imagine."

Short story is that Dad, fifty-nine, athlete-fit, clean-living health nut, got a virus that damaged his heart. The medical term is dilated cardiomyopathy. The virus weakened the heart muscle, so it can't pump as hard, and the damaged muscle is now slowly being replaced with scar tissue, which forces the heart to enlarge and eventually – or, more often, quickly – fail.

It's not that uncommon, and if the patient hasn't already dropped dead, it can be managed. *If* said patient is cool with modern medical practices and doesn't believe Big Pharma is an enemy that needs to be destroyed.

Mitchell Durant won't even take an aspirin. Before this, he'd never had a day of ill health, which he put down to his, frankly punishing, exercise regime and discipline around diet. Our father would have made a terrific Spartan.

So you can see how Doc Wilson's treatment plan might not have been so eagerly received.

"Dad pushed back, I assume?"

Ava's grin is rueful. "And Doc listened, because he's a good guy. And then he told Dad that if he didn't stop being a fool, he'd be dead in a week."

"Ouch. No wonder Mom cried."

My sister pulls up her knees and hugs them, an unusually vulnerable gesture for her.

"Thing is, he's right," she says. "Dad could die anytime."

That should be my cue to offer some kind of reassurance. Be the brother in charge, like I used to be. The man with the plan.

But the weight of it all presses down on me, black and suffocating. Before France, before the ass-dumping, I thought I *did* have a plan. I've always been methodical and organized, disciplined like Dad, and up until then, that had proved a winning strategy. I graduated from Harvard with a top degree, I turned the French winery around, I had a beautiful fiancée. I was in charge, in control, on *top*.

And then I wasn't, and the worst of it was that I didn't see it coming. My plan fell apart without warning and it shook me to the core. My confidence was dealt a body blow, and if I hadn't had the excuse to run home and look after Dad, I don't know how I would have handled it. Badly, if how I reacted to Shelby is anything to go by. One little unexpected moment and I hightailed it like a startled jackrabbit. So much for being in control.

And all this leads to a fact I've so far avoided thinking about. If Dad goes, which, if he keeps this shit up, he might, I can't take his place. I can't be the force that keeps our family together because I'm not the man with a plan anymore. I'm only pretending to be. And the truth I can't face is that my family don't know that. I'm pushing on, making it look like I'm in charge, and it's all a lie. I don't want to *think* about what will happen when they realize.

It's why I can't even for a second contemplate a relationship with Shelby Armstrong. If I fuck up with the winery, then that's yet another person I've let down, and my list of potential let-downees is way too long already. If I keep my emotional distance from her, then I can protect my heart from another hammering. I'll *care* but I won't be emotionally slaughtered.

But I have to admit that if things were different, if I felt less bruised and less like a fraud, then I would be doing all I could to win Shelby's affection. She's kind, funny, beautiful and – uncomplicated. I haven't had much experience with people like that. People who might make it possible for me to let down my guard.

Ava's standing, brushing dust off her jeans.

"You coming in?" she says.

"No, I'll sit a while longer," I tell her. "It's a warm night."

When she's out of sight, I reach for the bourbon bottle. There's a third left, and I pour it generously into my shitty plastic tumbler.

I'll regret it in the morning, but right now, Jack seems like the only friend I have.

Chapter Seven

SHELBY

I'm awake. The anxiety broke through before the alarm. There are five cats and one dog on my bed, two dogs on the floor beside it, and I have never felt more alone.

Or more foolish. Or more confused.

I didn't mean to kiss him but I did *almost* kiss him and from the way he reacted that was *not* a good thing. Which *is* a good thing because kissing Nathan Durant would be a huge mistake.

I'm not making sense even to myself.

Why would it be a mistake, Shelby? You haven't had a romantic relationship for … a really long time. OK, you've had a couple of flings, but you made sure to pick guys who were so easy-going they were also just as easy to leave. They kind of drifted in and out of your life, leaving a faint smell of surf and weed. You occasionally check their Instagram posts but it's like you're looking at a distant acquaintance, not someone you shared a bed with. The winery has been your only love affair these past years, but let's face it, it's a little one-way.

And you haven't answered the question: why would it be a mistake to kiss Nathan Durant?

OK, me – here's my best thinking for this hour of the night. If Nathan and I get involved, then people will take me even less seriously than they do now. They'll get all gooey about the romantic aspect and ignore everything I'm doing professionally. Cute lil Shelby, isn't it great she finally found a man? He's a Harvard graduate, dontcha know? They hooked up just in time for him to save the winery. Ain't love grand?

Ugh.

And then there's the small issue of my dad. The winery is his legacy, and *I* want Flora Valley Wines to *always* be associated with Billy Armstrong. I don't want some Nathan-come-lately stealing his thunder.

Also, Nathan's made it clear he's in this for the short haul. It's a business contract and once he's fulfilled it, he'll be onto the next one. Adios, as they don't say in France.

But then why do I still care that he didn't want to kiss me, even if I didn't really mean to kiss him? Why???? Answer me that, universe!

I wait. The line to the universe is busy.

I glance over at my alarm clock. Five-ten.

Jordan will be up but she's at some extreme camping overnighter where there's no cell coverage. Chiara keeps international spy hours, so she's almost certainly awake but

I'm not sure I want her to know what happened, even if nothing happened.

Come on, Shelby, that's dumb. She's one of your best friends of all time forever and ever. We look out for each other, us three – Chiara, me and Jordan. Always have, since we were kids.

I text Chiara: *U up?*

Immediately, my phone buzzes.

"Something wrong?" she asks.

"I don't know," I say. "I need to run it by you."

And I explain the almost kiss and his not happy reaction, and it doesn't sound any less embarrassing in the retelling.

Chiara doesn't laugh. She says, "Right. OK," decisively, as if everything is now clear. "This is good."

"It is?" I ask.

"Shel," she says. "You know that because I'm both curious and suspicious, I like to find out about people. Not all people, some are too dull to warrant the effort. A guy like Mr Durant, though, I *will* do my due diligence on."

"OK…?" My voice comes out all squeaky. Is she going to tell me he's a scam artist?

"Hold the worry-horses until I'm finished." Chiara is so bossy sometimes. "Now you told me that he's contracting with McRae Capital, so I called this girl I had a threesome with, who works there, too."

"A *threesome!*"

"You're so easy to shock it's not even sport. No, I'm

kidding. She did a bit of digging into Nathan's background and found a *very* interesting fact."

"Do I want to know?"

"It's for your own good. The winery he managed in Bordeaux? He got engaged to the owner's daughter. They met at Harvard, apparently, and he followed her to France. It's how he got into wine in the first place. They were together for nearly four years before getting engaged, and then, week before the wedding, she dumped him."

"Oh," is my not-very-intelligent response. "Poor Nathan."

"Yes and no," says Chiara. "Yes, it's tough luck to be left at the altar. But don't you get what that *means*?"

"Of course, I don't. I'm a moron."

"He's on the *rebound*." Chiara clears it up for me. "That's why it's a *good* thing that he did not kiss you. You do *not* want to be rebound girl, no matter how hot the guy is."

"Is that why you didn't flirt with him at Bartons?"

"Correcto. Guys who've been dumped – they compensate by becoming overly competitive. They put their dick in charge and set out to *prove* their manliness. Women become like pig buildings in an Angry Birds game, there to be knocked over. Highest score number wins."

"That metaphor's as confused as I am."

"The fact Nathan didn't jump your bones is a good sign that he's a decent human being," Chiara says. "But you should be wary. Rebound guys are more trouble than they're worth."

"So I should definitely just keep it professional?" Even

though Chiara has given me yet another reason not to become involved with Nathan Durant, I have to check, just to be sure.

"Absolutely," says Chiara. "Polite, matter of fact, focused on the work. After all, saving the winery's your priority, isn't it?"

Yep, I'm sure. I think.

In the background, I hear a man's voice. He sounds foreign. Maybe German? And impatient.

Chiara calls out, "I'm talking to my *girl*friend!"

To me she says, "That'll keep him guessing."

"Who's he?"

But Chiara's done advising. She wants to go play "hide the bratwurst" with the German.

"Stay cool, Shel, and you'll be fine. Focus on what's important."

"Love you," I say.

"Love you, too." And she's gone.

There's no point going back to sleep, but instead of thinking thoughts that are strictly professional, I think about how brokenhearted Nathan must have been to be jilted. The only time I've felt truly emotionally devastated was when Dad died. But though grief for him still punches me in the gut, it never makes me feel to blame. Whereas I'd take a bet that perfectionist Nathan is still beating himself up over what he'd see as his own failure.

I know what it's like to want to prove yourself. I can only hope he'll let us prove it together.

Chiara said to play it cool but my nerves are being very uncool this morning. I know Nathan's here because I heard the pickup pull in. He'll be in the office, I guess, where I can't delay being any longer.

The coffee's boiled. I pour two mugs and carry them out. Professionals start the day with caffeine, or if they don't, they should. Plus, I hope he takes it as a sign that we can reset and start again, with no weirdness between us.

His back's to me. He's staring at the calendar on the wall, on which I'm supposed to write important dates but don't because everyone at Flora Valley knows what they are anyway.

Hearing my approach, he turns. Wow, he looks a little rough. Wonder what he got up to after the event that shall nevermore be mentioned?

"Uh, I brought coffee," I say.

Top marks for being obvious, but whatever.

There's a slight hesitation. But then he says, "Thanks."

We're almost conversing. Good start.

And obviously up to me to continue.

"So I guess we should open the kimono," I say.

Where I got that phrase from, I've no idea.

There's a little twitch around Nathan's left eyebrow, but apart from that, his face offers no clue as to what he's thinking.

"Talk about what you've got in mind," I elaborate. "For the winery."

Am I right? Was that a quick show of relief? I wish I was as people-smart as Chiara.

"Sure," he says. "You want to talk here or in the house?"

I can see why he's asking. The office is a little ... crowded. The desk and shelves are covered with files that haven't been filed, as well as books, bills (ugh), memo notes, a half-eaten apple (how long has *that* been there), and a novelty mug I keep pencils in that says *White Trash Wine Glass*. A present from Jordan, who still thinks it's hilarious.

But the house is my personal domain, and I can hear Chiara telling me to keep a professional distance.

"Here's good," I say. "Let me just clear a space."

"I'll come back in an hour, shall I?"

Sarcasm! A welcome sign we're getting back on track.

As it happens, it takes me ten seconds. I lift a pile off the desk and place it on top of another pile on a nearby shelf.

I place a folding chair in front of the desk for me, and gesture for Nathan to take the seat behind it; hastily throw the half-eaten apple in the trash before he does.

"OK." I give him his cue. "What's the plan, man?"

He stares at me, as if trying to decide whether I'm having him on. Verdict goes in favour of me being sincere. Or else he can't be bothered wasting any more time.

"The standard ways that wineries make more money," he begins, "are to increase production, raise prices, and cut operating costs. Flora Valley's production is at capacity, and any new planting we might do would take at least five years to become useful."

"If we raise prices," I butt in, "we'll lose our existing customers."

"You're losing them anyway," he says. "Pre-orders are way down."

Can't deny that. Want to. But can't.

"Your operating costs used to be pretty low," Nathan continues, "but not since you lost your free family labour. Your equipment needs to be replaced, and if we are to have any chance of increasing production in the future, upgraded."

"Is JP prepared to outlay that kind of money?"

He's the only one in any position to do that, so it's a pertinent question.

"On condition, yes."

Here it comes. The plan I asked for – and am not at all sure I want.

"Flora Valley succeeded primarily because of the association with your late father. The downside of that is, the Billy Armstrong brand eclipsed the winery's own brand. Flora Valley Wines needs its own identity now. It needs to reinvent and relaunch. To a new range of customers."

There's no *way* I'm letting him erase my dad from our 'brand'. But if I put my foot down now, that's the end of it. I'll be patient, and I will *not* snap the handle off this coffee mug.

"Go on," I say, with remarkable calm.

"Today's wine consumers are a different breed from even five years ago," he says. "They're vastly more cost-conscious. That doesn't mean they want cheaper wine, but equally, they don't want luxury for luxury's sake. What they want is *value*. And that value comes partly from quality compared to price, but mostly from the experience they feel the wine delivers."

Oh, boy. I'm in a dinghy of ignorance adrift on a sea of jargon. And hating every minute of it.

"How can a wine provide an experience?" I ask, trying not to sound too snippy. "It's not a tour guide."

"No, but the *winery* is," says Nathan. "We need to bring people here, and we need to take the winery to them."

"Bring people here? You mean, like a tasting room?"

This doesn't sound completely terrible, but I'm wary.

"I mean exactly that. Why did your father never set one up?"

"I think Mom objected." I'm trying to remember. "She felt the winery intruded enough into our family life."

"Well, we need one now," says Nathan. "How do *you* feel about it?"

Good question. If I ignore everything else he said about Dad, I can give an honest answer.

"OK, I guess," I say. "It'll be … different."

"We need a website, too. Can't believe you've never had one."

"Dad used to call, and send emails out," I explain. "Thought it was more personal to talk to his customers directly."

The customers who *loved* him.

"Not a bad tactic," Nathan says. "But not efficient. And not broad reaching. Today's wine consumers do a *lot* of online shopping. Those we can't get here in person, we want here virtually. Our website will need to work hard."

I note the "we." But it's not enough to make me feel good about this conversation. He's basically saying that everything Dad and I have done up till now, has been wrong. And though I *do* know we have to change, I resent his wholesale dismissal of our years of hard work.

"Hey."

My thoughts must show on my face. Hopefully, not too plainly.

"This is not a criticism," says Nathan.

OK, my thoughts have come across loud and clear.

"Nothing you've done will go to waste," he tells me. "Flora Valley makes great wine, and that's ultimately all that matters. If we take these initiatives, we can make it a great business, too."

"We" again, and his expression and tone of voice are kind, sincere. I really believe he means it.

All Chiara's advice about being matter-of-fact and focused on the work go out the window. For the first time, I feel someone else has my back, and the relief of that is so immense, I think I might cry.

'Shit," says Nathan. Because would you look at that – I *am* crying. "I'm sorry. I didn't mean to upset you."

"You *haven't*—"

It comes out as a damp hiccup. I look around for a tissue box but the closest paper to hand is the stack of bills and though I'd happily blow my nose on them, Nathan might object.

A handkerchief appears in front of my face. It's white and crisply ironed. Like I've only ever seen in movies.

"Blame my mother," he says. "She slips one in my pants pocket every morning."

My laugh turns into a sneeze, and the handkerchief is no longer crisp. I'm not sure how much snot is acceptable in a professional relationship but it's too late now.

"Thanks," I say. "For this," I crush the handkerchief in my fist, "and for wanting this place to succeed. It means a *lot*."

I finally meet his gaze, and we offer each other a tentative smile. Nathan's a little trapped behind the desk, but he reaches out to give my arm a reassuring pat. The instant we touch, there's an electric flash of connection. At least there is for me. But maybe I'm over-sensitive all round this morning.

Perfect timing for a quiet knock on the door.

"Morning."

It's Cam. Using up one of his limited daily quotas of words.

I'm so full of weird conflicting emotion, I sound like a crazy person.

"Cam! Hi! Come in!"

He edges an inch further inside.

"This is Nathan Durant," I say. "The new manager I told you about. Nathan, this is Cam Hollander, maintenance man and cooper extraordinaire."

Nathan, still trapped behind the desk, reaches across, and Cam leans past me to take his hand.

"Good to meet you," says Nathan.

He doesn't seem to be full of any kind of emotion, let alone weird conflicting ones. But that's possibly because he's fully focused on Cam. Most men do this when they meet Cam. Might have something to do with the fact he's six-five and muscled like a Michelangelo statue. And that he carries himself like the former soldier he is, upright and alert. Ready to move in any direction.

Cam's current choice of direction is out the door again. He only came in because he knew he had to meet Nathan. Having done his duty, that's his people contact over for the day, he heads back to the shed in which he lives and works.

"Cam, how busy are you?" I ask.

He shrugs. "So-so."

There's no point in delaying with Cam or he'll disappear on you. So I plunge right in.

"How would you feel about building us a tasting room?"

Chapter Eight

NATE

So on the plus side, Shelby and I seem to be on a good footing. Luckily, she didn't seem to feel the same jolt I did when I touched her arm. Which I won't be doing again.

On the downside, she's just commissioned Cam, who I'm now calling Survivalist Ken, to construct the new tasting room, without pausing for a second to check with me. We haven't discussed what the damn thing will look like, or even where it'll be situated, so how will he know what to build? He looks like the kind of guy who doesn't much go for a lot of windows. Would prefer, in fact, that the whole place was buried underground, and was eighty percent armoury.

Given the potentially fragile nature of my rapprochement with Shelby, I intend to suck this up. But she and I will have to have a little chat about roles and responsibilities for the future. And I'll ask how much she's paying Cam the Commando. I don't want to find out he's stockpiling gold as well as ammo.

That's another task that's urgent. Getting the books in order. Getting them *out* of actual books and into an online accounting system. With properly organized account codes, so we don't get line items like "Hog care" and "Mom's herbal stuff," which could give quite the wrong impression in some quarters.

No time like the present. Shelby's gone back to work in the house, as this office wasn't built for two. Or one, for that matter. There's a phone here that connects to an extension in the kitchen, so I can call her if I have any questions.

Twenty seconds later.

"Has this computer ever been operational?"

"Did you plug it in?"

I'm a Harvard graduate and experienced manager. I'm also *heinously* hung-over, so it could be a fair call.

"Everything that should be on is on," I tell her. "Except the computer screen. That's still an attractive black."

"Sounds broken to me. I'm no expert, though."

"Is there a computer store in Verity?"

"No idea. I've never needed one."

"And yet you have a broken computer."

"First I've heard of it," she has the nerve to say. "I do everything on my phone, or on paper. Can't you use your laptop?"

The answer should be yes. As it happens, I left it at home, on the floor next to my dignity. Then again, it's a wonder I managed to put my pants on the right way around this morning.

I search "computer repairs" on my phone. There *is* one in Verity. It's called Byte Me. Of course it is.

"I'll take a trip into town," I say. "Need anything?"

"Are you buying?"

"Depends what you want."

On *my* list are super strength Advil, more coffee and possibly hair of the dog.

"Key lime pie from the Cracker Café," she asks.

"Is that the place with the stuffed alligator?"

"Iris is very proud of her Florida roots," Shelby tells me. "Rumour is she killed it herself. With her bare hands."

"I'll make a note not to skimp on the tip."

"Say hi to her from me," Shelby says and hangs up.

Growing up outside of Martinburg, we never had much reason to come to Verity. In this county, cute small towns are a dime a dozen. And Dad wasn't big on family outings that involved cruising main streets and eating in diners. He'd take us hiking, or trail running. If we went to the beach, we were expected to swim at least a mile before he'd countenance any sunbathing.

From the day we turned five, all the Durant kids had to compete in a sport. I picked track, Ava picked track *and* horse riding, Danny chose soccer and the twins tennis, because they could play it together. Weekends were a logistical operation to rival D-Day as we all went in separate directions. Looking back, I'm not sure how Mom felt about spending all day tag-teaming with Dad to drive us around. I never heard her complain.

"Your father wants the best for you," is what she said if any one of us complained about our relentless schedules, and the pressure on us to not only compete but also win.

Mom was the only one we'd ever voice any discontent to. Dad didn't respond well to whining. "Healthy mind needs a healthy body" was his mantra. Along with "Discipline is choosing between what you want and what you want more" and the perennial favourite, "Excuses don't get results."

I'd say it's fortunate that we're all genetically half Dad. None of us Durant kids likes to lose, and we're prepared to put the effort in to make sure we never do.

Still, as I pull up outside the Cracker Café in Verity's tiny, picturesque main street, I wonder what our childhood would have been like if we'd eaten pancakes as a family on weekends, instead of being scattered across the county, amped up on competitive nerves. Those parties around the fire pit, initiated by Ava the rebel, were the first time we kids had connected as a social group. First time we did anything together that felt like fun.

The bell above the door jingles as I enter the diner and the woman behind the counter looks up. She's sixty-ish, all sinews and wire like the gator-wrestler she's rumoured to be, gimlet eyes that alert to a bullshit tolerance of zero. This must be Iris.

She appraises me. I can almost see the words "city slicker" forming in her mind. She'll be checking my palms next to see if I've ever done a hard day's work. The gator Iris may or may not have strangled is mounted on a high shelf to my left, lying full length with its mouth open. It doesn't look as if it likes me, either.

"What can I do for y'all?" she asks.

"Coffee, thank you, ma'am," I say because I've been well brought up, and I don't want her spitting in my cup of joe.

"Nothing to eat?"

I know a threat when I hear one. Thankfully, I can say, "A slice of key lime pie to go. And I'm to tell you Shelby says hi."

My buttering-up tactic is a solid fail.

"You the Harvard fella come in to order her around?"

"No, ma'am." I should have shopped for the Advil *before* I came in for coffee. "We're a team."

"That gal's a hard worker," Iris informs me. "And generous as they come. 'Round here, we're a real community, and folks know we gotta pull together. When the big fires came, we all pitched in, helped those in need. Shelby Armstrong didn't know the meaning of the word 'tired'. She just kept right on until the last job was done."

I'm seriously considering putting my head in that alligator's mouth and slamming its jaws shut to put me out of my misery.

"I appreciate that, ma'am," I say. "I'm looking forward to working here."

"She loved her daddy, too." Iris fires a final shot. "Billy was a fine, upstanding man. His passing was a sad loss for us all."

Finally, she hands me a mug of coffee. Smells good. Not as strong as Shelby's, but anything stronger than that would drop you like a kick to the heart.

"I'll box up the pie," says Iris. "Sit wherever you like."

I'm speculating on whether that means she's softened a fraction, when the bell jingles again, and the door is shoved open with enthusiasm. In strides a tanned, athletic-looking blonde, wearing a climbing harness around her very short shorts, and carrying a safety helmet under one arm.

She spots me, and her face lights up.

"Oh, hey! It's you!"

I swear I have never seen this girl before in my life.

"You're Nathan!"

She holds out her hand to shake mine, and I switch the coffee mug to my left because I'm sure as hell not giving Iris the chance to take it away from me.

"I'm Jordan. Shelby's friend."

Have to say that's a relief. Until I wonder how she recognized me so easily. How exactly has Shelby described me?

"Chiara said you guys had drinks at Bartons last night," she says. "Rather you than me. I mean Ted's great and all that, but those cocktails are like what the hell, could I not just have a beer, right?"

"Right."

"Thanks for driving Shel home. Ted said you were—" She puts on a bad English accent "—quite the gentleman."

No aspect of my life will be private here. May as well accept that now.

"And you've met Javi and Cam, too." She rams home my point. "God, Cam, he's so hot. Love those strong, silent types."

Opposites attract, I guess. Though I can't see why she'd go for any guy who has recipes for roadkill.

"Jordan, honey, I've got your lunch order out back. I'll fetch it."

Iris is smiling. She likes Jordan. Jury's out on whether *I've* come up any notches in her estimation.

Thing is, I like Jordan, too. She's impossible *not* to like. Cheerful, full of energy, slightly chaotic. Like a basketful of Labrador puppies.

"What's with the gear?" I gesture to her harness and helmet. "Rock climbing?"

"Yeah. Got a summer holiday group of teens," she says. "Mostly boys."

Hope their hormones let them focus on the climbing or there'll be carnage.

Iris drops a giant box full of sandwiches and glazed donuts on the counter. If you didn't know they were for a group of teens, you'd think she was catering for an army.

"Thanks, Iris, you're a star."

I'm about to ask whether Jordan needs help carrying the box when she lifts it off the counter like it's made of air.

"You should come for a beer with us at the Silver Saddle," she says to me. "Friday's our girls' night but you can crash it, seeing you know us all now."

My alcohol-fuzzed brain manages to work out that "us all" means Jordan, Chiara and Shelby. I'd need something stronger than beer to keep up with those three. Guess I foresee another hangover in *my* future.

"Sure," I say. "Thanks."

Jordan smiles. "You know, Shelby was worried you'd be a total dick, but I think she kind of likes you now."

Seems my opinion on that subject is irrelevant, as Jordan shouts a cheerful goodbye to Iris, who's out back again, and heads toward the door.

I go to open it for her, but she says, "I got it" and proves that to be the case by deftly balancing the giant box in one hand and yanking open said door with the other. If any of those teenage boys do slip on the rocks, I suspect Jordan could lift them by the scruff of the neck, no trouble.

I watch her leave, then turn back to find Iris behind the counter giving me a hard stare.

"Pie." She pushes a much smaller box toward me. Nods at my mug. "Refill?"

The truthful answer would be yes. But the thought of sitting alone, with Iris giving me the evils from the counter and the alligator doing the same from the wall, is too much in my current state.

"I have to find the computer repair store," I tell her.

"Byte Me," she says, with ambiguous emphasis. "Next to Curl Up and Dye. Hair salon," she adds, in case I'm simple. "'bout halfway down."

I pay for the coffee and pie, and leave a generous tip that Iris ignores. As I walk out, I can *feel* her eyes burning holes in my back.

Luckily, the computer store is also next to the pharmacy,

and the repair guy is neither hostile nor overly chatty. He says the computer isn't worth fixing, so we negotiate a price for a new one, and a printer that doesn't take five minutes to spit out one page. The Advil kicks in as I head to the pickup, so by the time I make it back to Flora Valley, I'm a much happier human.

Or I am until I spot Shelby in a huddle with Cam the Mountain Mute on the rustic porch seat outside her house. I have her pie in my hand, but I can't bring myself to man up and give it to her. I don't want to see how close they're really sitting or hear what they're talking about.

What I *want* to do is punch Montana Moron in the head. I want to lay him out with one blow and line dance on his huge, unconscious body.

Shit. I've crushed Shelby's pie.

Shit and quadruple shit, I'm jealous.

Last time, I felt like this, I was in love.

Chapter Nine

SHELBY

I had to break it to Cam that Nathan will be a big part of the tasting room project. Cam doesn't like dealing with strangers. Any new customers he gets come through existing ones, and we're the go-betweens until Cam's comfortable with the new peeps. This has been known to take months. Most people don't mind, because of the quality of his work. He's an old-style master craftsman, with a real affinity for wood.

The most anyone's been able to glean about Cam's origins are that he grew up in Wyoming. He joined the army straight from school, did several tours of the Middle East, and was invalided out. Came to the Flora Valley area nine years ago and Dad was his first customer. That's it, that's all we know. No further details spilled through fireside yarns or drunken confessions. Of course, Cam doesn't ever have more than one drink, so there's that.

These days, he makes barrels and fixes pretty much

79

everything except the most technical equipment around here. Every weekend, he helps out with the local Riding for the Disabled. It's mostly kids. They love Cam. We *all* love Cam. None of us has a clue what makes him tick.

"I thought I'd ask Javi if he could rustle up some labor to help," I tell him.

We're sitting on the porch seat, which he made for Mom. If anyone *does* know Cam, it's Mom. But she'll keep his secrets. She's good at that.

Sometimes I wonder if Cam knew Mom was planning to sell up. All the time Dad was sick, she never said a word to me about the future. I didn't know about the artist's cottage she had her eye on. I *really* didn't know how hard she'd found our life here, how much of a toll the lack of money and all the effort Dad expected us to put in had taken. I didn't realize how important her art was to her, and what a wrench it'd been to put it on the back burner for so long.

I didn't know because she never said. At least, she never said it to me.

No point in asking Cam if Mom had talked to him. Might as well interrogate one of his barrels.

"How many builders do you think you'd need?" I prompt because that's what you have to do with Cam.

"Depends," he says.

On the design, the budget, the materials, and all that detail stuff, is what he means. It also means that he's open to working with others. I've spent six years learning to interpret Cam-speak.

"Boss man," he says next.

Which means Nathan's back. With pie!

I follow Cam's gaze, and yep, that's Nathan, but he's not coming my way. He's heading back to the office. At pace, like he's forgotten something. Or he's in a cranky mood.

Fig. I was feeling OK and now I'm not. I hate that.

"OK?"

I must have sighed. Cam's brown eyes show concern. He worried about me a lot after Dad died. I know because he did a lot of repairs without charging me. It was his way of saying I could rely on him. I knew that already, but it was nice to have it reinforced.

But Cam doesn't need to hear all my troubles. Or maybe I don't want him to feel obliged to help me sort them out. I need to stand on my own two feet.

"Got a lot to do," I say. "And a short window of opportunity to get it done."

Cam knows what I'm implying. Flora Valley Wines is up against the clock.

He stands and drops a big, rough hand on my shoulder. It's meant to reassure and it does. No need for words.

Cam heads away, and I sit on the porch seat until I can't put off Nathan contact any longer. Besides, I'm desperate for pie. I hope Iris added her usual avalanche of whipped cream.

The office door is ajar. I poke my head round and he's at the desk, going through the account books, frowning. I don't see Iris's usual take-out box anywhere, and it seems a little rude to make "Where's my pie?" my opening line.

So I say, "Hi."

Which isn't much better.

"Will the computer live?"

May as well keep making an effort.

He shakes his head, pencils a note on the pad in front of him.

"Does it want to be buried or cremated?"

OK, dumb jokes. But come on, buddy, play along!

There's no play in his steady look.

"I've already wasted a morning," he says. "These books are a mess. Can I get on?"

At first, I'm taken aback by the coldness in his expression. It's like when we first met, in JP's office. He was so aloof and uncommunicative. But not the way Cam is. Cam keeps his distance, but at least he *cares*. He cares about the winery and he cares about me. And for a moment earlier this morning, I thought Nathan did too. But now he's looking at me like I'm nothing, a waste of his time. It's the look a bunch of the investors before JP gave me, that made me feel like a stupid little girl. Is that how Nathan sees me after this morning? A stupid weak little crybaby? Now, I'm taken aback by how *angry* I feel. If he has a problem with me, why doesn't he come out and say it! And *why* does he suddenly have a problem? What did I do? For fig's sake, this morning he was kind! He gave me a clean handkerchief that his mom ironed! He said 'we' like we were a team! So how the fig *dare* he suddenly pull this superior thing-swinging act!

"No, you can't get on with the messy books," I tell him.

I grab the folding chair and plant my rear in it.

"Not until you tell me what's going on with you."

There it is again, that slight twitch of his left eyebrow.

"Nothing's—"

"Bull crap." It's the closest I get to real swears, and it only happens when I'm crabby. "You were fine this morning. Now you're not. What happened?"

"N—"

"Say 'Nothing' again and I'll stab you with that pencil."

I probably should pick it up if I want to make good on that threat.

Too late. Nathan's got it. He starts rolling it between his fingers.

"I can find another pencil here somewhere," I say. "Come back in an hour."

Not even a hint of a smile for that pretty darn good joke.

"Look," he says, while not actually looking at me. "You and I have totally different modus operandi—"

"Yikes."

"Ways of working," he adds.

"I do know words," I say. "I'm just allergic to jargon."

Now, he looks at me. Coolly. One eyebrow raised.

"Is that right?"

I fold my arms in a totally not defensive pose.

"Circling back so we can get on the same page going forward." I *might* be digging myself into a hole. "That kind of jargon."

Nathan nods, slowly. Picks up a sheet of paper and scans it.

"*Malolactic fermentation,*" he reads out. "*Tensile and incisive structure.*"

He scans further down. "*Chewy tannins. Volatile acidity—*"

"All right!"

Smarty-pants.

Nathan replaces the sheet of paper. He's still not smiling.

"As I was saying, you and I have very different ways of working, and I think we should establish a clear delineation of responsibilities."

I understand those words loud and clear.

"You mean – you'll do your stuff and I'll do mine, and we'll keep out of each other's way?"

There's that twitch above the left eyebrow again but all he says is, "Yes."

So much for 'we'. So much for kind. Looks like the only person round here that cares for me is Cam.

Who will object to being delineated?

"What about Cam?" I ask.

The twitch moves down to a muscle in the left jaw.

"I'll liaise with Cam."

'I don't think that's a good idea," I say. "Cam's used to me, and he'll take a while to get comfortable with you."

About a decade.

"And we have projects to get on with," I continue, " Like the tasting room."

Which was *your* idea in the first place! I don't add.

He sighs. It's *super* annoying. I'm getting angry again.

"Shelby, you're the winemaker. Everything to do with

making wine is your domain, and I respect your expertise. Everything else, including the budget, is my responsibility, and I hope you'll respect *my* decisions as well."

"So I get to make wine but I can't spend any money doing it?"

Now he's the one looking annoyed. Well, I wouldn't sound so petulant if he wasn't being so figging patronizing!

"Setting aside the fact that there's fuck-all money to spend, you can make requests for whatever you need, and I'll do my best to make it happen. No guarantees but I'll do what I can. If the request is reasonable, that is."

He just had to throw that in, didn't he? That little jab.

"Fine."

I'm leaving.

"I'll make my wine, you operandize, or whatever. And never the twain shall meet."

I'm at the door. Determined to have *one* more say.

"But if you want coffee, you can get your own from now on. And if Iris puts gator milk in it don't come crying to me!"

Chapter Ten

NATE

Shelby has given me a lot to think about. Such as – how do you milk a gator? Apart from carefully.

Come on, Nate. Stop hiding behind jokes. You acted like a complete heel just now and you know it. You hid behind a wall of corporate-speak instead of being honest and upfront. Shelby didn't deserve that.

But would being upfront have been any better? What should I have said – I'm shitting myself because I think I might be falling in love with you? It's not a statement to inspire confidence. I'm her boss, for one, which I just made abundantly clear in the most asshole-like way. But the truth is I *am* in charge and that means making decisions that are rational, not emotional. How could Shelby trust that I'll do what's best for the winery and not just what would please her? How could *I* trust *myself* to do that?

Then there's the whole knotty, gnarly mess of my previous relationship. And my reluctance to accept that I was the author of my own downfall. Now that the hurt of being jilted has subsided a little, I've been able to get a better handle on what kind of hurt it actually is. And I can tell you that it's not betrayal and it's not heartbreak. It's shame. Because I failed.

When I met Camille at Harvard, she was going out with a rich and successful older guy. I was nothing but a debt-laden student. I thought I loved her but I can see now that my feelings for her were more proprietary. She was mine, a prize. Evidence that I was a winner.

The guy she dumped *me* for was a musician. A drummer in some Norwegian death metal band. I didn't even know she *liked* death metal, that's how shitty a boyfriend I was. She dumped me because I put her second. Way, *way* second, aka last. I shut out all extraneous information, like requests for us to spend more time together, and focused entirely on the work. Because building up that winery was another prize to be won. A bigger prize than Camille.

In short, I behaved like an arrogant ass, and I got what was coming to me. Mr Perfectionist-Hates-to-Lose failed publicly and spectacularly. But it was my ego that got hurt, not my heart. And it might be my ego that's fuelling this bout of jealousy. Might be that I don't know what it even means to be in love.

As I said, none of the above exactly inspires confidence. If I were Shelby, I'd keep a wide berth.

Oh, yeah – that's exactly what I just forced her to do. Good job, Nate. Why not burn the winery to the ground like you have with the rest of your life? It'll save time.

Shit, and then there's Dad. Anxiety about him – and Mom – is my constant companion, along with the nagging feeling that I should be doing more to get him to see sense. But so far, my brain's stayed empty of bright ideas. Every medical fact we present to him, he counters with some spurious 'research' that he totally believes is also fact. And if he continues to blatantly ignore the toll his stubbornness is taking on Mom, the woman he loves most, then he'll be impervious to any emotional blackmail us kids try to pull on him. So what's left? He drops dead and we all stand around his corpse chanting, "We told you so"?

Which reminds me that I haven't checked with the twins to find out whether they actually did manage to take Mom to lunch. I should be getting on with the winery accounts, like I told Shelby, but right now, I want to talk to someone who doesn't think I'm a *complete* POS.

"We were just about to call you!" says Izzy.

My little sister always sounds bright and breezy, but the pessimist in me has to double-check. "Everything OK?"

"Mom refused to take time out for lunch, sigh, but she *has* agreed to come for a quick tea and scones at that cute new place down the road from us with the cows. You want to join us?"

"The cows?"

"The ones that you pour milk out of!"

"Iz, I'm no farmer but I'm pretty sure you don't *pour* milk out of cows."

"These ones you do," she tells me. "I'll drop you a pin. We'll be there at three."

I sit for a moment while my sense of duty fights my wish to not be anywhere in proximity to Shelby Armstrong. The pile of paper otherwise known as the winery accounts looks up at me accusingly, as does the new computer, now installed with the latest accounting software. I should be doing my job as boss. I should be operandizing, as Shelby put it.

Goddammit. I grab my pickup keys and check my phone to see where Izzy dropped the pin. It's a café called Potters, which seems to have nothing at all to do with cattle. But what do I know?

When I pull up outside, I *do* know that I should have asked who Izzy meant by 'we'. I thought she and Max were the ones taking Mom out, but Danny's Porsche is parked beside Mom's SUV and that means there's no chance Ava won't be here, too. I love my siblings, but I was hoping for a peaceful afternoon where the loudest noise would be the genteel clink of teacups on saucers. Instead, it's highly likely this will end with whipped cream splattered up the walls.

The café is one of those that brings to mind the word 'whimsical' and not necessarily in a good way. It's a riot of British-themed twee, with the centerpiece being an extensive collection of small porcelain animals all dressed in human clothing. Like mementoes of some miniature Island of Dr Moreau.

"Nate!"

Izzy calls me over to their table, on which has been placed a three-tier stand filled with tiny sandwiches, scones and cakes, as if they'd been baked for the porcelain animals instead of full-size humans. There's also a floral-patterned teapot and matching cups, and bowls holding sugar cubes, butter and preserves. And a milk jug shaped like a cow. Got it.

"About time," is Ava's greeting, after I've kissed Mom's cheek and sat down. "We weren't going to hold back much longer."

"Here, Mom," says Max. "Let me serve you before the horde descends."

"Who are you calling a horde?" says Ava. "And don't skimp on Mom's plate. You know there won't be a hope in hell of seconds."

"My point exactly," says Max.

"No squabbling, children," says Mom. There's a faint smile on her face, which is a relief to see.

"There'll be no squabbling at all so long as I get that mini macaron," says Ava.

"*I* want the macaron," protests Izzy. "You *know* they're my favourite!"

"Problem solved," says Danny, and he grabs said macaron and stuffs it in his mouth. "Mm-mm," he says, smirking through pink meringue crumbs.

"You're such a dick," says Izzy, but she's smiling. Unlike some of our other siblings, who will remain nameless, she's quick to forgive. And unlike one of those nameless siblings, she never does anything she needs to be forgiven for.

"You're looking a little pale and interesting there, bro," says Ava. "Hangover? Or something else?"

"Don't interrogate me," I reply. "I'm not in the mood."

Ava shrugs, but before I can find out whether that means she'll back off, Mom pipes up.

"Nathan, dear. Tell us about this young woman you're working with. Is her name Shelby? JP says she's a delight."

Of course, JP will have talked to Mom. There are no boundaries between McRae Capital and the family Durant. But I can hardly tell Mom to back off, so I give the answer I assume she wants to hear.

"Shelby Armstrong. Her dad Billy founded the winery. She's a talented winemaker."

"Thought you said she was a nut?" says Danny. "Like the worst kind of manic pixie dream girl?"

I'll kill him later. Choke him with pink macarons.

"Let's just say first impressions weren't favourable." My poker face is on full. "But she knows her stuff. Flora Valley Wines are top quality."

"Is she cute?" says Max.

I'll choke him, too.

"How does *that* matter?" says Izzy. "Why don't you ask about her *winemaking* skill instead of her appearance?"

"Because I want to know if she's cute," says Max, the wind-up kid.

"She *is* cute!" Danny, goddamn him, has been googling on his phone.

He shows the screen to Max, who whistles. "Cute as a *button*."

"You're both sexist pigs and I hate you," says Izzy.

"Do *you* want to see what she looks like?" Danny asks her.

"No!"

But Ava says, "Of course!"

When she sees the photo of Shelby, she gives me a curious look. Which I avoid.

"OK, *fine!*" says Izzy. "Give it here!" And she snatches the phone from Ava.

"Oh, she's so *pretty*," Izzy sighs. "Those amazing *eyes*. Look, Mom—"

Mom slips on her reading glasses and peers at the phone screen. "She seems like a very sweet young woman," is her verdict. "JP was surprised that she's still single. Said he thought she would have been snapped up by some handsome young man well before now."

I'm going to choke *myself*. Shove a whole three-tier cake stand down my throat.

"It'd be a bad choice for her to become *Nate's* girlfriend, though," says Max.

My gut feels like he's punched it with a cow jug. Why? What does he know?

"If Nate can't turn the winery around," Max explains, "that'd be a relationship-killer right there. Hard for love to stay strong when your dreams are in ruins."

"You underestimate Shelby," I say, without thinking. "She's held the place together all on her own *and* got investment. I won't be the only one working to turn Flora Valley around. We'll do it together. And we *will* make it a success."

"So you've changed your mind about her being a nut?" says Ava. She nods slowly. "Interesting…"

Mom says, "Of *course* you'll succeed. JP would never have asked you to step in if he didn't have complete confidence in you."

Mom means well, but I'm dying here. I can feel the eyes of all the little porcelain animal-people judging me. Gotta go, or I might start to hyperventilate.

"Sorry, team." I put on my calm voice. "I have to get back. Got at least another four hours of work ahead of me."

"Don't work too hard," says Mom.

She looks worried, and I feel like a heel. She has enough worries, already.

"Promise," I lie, as I kiss her goodbye.

As I get the hell out of the café, I can hear Max and Ava fighting over the untouched scone on my plate.

I make it about five miles down the road before I have to pull over. It's a quiet, rural area, nothing but trees and fields and the odd horse. I roll down the window and breathe in big gulps of clean, fresh air. And try to get my scrambled thoughts in order.

When Max said it was a bad idea for Shelby to be my girlfriend, I almost brained him with a floral teapot. When I said that she and I would turn the winery around together, I meant it. Because I want it to be true. I want to work alongside Shelby all day, and at night, I ... yep, OK, I want that. I want to remove her faded t-shirt and shorts and kiss every freckle on her naked body. I want her to look at me the way she looks at Survivalist Ken, instead of the way she looked at me today. Disappointed, hurt and rightly pissed off.

I don't think this is ego, because it doesn't feel like it did when I set my sights on Camille. I don't want to *win* Shelby. I want her to want me back. And maybe, eventually, after I've earned it, fall in love with me.

But I can't make her do any of these things. And I might have to accept that she never will.

I recall a saying of Ava's: *Today sucked but there's always tomorrow to punch in the balls.* It's not going to feature on any kitchen sampler or motivational meme site but right now, I appreciate its sentiment.

Better get back to Flora Valley Wines. I wasn't lying when I told Mom I had a *lot* of work to catch up on.

Chapter Eleven

SHELBY

I don't like being angry. I don't like holding grudges or feeling resentful. To me, that's always seemed a waste of energy. I mean, does *anyone* want their gravestone epitaph to be, *I'm glad I spent so much time hating on everything*? I'll probably wish I'd been more organized, but I'll never wish I'd been closer to friends and family. OK, maybe closer in a physical sense, but I talk to my siblings all the time – we have a group chat where we post ridiculous nonsense, and we know we can call each other up if we're in trouble. And though Mom's on the coast now, it's less than an hour's drive away. Whenever I feel the need to be blinded by every colour on the spectrum and drink tea that looks like it was swept up last Fall, I know I'll always be welcome.

The biggest reason I don't like being angry is that when it fades away, all I'm left with is sadness. I thought Nate and I were connecting but then he slammed a great big iron door between us called 'delineation of responsibilities'. I may not have to do the accounts anymore – thank you, thank you – but now it looks like if I want to communicate with Nate about anything, I'll have to slip a note under the office door, or tie it to one of the dog's collars and send it instead. It'll be like it was after Dad died, when despite knowing that everyone had my back, I'd never felt so alone.

I didn't cope with that too well, to be honest. I threw myself into working and stalking investors, but one morning, three months after Dad died, I couldn't get out of bed. Just ... couldn't move.

Cam was the one who found me. Called Mom, who was on an artists' retreat – her way of coping with the loss. She dropped her brushes and came back right away, bless her. Got our family doctor around, who diagnosed depression caused by grief and exhaustion, and put me on meds. Jordan, Chiara, and Mom took turns being with me, even though I was *terrible* company. And my siblings called every day.

When the meds kicked in, I felt a million times better. Good news for my minders, because I hadn't had the energy to shower for days, and I was *rank*. In a couple of weeks, I felt almost back to my old self, enough to get up and get going again. Stayed on the meds for twelve weeks, then eased my way off them. Our doctor said I shouldn't hesitate to go back on them if I felt I was struggling. So far, I've been OK.

But Nate suddenly putting up walls again has really knocked me. I feel small and vulnerable and a little scared.

Which is probably why I'm curled up on our couch with all the cats and dogs I could muster, and a big mug of hot chocolate to make up for not getting a piece of Iris's pie. I squirted so much ReddiWip on top that I can't actually get any liquid in my mouth without burying my entire nose in cream. I guess there are *some* advantages to being alone.

The sweet drink does its work and soothes me to the point where I can address the question that's still nagging away – why? *Why* did Nathan do this sudden about-face? What changed between this morning and when he came back from Verity with, as Iris would say, a burr up his butt? And why didn't he give me a straight answer when I asked him that exact question earlier?

PSA: a sugar high isn't real motivation. Like being drunk isn't real courage. Luckily for me, when I storm off to the office again and try to open the door, I can't – it's locked. I didn't hear the pickup drive off. Probably happened when I was squirting whipped cream out of the can; that sucker sounds like a tornado. But the pick-up's definitely not here. And neither is Nate.

I'm coming down off the sugar buzz, so my main frustration is that I can't ransack the office to find my slice of pie. Mostly, I'm relieved. If I can't get an answer from Nate, I can't be hurt if it's something I don't want to hear.

Like he doesn't want us to be friendly because then it'll be that much harder to tell me that the winery isn't going to make it.

Or like someone in Verity let slip about my breakdown. They would have meant well, probably did it to make sure

Nate looked after me. But if he suspected I was a flake before, now he knows that for sure.

OK, now I'm sad again. And if I have another hot chocolate, I'll throw up. It's gone four-thirty, so I don't expect Nate will be back again today. Guess I'll just get on with my chores. Feed the pigs, dogs, cats, and Dylan. Make sure the outbuildings are secure, though Cam will probably have done that already. Schlep back to the house. Spend the evening alone. Again...

Snap out of it, Shel. If you need cheering up, call your siblings. Call Jordan or Chiara. Call your Mom! You have *plenty* of people who love you. Count your blessings. And stop coming up with doom scenarios for why Nathan pushed you away. His reasons could be nothing to do with you at all.

I keep myself busy for another couple of hours. The cats and dogs inhale their kibble. The pigs go insane for leftover zucchini and ignore perfectly good lettuce. Dylan seizes the opportunity to snatch the lettuce from my hand and attack it for not being corn. As I guessed, Cam's made sure the outbuildings are secure, but I'm happy to walk around, as it gives me an excuse to enjoy the familiar scents and sounds in the soft end of day light. This is my home, the only one I've ever known. It's a cliché, but if I ever had to let Flora Valley Wines go, a huge chunk of my heart would go with it. And I'm not sure I'd ever fully recover.

All the more reason to keep my chin up, as Ted would say, and put everything I've got into making our winery a success.

My loop back to the house takes me past the office. There's a light on inside! I hastily check. Nate's pickup's here. Not a burglar. Good news.

What's he doing here at this hour? I know Harvard people work insane hours, but this isn't Goldman Money-Sacks, it's little old Flora Valley Wines. We work super hard in the busy times, but for the rest, we go with the seasonal flow. But it's possible that flow is a foreign concept to Nate.

Doom scenario #1 takes hold again. Namely that he's having to pull the hours because we're seriously in the cack. Fig. I need reassurance. Wish me luck – I'm going in.

"Shit!"

I've startled him. "Sorry. Only me."

Nate flops back in his chair, running his hand through his hair.

"I'm a little wound up," he says, with a quick rueful smile. "Been a day."

I edge closer and say, cautiously, "Anything I can help with?"

To my surprise, he doesn't go all stony-faced. His expression is more embarrassed, and I'm not sure how to read it.

"I owe you an apology," he says.

Now, I'm startled. "OK?"

"For the way I spoke to you. I was being a *connard*. That's French for asshole."

Nate picks up the pencil like he did this morning, staring at it as he rolls it round. The folding chair is still opposite his desk, so I sit quietly down. I don't want to do anything to break the mood. Whatever this mood is.

He looks at me, and the embarrassed expression is back, but I can see he's also filled with resolve.

"Shelby, do you know why I left France?"

Yes, but I'm not supposed to. I shake my head.

"I was engaged to be married," he says. "She dumped me on my ass, the week before the wedding."

"Ouch."

A hint of a smile. "Yeah, hard landing, that one."

"I'm sorry."

"So was I," he says. "I was the most sorry fucker you've ever seen."

"Nothing to be ashamed of."

He screws up his mouth. "Maybe not. But all the stuff leading up to that, I can *totally* be ashamed of. I – wasn't a committed boyfriend, let's put it that way."

It's out before I can stop it. "You did the boinky-boink with someone else?"

His eyes go all wide, like he's trying *really* hard not to laugh.

"The *boinky-boink*?"

Then he's gone, laughing loud and long, while I blush deep and red.

"Oh, man," he says, wiping his eyes. "And to answer your question, I did *not* do the ... thing ... with someone else. I just wasn't around enough. I threw myself into work and I neglected her. Simple and stupid as that."

'You probably thought she'd understand because it was her family's business," I say, blithely.

Then I freeze. Nate does too. There's a chilly little pause.

"You knew all this already." It's not a question. "Let me guess – Chiara?"

I bite my lip and nod.

"Is there anything Chiara knows about me that I don't know but really ought to know?"

"Almost certainly," I say.

He blows out a breath.

"I'm glad you told me, though," I say. "And if it helps you feel better, I haven't had *any* proper relationships."

"Why not?" He seems genuinely perplexed.

"Oh…" I'm blushing again. "I just … haven't had time. Or met the right person."

Or made any effort to look for them.

"Shit." He says it under his breath.

"I'm fine!" I say, because mostly, I am. "Don't worry about me."

He blinks, like I've brought him back from a whole other train of thought.

"Glad to hear it," he says, quietly.

We stare at each other for a moment. The lighting in here isn't great, and it's hard to tell if it's casting those shadows on his face, or if he's tired. Guess it's been a long day for both of us.

"You know," I'm taking a risk here. "I really believe we'd work better as a proper team, rather than being … delineated."

I spot a half smile and am half hopeful I haven't blown it.

"I had the same idea," he says. "What I said this morning – I had a reason, but it was a stupid one. That's why I owe you an apology."

He extends his hand across the desk. "Can we start over?"

I shake it overly hard because I'm *so* relieved. He winces.

"I need to get back to the gym," he says, shaking out his hand.

"There's a good one in Verity," I tell him. "Called the Jim-Nasium, because it's owned by—"

"A guy called Jim?"

"You'd think so, wouldn't you?"

I choose to believe he likes it when I wind him up, though he does have a *very* good poker face. A ridiculously handsome good poker face. I'm dying to ask what his stupid reason was, but I won't push my luck.

"Do you really have to work, or can you go home now?" I ask, instead.

It's like I've pulled out the workaholic bung and given him permission to deflate. He literally sags in the chair.

"Yeah, I should go home," he sighs. "The numbers are starting to blur together and that's a bad thing with numbers."

He stands, and so do I, He puts on his jacket, and drops his phone into a pocket. I still have a lettuce leaf in my own pocket, but he doesn't need to know that. I hold open the door as he switches off the inside light. The feeble security light is our only illumination, as we hover outside.

"I can bring you coffee in the morning," I offer. "I'll hold the gator milk."

To my astonishment, he bends and kisses my cheek. For a fleeting moment, I breathe in his scent, a hint of sweat and something spicy, and my body lights up like a Christmas tree. I almost, *almost* grab him and pull his mouth fully onto mine, but he steps back. And it's too dark for me to properly see his face.

But his voice sounds calm and normal, as he says, "See you in the morning."

And all I can do is say, "Yep, see you then."

Chapter Twelve

NATE

I deserve a medal. OK, only a bronze one because I *did* kiss her cheek. But what I *wanted* to do was pull her to me, kiss her full on the mouth, explore that sweetness with my tongue, gently bite those freckled lips, and...

Merde. My balls tighten ominously. I'm about to disgrace myself like some horny teen in his first clinch behind the barn. Which is not the explanation I want to give the highway patrol officer when I get pulled over for erratic driving. Focus on the road, Nate. Dying in a ditch with a hard-on is not how you want to go. At least, not today.

I make it back home without incident but also without *any* idea of how to deal with any of this. I can't deny what I feel for Shelby because thoughts of her consume me every hour I'm awake. Is this what love is? I thought about Camille all the time in those early days, but only because I was obsessed with winning her. My train of thought with Camille was on a single track. Whereas when I think about

Shelby, it's like I'm looping the loop on some lunatic rollercoaster and being thrown between heady exhilaration and sheer terror.

The exhilaration is more than sexual, though I can't deny I've imagined having her in every way physically possible. It's also the prospect of being with someone who, to put it simply, brightens my life. Someone who's kind and generous and funny. Someone I can laugh with, *relax* with. I never fully let my guard down with anyone, not even family – *especially* not family. But I feel like I can with Shelby. I can imagine us together on her couch, surrounded by cats and dogs, watching the log fire crackle away and just … *being* with each other. No expectations other than respect and affection. I can't explain how much I want this.

But then there's the terror. What if I can't change? What if I'm always going to be a control freak who keeps his emotions locked up tight? What if I won't have enough time for Shelby because saving Flora Valley Wines will require me to work my ass off? And what if I can't save it, no matter how hard I work? As little brother Max said – damn his eyes – it's hard for love to survive the destruction of your dreams.

So many what-ifs. I hate what-ifs. They peck away at my brain, and I can't shut them up, the pecky fuckers.

As I pull into our driveway, I wonder again whether it'd be better for my mental health if I checked into a hotel. But then, I remember – again – that the whole point is for me to save as much of my salary as possible in case the worst happens with Dad, and Mom needs help. She'll resist selling this place until she absolutely has to, but the cost of its upkeep is not insignificant to put it mildly. Dad's never talked about life insurance so we're only guessing that he's got some. He's always been financially prudent but that might be doing battle with his unwillingness to confront mortality. All the more reason for us Durant kids – well, mainly me – to build Mom up a nest egg. All the more reason to work my ass off to save Flora Valley Wines. And here we go round again.

I'm too late for dinner, and everyone seems to have retreated to their rooms. I'm not unhappy about that. In the kitchen, there's a note stuck on the oven in Ava's handwriting that says 'EAT!!!'. Which is ironic because my sister lives on protein bars and air, as far as I can tell.

Inside the oven, there's a foil-covered plate and under the foil, there's Mom's famous mac-and-cheese, and I'm suddenly so hungry I almost grab a handful and shove it into my mouth. But even though the kitchen is empty, I feel Mom's presence. I still wolf it down so fast I'm at risk of choking, but at least I'm using a fork.

I rinse my plate, load it into the dishwasher and grab a beer from the fridge. I'll drink it in my room because if I don't head up those stairs now, I soon won't have the energy to move.

On my bedroom door, there's another note in Ava's handwriting. 'NOW SLEEP!!!' Again, ironic coming from her. Ava's never outgrown her infant sleeping habits which according to Mom and Dad almost resulted in her being driven to the nearest mountainside and abandoned. My own sleeping habits, apparently, were perfectly regimented, which says all it needs to say.

As I close the door, I spy a third note. 'NO SCREENS!! NO ALCOHOL!!' On the bedside table, there's a glass of milk and a plate of Mom's chocolate chip cookies. And yet another note that says, 'YOU'RE WELCOME!'

I'm a grown-ass man and I can do what I want, but I set down the beer and pick up the glass of milk. And, yes, I do dunk the cookies in it. My token rebellion is to skip brushing my teeth. Sue me, Tooth Fairy.

Now, I'd like to be able to say that as soon as my head hits the pillow, I sleep like the dead. But this is me we're talking about. I lie here in the dark and let the what-ifs peck away at my brain until my own exhaustion calls time and forces the blackness to overtake me.

Chapter Thirteen

SHELBY

OK, so unlike the last time I almost kissed him which would definitely have been a mistake, *this* time felt like it would have been a lot *less* of a mistake. But I don't know why.

I still have Chiara's 'rebound guy' warning in my head, and the small technical issue of him being my boss hasn't got any smaller. So, what's different? Maybe it was because he apologized. It takes courage to admit you've been wrong. And he also admitted his reasons for being cranky were stupid, which is cute. Frustrating that I don't know what those reasons are, but I get the feeling that with time, he'd tell me.

I like that. I like that he thinks it's important to be honest. Honest people are dependable. And it occurs to me now that some important people in my life have fallen short in the dependability stakes. Dad, for one.

I loved my dad so much. *So,* so much. One of the reasons

I stayed with the winery was that I just had to be near him. Soak up his optimistic energy like I was a plant and it was sunlight. When he wasn't around, I felt … less alive. I guess that's why I crashed so hard when he died.

But the truth is – and I can hardly bring myself to even *think* this – he let me down. He promised that the winery would pass to me, but he never did anything about it. He put both Mom and me in a *terrible* position, one that could have broken our relationship. I have to be grateful that Mom believes clarity equals kindness, and so I was never in any doubt about how she felt or what she planned to do. But, and again this is hard to admit, she chose her own well-being over mine, and my siblings let her. Between them, they made it so I had to *fight* for a chance to keep ownership of Flora Valley Wines.

This is unfair, I know it is. It was never that simple. And I know without a shadow of a doubt that Mom and my brothers and sister love me dearly, and never want to see me suffer. But deep down inside me, there's a little seam of hurt that not one of them stood by my side after Dad died. I had to fight all on my own.

I'm no psychologist, but I can see why I might be attracted to Nathan Durant. He's honest and hard-working like my dad totally was. But I truly believe that Nate will do everything he can to save Flora Valley Wines. So, he's also a guy I can depend on.

And he's *hot*, oh, my Lord. He is *smoking*. Which is not the sole basis for a relationship but sure does add to it. The spot on my cheek where he kissed me is still tingling, and I swear his scent has lingered. It can't be the cats and dogs because they smell like cats and dogs, not like a hot sexy man.

The smallest dog is snoring with a cute whiffling noise, and I'd better sleep, too. No good decisions have ever been made at two in the morning. And tomorrow, I want to be bright and sharp for my first proper day as a member of the Flora Valley Wines Management Team of Two.

I hear Nate's pickup pull in as I'm putting the coffee pot on the stove. I text him *Java in five*, and test the waters with, *Kitchen or office?*

I'm surprised and secretly thrilled that he texts back immediately with *Kitchen*. No emoji or little xxes but this is Nate. He probably texts in full sentences with correct punctuation.

And here he is, looking fresher – and hotter – than he did yesterday. He's in a preppy blue polo shirt that makes his eyes look like the water in *Blue Lagoon*. And then I stop staring at him because I notice what he's holding.

"Is that a pie box?"

'It is," he says.

"With actual pie in it?"

"No, I'm giving you an empty container because I'm nasty and maladjusted."

I ignore the sarcasm because – pie!

He hands it over, and I have to check. Key Lime, with whipped cream up the wazoo. Iris, you are a goddess.

"Did you forget last time I asked?" I ask.

"Uh, no." He tugs on his earlobe. "But that piece had an – accident."

I put the pie in the fridge. "I'll save it for this afternoon."

"Your willpower is impressive," he remarks.

"*So* impressive that I might even consider sharing it with you," I say, and I *swear* I see a flash of colour highlight his (also impressive) cheekbones.

The coffee pot starts to bubble. I pour us a mug each, and when he's holding his, I clink mine against it.

"Here's to Flora Valley Wines and all who sail in her," I say.

"I'll drink to that," he says, with a smile. "Or I'll sip carefully. This stuff is like molten lead."

"I aim to please." I smile back. "Right. What do we need to worry about first?"

The morning races by. We head back to the office and Nate takes me through the accounting system, but not the actual accounts because he still has the shoebox of receipts to enter. And to be honest, I don't want to know how bad things are until I have to. I'm much happier when things are in their Schrödinger's phase – you can still be optimistic they're alive rather than know for sure that they're dead.

I tell him in return about my plans for the next vintage.

That gets him talking about the winery in France, and we get so immersed in our conversation, we forget to stop for lunch. I only realize I'm hungry when my stomach makes a huge gurgle. Thanks, stomach. Way to be professional.

"It's three-fifteen!" Nate checks his phone. "How the hell did that happen?"

"Wine is very interesting."

"Agreed," he says. "But we've only scratched the surface of the worry list."

'Is it really a worry list?"

I don't mean to ask this in a sad, small voice but that's how it comes out.

Nate looks at me like he's weighing up how much truth I can stand.

"We can do it," he says. "But we haven't got a lot of runway, so let's be as smart as we can." He hesitates. "I wish I could offer you a cast-iron guarantee, but it'd be bad for both our sakes to set unrealistic expectations."

"Thanks," I say. "I really appreciate you being upfront with me."

"You're welcome," he replies.

And we stare at each other. There seems to be some sort of electrical disturbance in the air. Either that, or the office wiring needs an overhaul.

"I almost kissed you yesterday," I tell him.

He makes a choking sound.

"Too upfront?" I ask.

If it is, it's too late now.

He clears his throat. "I have something to confess, too."

My heart jumps anxiously. Hope it's not something that'll make me cry.

"My stupid reason for getting all high and mighty yesterday," he says, "was that I was jealous of Survivalist Ken."

Who? Oh!

"*Cam*? What do you mean you were jealous of him?"

Nathan props his elbows on the desk and leans forward.

"I was jealous because he was sitting with you," he says. "And because you were looking at him with affection. And because he's big and manly and probably knows how to tame wild beasts. And because he's known you longer than a few days. And just … because."

Oh my, those eyes. So very blue. And that mouth. So very delicious. So very close.

"Do you want to come to the house for pie?" I ask him. "Or…"

I can't say it. It's not the sort of thing I say.

His jaw is tense, and his breathing has quickened.

"'Or' would be amazing, but—"

"My room is second on the left up the stairs," I tell him, quickly, to give neither of us a chance to rethink. "Give me a five-minute head start so I can clear out the animals."

I hop out of the folding chair. "You're not allergic to pet hair, are you?"

"No," he replies.

"Good news."

And I hurry on out the door, hoping like heck he follows on behind.

Chapter Fourteen

NATE

My grandfather always worried about going senile, but when he did, he had a great time. Lost *all* his inhibitions. Which, of course, wasn't so great for the rest of the family. The cops got a bit tired of it, too. Still, he died happy.

Now, it seems I'm following in his footsteps. I've gone insane and I couldn't give a fuck. I'm climbing the stairs to Shelby's bedroom and trying not to think about everything I'd like us to do. Don't want it to be over before it starts.

Second on the left. Easy to spot. It's the door with five cats outside it looking pissed. The dogs passed me on their way down the stairs. They've got outside stuff to get on with. Enjoy, hairy buddies. I don't intend to go outside again for a good long while.

Door's shut. Because of the cats. As I put my hand out to open it, I have a sudden attack of nerves. My ex-fiancée was only the fourth woman I'd ever slept with, and the one I lost my virginity to doesn't count because I don't remember enough about her. So call it three women. I'm twenty-eight. That's pathetic.

My excuse is that between study, track competitions and training, I never had much time to hang out with girls. I didn't do frat parties. I was serious and responsible, and right now I want to punch my younger self in the face. Why didn't you sow more oats, you idiot? Put some hours in?

The door is opened for me, and Shelby's face, eyes huge, peers round it, while her foot fends off two cats, determined to get back in.

"Second thoughts?" she asks, punting a third cat into the hall.

"Nerves," I confess.

"Me too."

"I'm going to come in, though."

"Good," she says. "Now, I don't have to suffocate my humiliation with pie."

I slide past, as she does some kind of karate footwork that blocks three cats at once and slams the door.

"Sorry," she says. "I've got into bad habits, living alone. Let the pets take advantage of me."

"You don't let the goose in here, do you?"

"Nope. Pigs neither, you'll be pleased to hear."

"I brought – um, supplies."

I take the foil packs out of my pocket, sheepishly, like a schoolboy.

"Good thinking," she says. "The ones I have might be expired. It's been a while."

We've been standing like store dummies. I move towards her.

"I'd like to take advantage of you now, if that's OK?"

"*Totally* OK," she replies.

Then we sort of launch ourselves at each other, and start kissing, and I wouldn't give a damn if the goose *were* in here. I'm too blown away to care.

We kiss deep and slow, her body melding into mine, her hands around my neck so she can pull my mouth down onto hers. My own hands are cupping her rear, both to lift her further up—she's nine inches short of my six-foot-one—and to keep her tight against me. And I wasn't imagining it the other night. She's humming like a horny swarm of bees, and it's the most erotic sound I've ever heard.

My cock is insanely hard, and the pressure of her soft, warm body is almost too much for its tiny non-brain to handle. But I refuse to rush this. I want to explore every freckled naked inch of her, from top to toe and all zones in between. My cock can wait in line behind my tongue, mouth and hands. It'll get its turn.

OK, seems my desire not to rush isn't mutual. With magician-like deftness, Shelby's undone my belt and zipper. Now her hand is inside my pants, and my cock is straining toward her fingers, like a divining rod. I can't let her get a hold. I don't trust the *fils de pute* to show any restraint.

I grab her wrist. "Not yet."

"Why *not*?" she says, breathlessly. "I want you inside me so *bad*."

Bordel de merde, that does *not* help.

"It'll happen," I say. "But let's just … work up to it."

She frees her hand and slips it under my shirt, causing my ab muscles to have a minor conniption.

"You feel so good," she murmurs. "Can I at least get you naked?"

"That I have no problem with," I reply.

And we do our best to rip each other's clothes off before sheer practicality intervenes, and we focus on stripping ourselves.

There we are, naked as jaybirds, and *nom de Dieu*, she's perfection. Sugar dusted skin, copper lights in her hair, and the soft, full roundness of her breasts and ass.

I wonder how she sees me, if I match up to her expectations. Her amazing blue-green eyes are all drowsy with desire, so I guess I'll take that as a positive sign. I want to satisfy her to the hilt and beyond. I want to make her soar.

We're on the bed now, and she's pulling me down, arching into me. It's all I can do not to give up and slide right on in. Instead, I maneuver down the bed, kissing her warm skin all the way until I've reached my destination.

As my tongue delves into her sweetness, her whole body goes taut, and the sex-bee chorus starts again. I have to reach down and give the base of my cock a threatening squeeze. Behave, you *salaud*.

Her hands twine in my hair. I slide two fingers inside her and run my thumb up to where my tongue is, and back down. I hear her gasp, feel her buck beneath me. This is incredible but it's also goddamn torture.

She tightens her hold on my hair, and whispers, "Nate, please. Get up here."

Fuck it, I want to see her come. I want to be inside her, watching and feeling every second of her orgasm.

I wipe my mouth on the sheets and grab a condom from beside the bed. It better not be stubborn about rolling on. I have a moment here and I intend to seize it.

On. And Shelby has her hand around my cock, guiding me in, all the way in, and as we move together, her eyes widen with what I sincerely hope is pleasure.

"How can you feel so *amazing*?" she breathes. "Why is this so *good*?"

I'm incapable of answering. I'm lost, drowning in her. I drop my mouth to her breasts, take her nipples gently, slip my thumb back down in between us, add its strokes to the movement of our bodies.

Her eyes close, her head tips back and she pushes against me harder, more urgently. I don't want to blink in case I miss a moment.

And then I feel the heat radiating inside her, the sudden tautness in her body and I thrust faster, deeper, to send her over that edge. There. She shudders, gasps and clings to me as the orgasm rips through her.

My cock is gripped by pulse after pulse, and it's a bonafide miracle that I don't explode along with her. As she starts to relax, I slow my movements, gazing down on her, no doubt grinning like an idiot, until she opens her eyes again.

"Oh." She pulls me down, kisses me hungrily, greedily. Murmurs against my mouth, "Oh, wow."

It occurs to me that I am absurdly happy. Cock-a-hoop, as the saying goes.

But then Shelby frowns.

"You're still—"

"What?" Do I want to know?

"Uh – hard," she says, blushing. "Didn't we both—?"

I'm laughing with her, not at her, I swear.

"No, just you," I say. "I'm OK. Happy where I am."

It's true. Her pleasure was what I wanted, and it's what I got.

"That's ridiculous," she says. "You'll do yourself an injury."

"That's a myth," I say. "No one's actually died of blue balls."

"But – don't you want to?"

I bend to kiss her. "No rush."

"Hmm."

There's a glint in her eye, and she starts to move under me, bringing me deeper into her. My breathing becomes a little ragged.

"And what if I did this?"

She places her hands on my ass, runs a finger downwards and—

"Shit," I mutter.

And then I don't know *what* she does, but now all choice in the matter is gone. I let go, give myself up to the bliss of fucking her as hard as I can, until I'm consumed by a knife-edge pain-pleasure that makes me shout out loud.

Now it's me who's drowsy. Can barely lift my head off the pillow beside hers. But she's nudging me in the arm, and I'm forced to.

"Don't stop," she says.

"What?"

"Don't stop *moving*," she whispers urgently.

"OK?" I'm dazed, but still hard enough to comply.

Holy shit, three seconds later, she's coming again, and it seems to go on for*ever*. I'm torn between elation and concern that the condom is slipping.

Just when I think I'll *have* to pull out, she shudders to a halt.

Quickly, I extract myself. Condom's still on, thank you, thank you.

"Sorry," I whisper.

Pretty sure she can't hear me. Mind you, I've no idea how long *I* spent in that post-come stupor, so who am I to judge?

It's the scratching on the door that finally rouses her.

"Stupid cats," she mutters. "Go away."

"Feeding time?"

She's wide awake now. "What time *is* it?"

I removed my watch. No idea where I put it. Lean over the side of the bed, and dig my phone out of my pants pocket.

"Five-fifteen."

She sinks back into the bed. "Oh, that's OK. They don't officially starve for another fifteen minutes."

I'm on my side, propped up on one elbow. Shelby's colour's still high, and her hair is spread across the pillow in messy red-blond curls. Her lips are plump from all the kissing, and she's smiling fondly and contentedly at me.

I have fallen very hard indeed.

"Do you want to help me feed the pigs?" she asks.

"Sure," I say. "Got to be a first time for everything."

Chapter Fifteen

SHELBY

I've never fed the animals alongside a man I've just had spectacular sex with. But, as Nate says, there's a first time for everything.

Good thing he's there, too, because I'm a little ... unfocused. My mind is back in bed, reliving the feel of him, his hands, tongue, and ... I can't call it a thingy, that's ridiculous. It's a cock, that's what it is. Not that I will ever speak the word out loud.

His voice cuts in. "That bag says 'Pig pellets'."

I check the label. "Correct."

"So why are you about to pour them into the dogs' bowls?"

I check this, too. Also correct.

"I might not actually be concentrating," I tell him. "Owing to my mind being full of really *quite* filthy thoughts that all involve you."

Nate removes the pig pellets from my arms and inserts

himself in their place. We kiss for – no idea how long. Who cares?

Well, the dogs do. They're outside the back door whining. The cats have got their food already, so they have no further need of their human slaves.

Reluctantly, I break our kiss, hand Nate the bag of pig pellets, while I pick up the dog chow and fill the bowls. I've got balancing three of them down to a fine art.

"Why don't you leave the bowls outside?"

Nate tucks the pig pellets under one arm, as he holds open the back door.

"Pest control," I explain. "We don't use chemical stuff – sprays, poisons, etc. here, so it helps not to give the little blighters any encouragement."

"Blighters?"

"Ted word," I explain.

"Hmm," he says, using the tone Ted often inspires in other men.

The dogs attack their food like hairy hoovers, so I start to walk towards the pigs.

Beside me, I hear Nate say, "Is he gay?"

Second most common Ted-related question, after "Could we drink at the Silver Saddle instead?" Both uttered in that way that wants to be hopeful but knows defeat is inevitable.

"Nope. Lot of girlfriends. At least, I think so. When they all look exactly alike, it's hard to tell."

"Has a type, does he?"

"Is shiny a type?"

"Shiny?"

"You know – gleaming teeth and hair and jewellery. Like the Martinburg ladies back when they were their first husbands' mistress."

Nate shouts with laughter. I realize I haven't seen him do that much. His humour's been more of the dry kind.

I like making him laugh. I like *him*, very much. And not just because of the orgasms. But I'm not entirely sure why he should be attracted to me. My very few exes were all decent guys but not … Nate-level. What I'm trying to say is that men like Nate Durant don't come into my orbit. I get homegrown, not Harvard. Board shorts not business suits. Guys my mom would describe as "pleasant looking."

"You are *extraordinarily* handsome," I tell him.

He frowns, like it's a weird thing for me to say.

"You must get that all the time?" I may be digging a hole here.

"Not really," is his response.

Perhaps feeling he owes me more, he adds, "I was brought up not to put any store by looks. My father thought it was lazy to trade on them."

We've reached the pigs. Nate hangs back, I notice. A lot of people do, surprised at how large they are. Both our Vietnamese pot-bellied pigs top the scales at around one-seventy. I doubt fit, lean Nate weighs much more. And he's outnumbered two to one.

I dole out their pellet portion. Haven't had time to sort the food scraps, so they'll get those in the morning.

"Do they have names?" Nate hasn't come any closer.

"Ham Solo and Luke Skyporker. Don't blame me. It was my brothers."

I sense his hesitation, and though I'm not usually good at decoding signals, I think I know its source.

"We should sit down and fill in our background details," I suggest. "Over dinner, maybe? I could rustle something up."

"*Rustle?* What? Pork and beans?"

"Hush your mouth!" I nod toward the pen.

Nate peers at the pigs rootling around for the last pellets.

"Pretty sure they're not that fussy," he says. "They'd eat *you* if you dropped dead in there."

He picks up the pellet sack, and we stroll back to the house. I'd walk closer but Nate keeps looking around, including behind him.

"That goose hates me," he says, when he catches my expression.

"Dylan won't attack. He lost his mate a few years back, and geese only get aggressive when they're protecting their young."

"What if he's found a *new* mate?"

"Nope. Geese mate for life. There'll be no more Mrs Dylans."

"I want to feel sorry for him," says Nate. "And yet..."

Back in the kitchen, clean and scrubbed, and yes, all right, after more kissing and a bit of sexy fondling, I check out the fridge, freezer and cupboards. There's a selection of separate ingredients, but none I can see that combine into anything that could be described as dinner unless you'd just crawled out of a desert.

"Might have to go to town for pizza," I say.

"Let me look," he offers.

"Don't tell me you can cook?"

"OK."

He's already placed a collection of packets, jars and miscellaneous produce on the counter.

"Did you say your mom has a herb garden?"

I take him to the back door and point.

Twenty minutes later, I have a dish of spaghetti in front of me, made with peas, garlic, lemon zest and basil. Oh, and a hit of chilli.

"You're a magician," I tell him. "Want some wine?"

He makes a face. "I think I'm still hungover from two nights back."

Interesting news. Explains the rough look the other morning. I wonder what kind of drunk Nate Durant is? Myself, I'm exceedingly merry. And then I'm unconscious.

Don't get the wrong impression. Lack of money and an oversupply of work mean my opportunities to imbibe irresponsibly are few. Plus, Dad was very anti-drinking for the sake of getting drunk. Considered it a waste of good wine.

Besides, I don't need alcohol to be buzzed right now. I can't remember the last time I was this happy.

Then I notice Nate staring across the table at me. And he doesn't look like he's any kind of happy.

"I don't want to compromise you," he says.

Not one for the preamble is our Mr Durant.

"Compromise?"

"With the business. I don't want to make things difficult for you."

I lay down my fork. I've eaten most of my pasta anyway – it was figging delicious.

"How would it be difficult?" I ask, cautiously.

"If I have to … override you," he says. "When we disagree."

"You don't know we'll disagree."

The corner of his mouth lifts, but his tone is still serious.

"That remark proves just how different we are. Which means we'll *definitely* disagree."

I don't like where this discussion is heading because it reminds me that we're not technically on an equal footing when it comes to this business. It was exhausting enough having to fight to keep Flora Valley Wines. I don't want to have to fight to prove myself every single day. "Explain," I demand.

"You're optimistic," he says. "And I err on the side of pessimism. You're prepared to sail along and hope for the best, while I constantly anticipate and mitigate risk. You have organic, fluid systems, and I want everything locked down and in writing. And that's just for starters."

"Well, then," I say. "We complement each other. Don't we?"

What was meant to sound reasonable and confident came out more like a plea for reassurance.

Nate looks as though he intends to rebut.

But what he says is, "I'm not always aware of how I affect people. I can be overbearing, and when I've got a goal in my sights I tend to focus only on that. Everything else becomes noise, and sometimes everything else includes people I care about."

And suddenly, I'm not defensive anymore. I'm touched. He *wants* this to work out. He wants *us* to work out. He's doing what he does – anticipating risk, so he can enrol me in the mitigation of it.

"Should we have a code word then?" I ask.

"Code *what*?"

He'll have to get used to my comments from left field.

"If you're being a douche, I can say the word, so you'll know you need to stop."

"Is 'douche' one of your acceptable swears?"

"I don't have many. Make the most of it," I say. "Well? Code word or not?"

"Jesus."

I nod, slowly. "Could work."

He's grinning now. "Did you get the inspiration from BDSM?"

"Don't be ridiculous," I say. "Only time I've been tied up is when I got tangled in a sports bra."

"You," he states, with affection I'll choose to believe, "are a piece of—"

"Pie!" I just remembered. "We can have pie for dessert!"

I fetch the pie, and a second spoon, which I offer to him.

"Want some?"

He tries a tiny amount, and his eyes widen.

"*That*," he points with the spoon, "is fucking amazing."

And then I do something I've never done in my life. I stick my finger in the pie and curl it into my mouth. And I suck on it, slowly, with my eyes all the while on Nate.

Whose own eyes darken instantly.

"*Nom de Dieu*," he mutters. Which I guess is French.

I stand and scoop up the pie box. Then I do a wiggle walk out the door. I hear his chair scrape as he pushes it hastily back.

We reach the bedroom – I kept the door closed, so no cats. In seconds, we're naked and I'm lying on the bed, placing a dollop of cream and pie on each breast, watching Nate's cock reach an impressive full salute as he stands above me.

"Holy shit," he says.

That's *not* French. I know that much.

He lowers himself over me, and slowly begins to lick the pie off my skin. My nipples are so sensitive, they're almost painful. I do *not* want him to stop.

But then my breasts are clean of pie. The box is next to me, and propping himself (athletically, I have to say) above me, Nate scoops pie with his own finger and hovers it around my lips. I take his hand and guide his finger into my mouth, sucking its whole length, slow as I can.

His eyes close, and he stifles a curse word (language indeterminate). Having felt like he was the one in total control earlier, I am *relishing* this sense of power.

With a quick, sneaky manoeuvre, I manage to overbalance him, so he's forced onto his back. And before he can protest or shift, I have a scoop of pie and I'm straddling him with evil intent.

There's a fractional second where I can see him mull his options. He chooses wisely, lays back in surrender on the pillow, and lets me get down to it.

"Shit," I hear him mutter, as I spread Iris's best key lime and a whole lot of cream over the head and down the shaft of his cock.

I follow the pie with my tongue, and his whole body tenses. I take the base of the shaft in one hand and work my tongue up and down the underside ridge, flicking it over the head, which makes his cock jump like it's afraid I'll hurt it. I won't. Maybe a *little* nip just so it knows who's in charge.

"Fuck … Shelby…"

It's a feeble protest, and I ignore it. I place the head in my mouth, just the head, and start to tongue and suck it. My hand slips down to his balls and I cup them, because balls need love too.

He's making some kind of noise up there, but I can't make out actual words.

I should stop tormenting him, fun though it is. I take him all the way into my mouth and apply myself seriously to making him even more inarticulate.

When I think he's good and ready, I wet my index finger, slide it along the cleft of his ass, and start paying attention to the most sensitive spot, while I continue to ply his cock with my mouth, and gently fondle his balls. Women are so good at multitasking.

His fingers twine in my hair.

"*Shel...*' he whispers. "Seriously, I'm ... *fuck...*"

I feel his balls tense, and then it's all on. I take him deep as I can as he pushes into me, and I take the whole load, while he shouts loud enough to wake people in New Zealand.

Then I have the pleasure of sitting straddled above him, watching him lay there, eyes closed, ripped abs heaving as he gets his breathing under control. I might have also stolen a little more pie, because waste not, want not.

Finally, he opens his eyes.

"You," he says, still a little breathless, "are—"

"Say it in French," I demand, because right now, I am the triumphant queen.

He runs his hands along my thighs, and OK, yes, I make a little inarticulate noise of my own as his fingers near my queenly throne.

Then, in a sneaky manoeuvre of his own, he grabs hold of either side of my butt and pulls me up right up toward him.

"You know what?" he says, his face about an inch from my regal dominion. "I think we should continue with the Latin terms."

The only Latin I know is "Hallelujah", if that even *is* Latin.

But – oh wow – how about I look it up later?

Chapter Sixteen

NATE

Three things I know for sure: I'm in love with Shelby Armstrong, I still hate that goose, and I can never go back to the Cracker Café, because I swear to God that Iris will know just by looking at me what we did with her pie.

This morning, Shelby and I were so worn out, we mutually agreed to defer any more sex until this evening. We tag-teamed the shower, and Shelby found me a clean pair of underpants, left behind, she said, by one of her brothers. I hope that was the truth. Wearing her late father's Hanes would be seriously weird.

Over breakfast, we did what we'd intended to do before we violated Iris's pie. She told me about her family – two older brothers, Jackson and Tyler, and her younger sister, Frankie. They've all gone on to careers that are nothing to do with wine and live in three different states. Shelby talked about them with affection, but it must have been hard for her, being the only one who loved the winery enough to fight for it.

It struck me how brave she'd been, dealing with her dad's death and the shock of him leaving no will, and then cold-calling endless investors. Never giving up, despite knockback after knockback. Takes courage to be that optimistic. Much easier to assume everything will fall to shit, because then you have the satisfaction of being right even when you've failed. Philosophy 101, courtesy of Nathan Durant. You're welcome.

I told her the basics about my family. Downplayed my father's illness. When you've lost your own father, you don't want to be triggered by someone else's being at death's door. Shelby said she hoped she'd get to meet my siblings before they all headed home again. My initial reaction was resistance because who knows what they'd tell her about me? Right now, I feel like I'm a king in her eyes, and I'd like to preserve that illusion as long as possible.

Might have been because we were floating on a rosy post-multi-orgasmic cloud, but we had a productive day. Researched local web designers. Chose the one Shelby went to high school with because that's how it is around here. Finally got all the accounts online, which has to win the award for the world's most tedious yet crucial job. Sketched out a plan for the tasting room, worked out what consents were needed, did a back of the napkin budget. Shelby took our thinking to Cam the Commando and, apparently, he was enthusiastic about the project. Hope he didn't strain anything getting all excited.

Yeah, I'm still jealous. Yeah, I know that's childish. But fuck him.

We took a late lunch. Broke our agreement to wait and had sex in the kitchen. I lifted Shelby onto the counter, she wrapped her legs around me, and we went from there. No pie was harmed. Though my knees were pretty shaky afterwards.

All in all, a good day. Until five minutes past four, when I got a call from Ava.

Shelby saw my face. Didn't question why when I said, "I have to go."

She trusts me. I hope like hell I will never have cause to let her down.

So now I'm entering the Martinburg district hospital, where Dad's been admitted. According to Ava, he decided to go for "a little jog."

"Doc Wilson said he could do moderate exercise." Ava's frustration was clear. "So Dad went out, *we* thought, for about twenty minutes. Only he failed to mention that *his* idea of moderate exercise was a fricking 10k trail run. He collapsed about 6k in and is not dead only because a mountain biker saw him go down and called 911. Who, fortunately, were there in five minutes."

"Did his heart fail?" I asked her.

"Arrhythmia," she replied. "Heartbeats have a rave party. You pass out."

"I thought he was told to wear a heart monitor when he exercised?"

"Are you new here?" she said. "When has Dad ever done what he's told?"

I forgave her for being shitty. I'm feeling pretty irate myself. Pity Dad's in the hospital. Don't think medical professionals look kindly on you if you slap a man on his sickbed.

Whole family's here, clustered around Dad's bed. Ava's the only one standing, and the only one who looks angrier than she does upset. Danny has his arm around Mom, who's leaning into his chest, and the twins are on her other side, hugging her and each other.

Dad himself is hooked up to a barrage of medical equipment, which he will no doubt resist when he wakes up. I guess he's on the dreaded medication, too. Which is why he's merely unconscious and not laid out on a slab.

There's not much room, so I hover in the doorway. Danny glances over, nods in acknowledgement. Twins and Mom haven't even registered I'm here. Ava gives me the once over and raises an eyebrow. Probably noticed that my shirt needs pressing and that I'm wearing the same clothes I left the house in yesterday morning. Bar the underwear, of course, but I'm happy for her to remain ignorant of that fact.

Danny gently nudges Mom, to let her know I'm here. She raises her head to give me a wan smile, and I'm struck, not for the first time, that she looks more like Danny's older sister than our mother. She and Dad met when they were nineteen, and even distraught as she is now, Ginny Durant, née Adams, doesn't look much more than thirty-five.

Whereas Dad looks about a hundred-and-nine – gaunt and grey, and seriously unwell.

Izzy and Max know I'm here now too. Izzy smiles, and Max rolls his eyes. It's a show of solidarity, bringing me into the group. But I know I'm here too late. Everyone was already at the hospital when Ava called me. I wasn't on the spot like they were.

I recall Max joking about something he'd seen on the internet.

"The fuckening," he'd said. "It's when you're having a great day but you don't quite trust it. And then, sure enough, shit happens. And you go, 'Ah, there it is. The fuckening.'"

The progress Shelby and I made today, the glow of us getting together and having the most pleasurable, joyous sex of my life – all of it may as well have never happened. I'm plunged into this black stew of resentment and anger, primarily at myself for not checking in as I've done every day since the family all arrived home. I didn't call Ava last night, or this morning. I didn't let anyone know I wasn't coming home. OK, I'm a grown-assed man, not a kid, but I had a duty and I reneged on it, if only for a day.

A day, of course, when it all fell to shit. I wonder who led the charge to mobilize the family, Ava or Danny? Did it even matter that I wasn't there?

I feel this urge to take control, to claw back some standing, create some reason for being here.

But my moment's lost.

"Howdy."

Doc Wilson's the only man I know who actually says "Howdy." When he's stirred up, he says, "Boy howdy" and "Dang." He and Shelby would get along great.

Shit. I don't want to think about Shelby. My mind's too fucking conflicted right now.

"Ray," says Mom.

Her face has lit up. She's so pleased to see him. So's the rest of the gang.

I shift aside to let Doc in the room and cram against the back wall next to Ava, who's still looking pissy.

"Ginny." Doc bends to give her a pat on the shoulder. "What are we going to do about this dang fool?"

"Pull the plug," Ava mutters next to me.

She doesn't mean it. She's frustrated, as we all are, at Dad's stubborn refusal to accept reality. For someone always so driven by tangible, measurable success, he's been absurdly resistant to taking what seems like the obvious path to his recovery. Sure, he has his quirks regarding modern medicine, but when he was first diagnosed, we'd all assumed that his desire not to drop dead would prevail over any weirdness.

Seems you can convince yourself of anything if you try hard enough.

Doc's reading Dad's chart.

"Mitch, you are one lucky S.O.B.," he sighs.

Wow. S.O.B. Doc's *really* riled.

This would be my second chance to step in, but it seems today's not my day.

"They're talking about inserting a device called an ICD

to manage the arrhythmia," says Danny. "But Dad'll refuse to have any kind of invasive procedure."

"Can we force him?" Ava gets straight to the point.

"Well, now, that's a whole can of snakes right there," says Doc. "If your father's of sound mind, then he has the right to refuse even life-saving treatment. No physician can force him to do otherwise. It's unethical and illegal."

"So we'd have to prove he's nuts?" Ava persists.

"Ava," Mom remonstrates gently.

"Mom, seriously! If we *don't* find some way to force this lunatic to see sense, then he'll die! I'm sorry to be so blunt, but come on! We *all* know it's true."

"Does having alternative views on medicine indicate an unsound mind?" Danny backs Ava up.

"Not usually," says Doc. "You could try testing it in the courts, but…'

"That could take years," says Ava. "He'd be *long* dead before we got a decision."

Doc winces at Mom's expression. He's a plain speaker himself, but there's such a thing as being *too* plain.

Come on, Nate. Step up.

"Surely, if it was another emergency, the doctors would *have* to save his life?" I say. "Isn't that in their code of ethics, too?"

"It is, son," says Doc, immediately making me feel about ten years old. "But with a condition like this, emergencies aren't always … retrievable. It was sheer luck that your father received prompt medical attention today, and that it was arrhythmia and not anything worse. Though it *could* have killed him. Let's not kid ourselves about that. Drugs and a defibrillator aren't always close by."

"So waiting for an emergency's not a plan, either." I state the useless obvious.

"I'm sorry." Doc's speaking to us all now. "I'll talk to him again. Try to convince him that proper medical treatment is for the best. Remind him he has a family to think of. The man has a duty of care to you all, even if he can't see straight when it comes to his own fool self."

Danny stands and shakes Doc's hand. "We'll call you when he wakes up."

"Thank you, Ray." Mom stands, too, and gives Doc a kiss on the cheek.

"My job, Ginny." Doc pats her on the arm. "Plus, I like a good fight. The more bone-headed my opponent, the better."

He nods to all the rest of us in turn. "You take care now and mind your mother takes care, too. Your health is just as important as your father's. I don't want to be seeing any of *you* collapsed in a heap in my office, you hear?"

"Yes, sir," we all say, with varying degrees of conviction.

I shift again to let him out, and he fixes me with that direct look of his.

"Any issues, you come see me, all right?"

I guess he means about Dad. Or Mom – he's made no secret of being worried about her. And he's talking to me because I'm the eldest, and ostensibly the one in charge, though I haven't felt like that today.

"Sure, Doc," I say.

Soon as he's gone, the air goes out of us. We don't have Doc's conviction. None of us has a fucking clue what to do with this guy lying on the hospital bed.

Looking around, I can see how tired and stressed my family are. And I owe them – for being absent without leave, and for having a good time while they had to deal with this crap.

"Hey, Dan," I say. "Why don't you guys go get something to eat. I'll stay here."

He nods, to show he appreciates the offer.

"Mom?" he says. "Come on. There's a Denny's right next door. Nate will text us if anything happens."

"I'm *starving*," says Izzy. "Is that wrong?"

"Yes," says Max. "You're a terrible person."

Izzy aims to give him a dead arm. Durant revenge of choice. Max dodges it easily.

"Does Denny's serve alcohol?" asks Ava, as the group heads past me out the door.

"No, but you can have a cake batter shake," says Dan. "With sprinkles."

"That's dis*gust*ing. I love it."

Mom pauses in front of me, gives me a quick smile. "Thank you, sweetheart."

If Doc made me feel about ten years old, she makes me feel half that age.

Then they're all gone. The room is empty, apart from me, and my reluctantly intubated, unconscious father.

I take the chair vacated by Mom, which is closest to his bed.

"Evening, Dad," I say.

Who knows, he might be able to hear me. And he was always a stickler for manners.

My mobile has to be switched off in here, so if I need to text the others, I'll have to step into the waiting room. Won't know until then if Shelby's texted or called.

Not that I have any idea what to say to her. Or rather, *how* to say what I need to tell her. Because it's become starkly clear to me that until this situation with Dad is resolved, one way or another, I can't let my attention be divided.

Like Doc Wilson said, duty first. I have a duty to my family, to Mom, in particular. I have a duty to JP to get a return on his investment in Flora Valley Wines. Those are my top priorities.

Which means, strong as my feelings are for Shelby, I'll have to put what we have on hold. There's no way I'm making the mistake I did in France. If I can't give Shelby the attention she deserves, then we'll have to wait until I can.

And if she isn't prepared to do that, then ... I don't know.

I sit and watch Dad. Try not to think about the rest of my family carb-and-sugar-loading in a manner that *would* give Dad instant heart failure if he knew. The kid in me wants badly to be with them, but the adult in me overrides. It was my decision to stay here. Live with it, Nate.

Of course, my traitorous mind switches straight to the other person I crave to be with. Shelby. And I'm swamped by a wave of regret and need that's so bad, I feel like I want to throw up.

I try telling myself that I'll still see her almost every day, but that makes it worse, not better. I want her like an insane man, even sitting here in a room that smells of disinfectant and boiled cabbage. Couldn't even keep today's promise to wait a few short hours before we had sex again, so how the hell will I keep my hands off her for … I don't know, could be weeks?

And how will I explain to her that it's because I love her that I need to do this? It might seem to her like just the opposite. I know *I* wouldn't react too well in her situation. We all know how great I am at handling rejection.

But Shelby's not me. She's nothing like me. She's loving, open, generous and kind.

I'll just have to trust in her. And hope.

Because given what my life is right now, I don't have a choice.

Chapter Seventeen

SHELBY

I remember the day Dad found out he had cancer. Our long-time family doctor came round to the house, and from the look on her face, we immediately knew the news was bad.

I remember how I felt, too. Now, having read about grief stages, I understand about denial, anger, bargaining etc., but at the time, sitting there in our kitchen, there was only shock and numbness. Dad had always been so *robust*. Big, blond and broad-shouldered, like a clean-shaven Viking. He was a *poster* boy for health and vitality. When he smiled, I swear you could see one of those sparkle effects they use in commercials. No part of me could comprehend that he was terminally ill.

This morning, though, I'm right back there with those feelings of shock and numbness, and *complete* lack of comprehension. When Nate had to take off yesterday, I figured it was because something had happened with his own dad. I could tell he'd been holding back when he mentioned his father was ill, that it was probably worse than he implied, but he didn't want to upset me. Nate's a serious individual when it comes to doing the right thing – not hard to pick *that* up. Up till this morning, I appreciated that quality in him. Now, I don't know whether I want to cry or kick him in the pig pellets.

"What do you *mean*, you want to call it off?"

I'm sitting right on the edge of the folding chair in the office, and it's digging into my legs. I can't shift because I'm rigid with disbelief. Less than a figging day ago, this guy and I could not get *enough* of each other.

To be fair, he doesn't look happy about it. Looks like he hasn't slept at all.

"I *don't* want to call it off," he says. "I want to put it on hold."

"I'm not a *phone* call," I object.

Sitting across the desk from me, he draws his hands down his face. I can see this isn't easy for him, but at least *he* understands his reasons for doing it. Whereas I am completely in the figging dark.

"Nate, help me out here," I say. "What's going on?"

He hesitates, glances away, up at the poster Mom pinned on the office wall. It's got an illustration of a whale on it and the words *Dream Big*. Pretty low-key for Mom. Her favoured decorative motif is a mandala, in more colours than exist in nature.

"I'm stuck," is what he says, eventually. "Between responsibilities. To my family. And to here – this business."

From looking like an illegal dumping ground two days ago, the desk is now almost bare. All that's on it is a jotter pad, a sharpened pencil, and the new computer. Nate likes things tidy.

"I don't want to have to put them first," he goes on. "Before you."

OK, finally – a glimmer of understanding.

"You don't want to risk losing me like you did your fiancée?" I venture. "Because you can't give me enough time and attention?"

He nods. Why *he* couldn't have said that, I may never know. But then there's a lot about Nate Durant that confuses and frustrates me. Number one, why he feels compelled to make life so *complicated*.

I prop my forearms on the desk, lean towards him.

"Nate, I'm not your fiancée," I say, gently. "I'm me. I know what it takes to run this business, so I will never be unrealistic in my expectations of you. I know that the last day-and-a-half was *not* normal and that from now on we'll have to knuckle down and spend more time working than we will with each other."

I have to shift position on the chair because it's cut the circulation to my legs. Nate's watching me, attentive but wary.

"And whatever's going on with your family," I continue, "we can deal with it. *Together*. If you need time off here, I can cover for you. Yesterday, we proved we could be a team. Why can't you bring yourself to have faith in me?"

"I *do* have faith in you," he begins. "But—"

But—? I don't want to hear, "But—"! Why is it so figging hard for people to trust me? To see that I *do* have what it takes? I'm so angry at Nate right now, and I suspect a lot of that is delayed anger at everyone else who's underestimated and patronized me. What comes after this "But—" had better be good!

"I'm no good at doing things half-assed," he says. "If it were just the business to juggle, then, yeah, I could agree to see how we go. But the family situation … I can't take my eye off the ball there. I'll *have* to spend more time at home. No more … staying over. I might not be around much at all…"

His hand moves forward, as if he wants to reach for mine. Instead, he picks up the pencil. Gives me a look that's half-pleading, half-adamant.

"Shelby, I care about you. Which is why I never, ever want to promise you something I can't deliver. And I wish I could give you some kind of timeframe, but I don't have one. I haven't a clue how things with Dad are going to pan out."

He sticks the sharp point of the pencil into his fingertip, winces slightly, but doesn't take his eyes off me.

"Can you – is it too much to ask you to wait? Until I can do this right?"

OK, so I have to remind myself how much I value honesty. And I can see Nate is being honest here. I can see how genuinely conflicted he is. I have empathy for him, too. I know what it's like to have a family in crisis, how afraid and unhappy it makes you. The uncertainty of it all is *so* exhausting.

Then again, I also want to twist his head off and shove it up his butt. Why is it so *impossible* for him to just go with the flow a bit more? To trust in the universe, as Mom would say. Trust in *me*?

"Nate, you're forcing me to decide between waiting around for you and calling it off right now."

He winces again, but can't deny it's the truth.

"I can't make that kind of decision at a moment's notice," I tell him. "You'll have to give *me* time, too."

He takes a deep breath. "That's fair," he says.

His voice is even, but he looks like he's discovered another rotten apple core in his desk drawer. I suppose it's a small triumph that he's not using his poker face. That he's prepared to let his guard down at least *that* much.

"I'm sorry," he adds, to my slight surprise. Nate's always struck me as someone who doesn't feel a need to justify doing what he believes is right. "I don't want to hurt you."

"I know," I say with a sigh, because he means it. "But I *am* hurt, and I'm no good at pretending otherwise."

And then I run out of strength for more words, so I get up and I leave him there alone in the office, and the hurt, angry part of me hopes he stews on his stupidity – my word but the correct one – for a good long while.

I get in the Flora Valley Wines truck and drive straight to Verity and the Silver Saddle, and I call my besties on the way and order them to meet me there. I don't give a fig if it's only lunchtime. I need to be with people who care.

"Another," I say to Brendan, when he insists on taking away my empty glass.

"Things looking up?" he says, with a cynical tone that he can go bite on.

"Nope!"

I expect him to leave, but he doesn't. He stands there until I glance at him again.

Brendan's standard factory-mode expression makes troublemakers and loud drunks hush instantly and back away slowly. It could probably make a rearing grizzly drop down and do a rapid U-turn. Right now, though, his face looks almost … kind.

"Anything I can do?" he says, in a soft voice I frankly did not know he possessed.

"Uh oh," I hear Chiara murmur. "Incoming."

"Huh?" says Jordan, whose powers of observation are not so uncanny.

I burst into tears. Big, fat ones, accompanied by snot and sucking sounds.

"Shit," I hear Brendan sigh.

A cloth is shoved into my hands. His bar cloth. It's not all *that* clean but it's not like I'm going to make it any cleaner. I sob right into it and have no intention of stopping anytime soon.

Jordan has both arms round me. She kayaks; she doesn't mind excess moisture. Chiara might pat me on the shoulder, but only if she can guarantee no snot has leaked onto it.

Eventually, like a clockwork toy that's smashed itself into a wall too many times, I wind on down to a hiccupping sniffle.

Like magic, a glass of what looks like a very decent pinot grigio appears in front of me.

"On the house," says Brendan, but not in his kind voice, just in case it sets me off again.

I offer him back the bar cloth, but he refuses, and walks off before any emotional shenanigans can resume. Jordan has to twist her neck just about full circle to perv at his butt, the weirdo.

"So," Chiara has given me a grace period. Now it's down to business. "Does crying mean you intend to give him a chance?"

"Why would it mean that?" says Jordan. "Can't she just be upset about him being a dickwad?"

"That would be *angry* crying," explains Chiara. "Totally different from sad crying."

We sit in awe of her wisdom.

"I don't *know*," I say, hopelessly, because that's how I feel.

"Do you love him?" says Jordan.

"I've known him less than a *week*," I protest. "I don't even know if he has a middle name!"

"Mitchell," says Chiara, immediately. "After his father."

"Sexy," says Jordan.

"His *father*?" I say.

"No, the *name*, idiot. Not as sexy as 'Brendan' though."

"But you think you *might* fall in love with him," says Chiara, relentlessly.

"Yes," I admit. "I was definitely well along that track before this morning. But why does he have to make this so *difficult*?"

"Some people are naturally cautious," says Chiara. "I'm one of those people, whereas you and Jordan are not. You're the kind who think nothing's wrong with rocking up to a battered panel van scrawled with the words 'Free candy'."

Jordan and I exchange a look. It says, "She's got us."

"Add to that a perfectionist nature," Chiara continues, "and you've got the textbook formula for heel-dragging and compartmentalizing."

"Plus his dad's ill," adds Jordan. "That can make you *totally* freak out. Oh, shit. Sorry, Shel."

"What for? You're not wrong."

"Think that might be at the heart of it," says Chiara. "Fear of what's going to happen if his dad gets worse."

Chiara should start practicing as a psychic. She'd make a fortune.

"Could be," I reply. "Like I said, I don't know him well enough to be sure."

"And even though you don't know him well, you still have to decide," says Chiara. "What's it going to be, Shel?"

"Come on, Kiki, don't pressure her," says Jordan, the defender. "She should sleep on it, at least."

"I should," I agree. "And right now I will drink on it."

I take hold of my glass – great colour and nose; where the heck's Brendan been hiding *this*? – and I raise it in a toast.

"Here's to the right answer coming to me in a dream," I say. "Cheers!"

"*Zum Wohl*," says Chiara.

"German?" I ask, pointedly.

"I'm a woman of the world," says Chiara, unabashed. "I've also learned that the German for a woman's nipples is *brustwarze*. Translates as 'breast warts'."

"To breast warts!" says Jordan, loudly, possibly to get Brendan's attention, a ploy she should know by now is doomed to failure.

We clink glasses, and I manage the first smile of the day.

Won't be smiling when I'm in bed alone tonight definitely *not* sleeping, but that's in the future. I'll deal with that when I absolutely have to, which right now, seems like the perfect guide to better living.

Chapter Eighteen

NATE

I f there's anything in this world guaranteed to keep you humble, it's coming home as an adult and sleeping in the bed you had as a kid.

OK, so the room has changed dramatically. After I left for France, Mom painted the once blue walls a pale sage green and hung watercolours of flowers in place of my posters of Filbert Bayi, Seb Coe and Mel Sheppard, the first American to win an Olympic gold for the 1500 meters, my track event of choice.

She got rid of my old desk and put in an antique sewing table, covered it with a vintage lace cloth, and set a jug of flowers on top. The bed she kept, but now it's got a floral quilt on it in place of my Golden State Warriors duvet, and a whole lot more pillows than any human with a normal number of heads needs.

All but one pillow is on the floor. I lie back on the last and try to make out the spot on the ceiling where I tossed half an Oreo up to see if it'd stick. I was seven, what can I say? It did stick, for about half a second. Left a faint oily mark that I stared up at on many an occasion during my childhood. Can't see it now. Mom probably repainted the ceiling, too. All traces of me have been eradicated.

I joined the family this evening in Dad's hospital room again. He was ... OK. Doc Wilson had been around that morning and maybe some of what he'd said had sunk in. Or maybe Dad was still feeling too weak to argue. On the way home, we stopped at In-N-Out to get more illicit burgers and fries to go. My bag's still sitting on the kitchen counter, untouched.

I could have stayed and hung out with everyone in the kitchen. Max insisted on making a pot of Darjeeling, because he's a sophisticated New Yorker now, and Mom brought out cookies that she'd somehow found time to bake.

I excused myself, citing work to do, which wasn't a lie, but wasn't the real reason I had to go. Real reason was that I couldn't stop thinking about what Shelby was up to, how she felt about me now, whether she'd *ever* forgive me. I couldn't stop picturing her lying there in bed, flushed and happy, smiling up at me like I was the greatest lover on earth. Which is exactly how she made me feel.

So what the *fuck* am I doing? Is it the height of stupidity, or arrogance, or both? Because we know how I can be when I get set on a path. Once I've decided it's the right way, I won't be deflected. I've already found out once what that cost me.

This morning, I was nervous but convinced that putting our relationship on hold was the right decision. And while I think Shelby *did* understand my reasoning, she was clearly less than thrilled. Can't blame her for refusing to give me an answer right away, but it makes for an uneasy wait, to understate it a million-fold. Waiting opens the door for Mr Doubt, and his good friends, Mr This Doesn't Look Good, and Mr Have You Been a Complete Fucktard Yet Again?

Someone knocks on my bedroom door. Quick and impatient, which can only mean one person. Ava.

Hastily, I haul my ass off the bed, and shove my laptop onto the sewing table, so it looks like I *have* been working, instead of searching for old traces of Oreo while wallowing in self-pity.

Opening the door, I see Ava with two glasses in one hand and bottle of single malt in the other.

"Dad might not touch a drop," she says, "but he knows how to stock a liquor cabinet. This is twelve-year-old Macallan. Want some?"

Don't get the impression that my sister is lush. When she's working, which is pretty much all day every day, she's a Spartan just like Dad. It's why she never became a professional jockey, she once told me. Too many meth heads. Bad path for an ambitious Durant, who can't bear to lose.

Ava sets the glasses on the sewing table, and waves the bottle at me, enquiringly.

"I haven't eaten," I admit.

"I know," she says. "One reason I thought I'd come check on you."

She has more than one? Thought I'd done a pretty good job of pretending to be same old steady Nathan.

"Want me to fetch your burger?" she says. "Pretty sure it'll be a lump of congealed fat by now, but—"

"I'll pass. Thanks."

She's rummaging in the back pocket of her exercise top. Activewear is Ava's default uniform, though she does possess good clothes. It was her dress I borrowed. I don't want to think about how incredible Shelby looked in it.

"Here. Protein bar."

Her body heat's softened it to the consistency of plasticine. What the hell. I really *do* want some of that whisky. I unwrap the bar, take a bite.

"What flavour is *this* supposed to be?"

"Goji berry and cashew butter."

"Jesus."

Ava grins and pours two glasses. She looks around and ascertains that there is no seating except an acutely uncomfortable antique sewing stool, so hops up carefully on my bed. Hands me up my glass, so she can reach over the side and grab an extra pillow.

"I think Mom heisted a pillow factory," she says. "My bed's disappeared beneath at least a hundred of them."

"Did she paint your walls, too?" I ask.

"Primrose yellow. Would have taken plenty of coats to cover the black."

Ava had a phase in her mid-teens. Was the only

competitor with a purple mohawk and black lipstick. Dad would have cared more if she hadn't won every track meet that year.

I get on the bed next to her, and we sit side by side like an old married couple, holding our glasses, into which she has poured a generous measure of whisky. I use the initial mouthful to wash away the taste of cashew berry. Then I take a proper drink.

"Damn," I say. "That is *good*."

"Agreed." Ava nods.

Then she says, "So how are you, big bro? Hanging in there?"

If hanging means by your fingertips from a cliff edge, then sure.

"I'm OK," I say.

"Ha, ha, bullshit," is her response.

Which, of course, immediately gets my back up. Ava and I, in particular, used to scrap a lot as kids. Needling each other until we finally got a reaction. I'd say our score on those battles was pretty much fifty-fifty. I'm not about to cede a victory this early in the piece.

"Got a lot on with the new job." I keep my voice level. "The winery needs a drastic overhaul."

"And Dad's being a nutbar. Which doesn't help."

"Guess not," I admit cautiously.

"Plus his shit has totally eclipsed *your* shit," she continues.

Her casual tone jolts me into instant alert. If I were smart, I'd say nothing. But the whisky has found its way into my bloodstream. Goji butter is no defense against twelve-year-old triple-cask-matured single malt.

"*My* shit?"

My sister gives me the side eye.

"Don't get all huffy," she says. "This is coming from a place of caring. I've been worried about you."

"OK…" I'm not yet convinced. "But what do you mean by 'my shit'?"

"I mean what happened to you in France," she replies. "We were about to fly over, watch you get hitched, and then whammo – it's off. And, like, all of two weeks later, Dad hits the deck and so all our attention went to him. I don't think *any* of us asked you about what happened, or how you felt about it, did we?"

"Hardly surprising," I say. "Dad has a potentially fatal heart condition."

"Really?" Ava's giving me the side eye again. "You cancelled your *wedding*. You quit a job that you loved and left a place you'd called home for four years. Are we so useless that we couldn't have remarked on at least *one* of those events?"

I take another decent slug of whisky. Not up to me to comment.

"Well, on behalf of the useless Durant clan, I'd like to apologize," Ava says. "And better late than never, I'd like to ask how you're doing."

"Thanks," is all I feel like replying right now.

"Nate," she says, in a warning tone. "Talk to me."

"And what's *talking* about it going to achieve?" I say,

with more heat than I'd intended. "Won't change what happened. Won't make it any better. Won't stop me feeling what I'm feeling. So why bother?"

"It wasn't you who called it off, then, was it? The wedding?"

Fuck, she won't give up. Never has, never will. What the hell, may as well get it over with. But Ava will be the *only* family member I tell. I swear on my grandfather's grave.

"No," I say. "She left me. For a death metal drummer."

A pause. "Norwegian or Swedish?"

"There's a difference?"

"Oh, yeah. Swedish is more melodic, with a lot of grindcore-based riffs and stuff. Norwegian's more accurately black metal, much more grimy and lo-fi."

Now, I'm giving *her* the side eye.

"What?" she says. "I like metal!"

"He was Norwegian," I tell her. "Name sounded like Ass-Bjorn."

"So how long had the stick-man been sticking it to Camille?"

A wave of nausea rocks through me. Can't tell if it's shame or anger or regret, or a putrid stew of all three. Might also be whisky on a near-empty stomach. There is that.

I saw Ass-Bjorn only once, when he came around to pick up my ex-fiancée and sweep her away to the fjords or wherever. Big, bearded guy. Looked like he'd been dropped on his head as a baby.

"I know nothing about timeframes," I inform Ava. "Camille didn't tell me and I didn't ask."

"I guess the winery owner didn't have too much issue with you quitting, given that he was Camille's dad," she says, like she's aiming for a black belt in mental torture.

"He understood."

Not entirely. Anton was upset about the whole wedding fiasco, but was more distraught that I wanted to quit. He'd come to depend on me. Originally, I'd had no intention of leaving him high and dry without a manager, so I'd offered a six-month notice period, even though every day there, with all those reminders of my humiliation, would be hell. Then Dad's heart condition was diagnosed and expedited matters to the point where Anton basically shooed me out the door. The French are big on putting *la famille* first.

To my surprise, Ava leans her head against my shoulder. She and I inherited Dad's reluctance to show physical affection, whereas Mom, Danny and the twins are serial huggers. They joke that with Dad, Ava and me, it's like embracing robots that need oil.

"I'm really sorry, Nate," she says. "You've had a rough time."

Weirdly, that does make me feel better.

"I'll get over it."

"Course you will. You're a Durant. When the Grim Reaper comes calling, no way we'll go unless we take a piece of him with us."

I smile. My face muscles have been tense for so long, it feels unnatural.

"So how are *you*?" I ask my sister.

"Ha, not a chance, pal." She hops up off the bed. "I'm done with this emotion shit for tonight."

Goddamn, she got the better of me. And to add insult to injury, she's stoppering the whisky and getting ready to carry it away with her.

"You could leave that here," I suggest.

"Not after the other night," she says. "You couldn't even form words. Lucky I'm strong, or you'd have been sleeping on the porch."

I thought I'd made it up to bed on my own after my Jack Daniels binge. Seems not. Wonder what other mortifications are yet to be revealed?

She slips the glass from my hand, brushes the scantest kiss across my hair.

"Night, bro," she says, as she shuts the door behind her. "Don't let the bastards grind you down."

I ponder her words. Seems like good advice.

Then I picture Shelby's face this morning, and how she couldn't hide how badly I'd hurt her.

Guess that advice doesn't work so well if one of the bastards happens to be you.

Chapter Nineteen

SHELBY

A part from that awful time where I couldn't get out of bed, I've been used to knuckling down, even when I don't feel like it. When you run a small family business, jobs always need doing, no matter whether you're tired, unhappy, or stressed out of your mind. If *you* don't do what's required, either someone else is forced to pick up the slack and work overtime, or it all starts to fall apart. If you want to go out of business pronto, that's the way to do it.

So even though I've had no sleep, and I'm dreading seeing Nate because I still have no clear idea what I'm going to say to him, I get up and get ready, same time as I always do. I may not be looking forward to the day, but that's not going to stop the day from happening or make the to-do list magically shorter.

Still, the instant I spy the silver pickup parked beside the Dodge, my heart and stomach decide to exchange places, making me simultaneously sick and dizzy. That free glass of pinot grigio was my last, so I can't blame alcohol. Nope, this is pure nerves. The nauseating kind that normally comes before doing something terrifying, like bungy jumping or ordering a drink from Brendan.

Deep breath, Shelby. It's not going to get any easier if you put it off. And you're *way* too old to spend the whole day hiding in a blanket fort, as awesome as that sounds.

In keeping with my tear-the-wax-strip-off-quickly-and-stifle-a-scream philosophy, I knock only briefly on the office door, and step right on in.

Nate's sitting behind the desk. Surprised to see me, he stands up in a hurry and nearly tips the whole thing over. Before this week, that would have meant a landslide of paper and files. This morning, the pencil rolls a little to the left.

"Hey," he says, taking the word right out of my mouth.

I extemporize. "Hi."

Then we stare at each other. Until, as is traditional in such circumstances, we both start speaking at once.

"I—"

"Th—"

Following the ritual to a T, we both say, "Go—"

"No, you go—"

And grind to a halt again.

"I'm sorry." Nate leaps headlong into the gap. "I should never have put you on the spot like that. It was a dick move."

"But it wasn't a stupid thing to ask," I tell him. "You've got a lot on your plate, and I know how emotionally draining family issues are. *I* haven't even *thought* about having a relationship since Dad died. Except, of course, with you…"

Nice hole you're digging, Shelby.

"So what I'm saying," I continue, hurriedly, "is that I'm OK to wait. I accused you of not trusting me, but I also need to trust that *you* know your own mind. So if you say you need time, I shouldn't question that."

I didn't know I was going to say that when I walked in. But I've said it now, and it rings true to me. Nate Durant *is* worth waiting for. Just … not forever, if you get me. I'm not up for some dying-in-a-cave scenario, like in *The English Patient*.

His shoulders sag and I can't tell whether it's disappointment or relief. But then he strides round the desk and pulls me into his arms. Only an embrace, no kissing. I wrap my arms around his waist, lay my head on his chest and breathe him in. Unlike Ted, Nate doesn't seem to go in for cologne or aftershave, so he smells like himself, manly musk with a hint of laundry detergent and … is that *cookies*?

"You are the greatest thing to ever happen to me," he murmurs into my hair. "And I will *not* fuck this up, I *swear*."

"Can I ask you one question, though?" I say.

I feel him tense.

"I can't be sure about timing," he says. "I don't want to overpromise and disappoint you."

"That's not the question."

I raise my head. He's frowning down at me.

"OK?" he says, warily.

"My question *is*: why do you smell of cookies?"

He nods, slowly. "Because I missed out last night, so I stole what was left this morning and ate them for breakfast."

"Can't believe your family left cookies uneaten," I say. "What kind of weirdoes are you people?"

"Weirder than you can imagine," he replies. "Though I *am* the only one who ate six cookies for breakfast."

I smile up at him. "I think we must have been separated at birth."

He seems to be battling between smiling back and frowning. For a second, I think he's going to kiss me, and my whole body fires up in anticipation.

But Nate's got a lot of self-discipline – I know *that* about him by now – so all he does is tighten his embrace for a moment, and then step back, with a last gentle touch on my upper arms.

"A part of me feels I ought to say I don't deserve you," he says. "But a way bigger part wants to prove that's one hundred percent wrong."

I *also* know that he can be super intense. And that worries me, just a teensy bit.

"Nate, the whole point of me giving you time," I say, "is so you *won't* become stressed out of your mind trying to juggle everything."

His face, which has been unusually demonstrative, closes up like a clam. Does he think I'm insulting him? Or that I'm not as into this as he is? I wish Chiara were somehow spying on us behind a two-way mirror, so she could give me instructions through a hidden earpiece.

I guess I should just be honest.

"If I had it my way," I tell him, "we'd be doing it right now on that desk."

Left eyebrow twitch. I've triggered a reaction, though its epicenter is probably a lot lower down.

"But, given that's not going to happen," I continue, "I want things between us to be as relaxed as they possibly can. I don't want you trying extra hard or worrying about me, because that's pressure you don't need." I pause. "Am I making any kind of sense? I'm not sure."

"You are," he replies. "I just ... I don't want you ever thinking I'm not fully committed."

I shouldn't smile, but I can't help it. "Nate, no one who'd met you for five *seconds* would be in any doubt about your level of commitment. To *anything*."

His poker face is on its maximum setting.

"Are you saying I'm uptight?"

Bite your lip, Shelby, or you're going to burst out laughing.

"I'll have you know," he says, "that I've been granted membership of the Can't Pull A Needle Out of Our Asses With a Tractor Club. It's seriously exclusive. You have to sit a test. Like Mensa."

Figure it's OK to laugh now, so I do.

"Shit," he says, but he's smiling. "Guess I'll be able to count on you to keep me grounded."

"And don't forget our code word," I remind him.

"Though 'Jesus' might give the wrong impression in some quarters. How about 'cookie?'"

"'Cookie' will give the *right* impression?"

"It's kind of like the word 'squirrel' is to dogs," I explain. "Instant universal distraction."

He mulls it over.

"Will it be a reciprocal code word?" he asks. "One *I* can use when you're being incredibly irritating?"

"Don't you mean 'if'?" I say.

"No."

Didn't even hesitate, the swine.

"OK," I say. "But we *both* have to agree to abide by it. There will be no ignoring or overriding of the cookie warning. Deal?"

I stick out my hand.

"Deal," he says.

We shake, and he winces again, flexing his hand as if checking for damage.

"How the hell does someone your size have hands that strong?"

"Years of vine work," I say. "Pruning, harvesting, tying, etc."

"You and your friend, Jordan, should start an all-woman wrestling team."

I adopt my most innocent-evil look. "I'd rather wrestle you."

"Stop," he says, in mock warning.

"But not in whipped cream because I'd just want to eat it."

He points at the door. "Out."

"Jello?"

"Out!"

I practically skip out, buoyant with relief that Nate and I are on good terms again. What I would have done if it had all turned sour, I've *no* idea. Lucky break for me, then.

Kind of incredible to think that a week ago today was the first time Nate and I met. In a short seven days, I've gone from resenting his presence on the planet to ... what? Guess we're lovers on hold, if such a category exists. On hold until the situation with Nate's father resolves itself one way or another.

The sudden realization of what that means brings me up short in the middle of the path. One way is that his father's health improves. Another is that it ... doesn't.

How could I have been so dense not to pick up on that? I suppose I was so shocked by Nate's suggestion that we take a break that it never registered. And I got bushwhacked by the relationship-on-hold convo, and never got around to asking why he'd had to make an emergency dash to the hospital.

Sheesh, I don't even know exactly what's *wrong* with Nate's dad. Only that he's suffering from a non-specific condition known as "ill". But if all the family came home to be with him, it seems clear now that he's on the "very ill" side of the register. You don't come rushing to your dad's bedside if he has a case of poison ivy. You don't put a budding romance complete with scorching sex on pause if you haven't got something *really* big to worry about...

I feel very bad about not asking. I feel worse because I suspect Nate didn't give me details in the first place out of concern that he'd upset me, by triggering memories of my own dad dying. He was mindful of my feelings, and yet all *I* could do yesterday morning was think of myself. That makes two of us thinking of me, I suppose, but only one of us is a selfish cow.

I could go back and ask him now, but do I really want to know? Do I want to retreat back to my old self, with my head in the clouds? Or is it time to step up, and be a mature lady?

"You OK?"

I've also been standing still on the path for too long. Cam's come to check on me and use up valuable words in doing so.

"I'm fighting the urge to be in complete denial," I tell him.

Cam scratches the back of his head, which means he's relieved it's nothing worse.

"Is there a hospital near Martinburg?" I ask.

He doesn't blink. He's used to my left-field requests. "Yup."

"It's not for me," I assure him. "I'm fine. I'm doing some sleuthing."

Dylan the goose comes waddling up. Cam automatically reaches down and strokes his neck. If Dylan were a cat, he'd purr. I hope Nate doesn't catch this little interaction. He's irrational enough about Cam as it is, bless him.

"Putting in an oak order," Cam says.

Cam gets most of the wood for his barrels from a forest in the back blocks of the Appalachians, and the rest from one in the Limousin area of France. Both are privately owned and supply only to Cam, for reasons that are as mysterious as everything else about him.

Some pinot noir vintners will only use French oak, but Dad liked the creamier flavour that American oak imparts, adding a little bit of French oak for silkiness and spice. Vintners can also get extremely anal about the proportions of new versus old oak, and the levels of "toast," which is when the barrel has literally been toasted over a flame to release other aromas from the wood, namely vanilla.

Dad would simply tell Cam his vision for the wine and leave it up to him to decide the makeup of the barrels. I've seen no reason to change that.

What Cam's asking is if I need any new barrels. Obviously, it costs money to replace the old ones, but after too many years, they stop adding flavour to the wine. Dad also used to leave it to Cam to decide when a barrel needed to be retired. I've seen no reason to change that, either.

But now, I'm no longer in charge of the money.

"Go check the inventory," I tell Cam, "and give me a report, and a cost estimate. I'll take it to Nate."

"Written?"

"Yeah." I make an apologetic face. "Sorry."

He winces, but it's probably because Dylan has pecked his hand, annoyed that he's paused the stroking.

"K."

Cam fishes a piece of dried corn out of his pocket,

because what else would he have in there? He holds it out for Dylan, who honks impatiently, and Cam heads off like a giant tousle-haired Pied Piper, a greedy goose flapping after him.

For a moment, I have a pang of concern about this new regime. The fluid, organic systems Nate has issue with have worked pretty well for us for years. This winery has always run on give and take. OK, sure, we weren't making enough money, but we could have lost way more if people hadn't been so willing to help. They did so because they knew we'd do what we could for them in return.

I hope Nate's need for order and certainty doesn't crush that spirit. We'll still need a solid amount of goodwill to see us through this coming season, at least.

But that can wait. Time now to find out if one Mitchell Durant is in Martinburg hospital, *and* if I can be cunning enough to get the staff to spill what's wrong with him.

Maybe I should enlist Chiara? She's way better at subterfuge than I am.

I text her: *Want 2 tell sum lies 4 me?*

Im ur woman, she texts right back. *Tell me what u need.*

Chapter Twenty

NATE

I am the luckiest guy in the world.

Also the most relieved and amazed.

In fact, my luck is so unbelievable that my natural pessimism is forced to kick in. Luck this good must be a mirage, surely? I must have imagined that conversation with Shelby. Or when I heard her say she was willing to wait, she was actually telling me to fuck right off.

Sometimes, my brain is a serious scumbag.

I use a tactic that usually works when my brain's being a dick – crunch some numbers. Numbers are solid, reliable, and consistent. Numbers are the same every time. They don't mess with your mind by changing around.

However, they *can* mess with your mind if they paint a financial picture that's darker than Ava's old bedroom paint scheme. Now that I've got the accounts and banking online, including the shoebox of receipts and the pile of invoices, I can get a real idea of where Flora Valley Wines stands.

And after a solid ninety minutes of spread-sheeting, I can safely say that Flora Valley Wines is standing on the financial equivalent of a frayed tightrope strung across the Grand Canyon with the knots unravelling at each end.

Shit. It's worse than I thought. More worryingly, it's worse than JP thought. He knew the last set of accounts showed the winery was barely solvent, but those were for the *last* financial year, and we're already well down the track of this one. I'm surprised JP didn't push Shelby for an up-to-date balance sheet. My feeling is he was so taken by her, and such a fan of her father, that he let his normal caution slide.

He had *me* by then, too. Being Dad's old friend, not to mention Ava's godfather, he'd kept tabs on all us Durant kids. He knew what I'd done with the winery in France before I contacted him looking for work, and for JP that must have seemed like serendipity. Saw me as the perfect guy for the perfect investment. I could make a joke about rosé-tinted glasses, but right now, I feel very far from laughter.

And there we have it. In only ninety minutes, I've gone from the luckiest guy in the world to one facing a battle I'm not sure I can win. Anton's winery in France just needed tweaking – improved logistics, and smarter sales and marketing. I persuaded him to shift to varietal marketing rather than the traditional labelling by regional *appellation*. The French are big on *terroir*, the land where the grapes were grown, rather than the type of grapes themselves. They won't even display the name of the grape on the bottle. But varietals are what international buyers want. It was a simple switch to make, but it launched us to a new level.

I can't perform that same magic trick here. But I have to pull *something* out of the hat. Shelby's livelihood depends on it. Our relationship depends on it. No matter what happens with Dad, I haven't a hope with Shelby if I let this winery fail.

Deep breath, Nate. Focus. Think smart and fast.

Two hours later, head aching from hitting brick walls, I'm forced to admit I have no option. The only way we can get through this season is if JP tips more money in. I have to call him. It's Friday. Maybe he'll be in a happy Friday mood.

It's 4pm and I'm sitting in his office, feeling like Oliver Twist. Please, sir, may I have some more? Yes, sir, I know I outlined a sound five-year plan for Flora Valley Wines that you approved, but let's just say we didn't have all the data.

I could also point out that he should have done more than a cursory due diligence to start with. But I'm aware that people are more likely to be generous and open-minded if you *don't* accuse them of being negligent.

"Nate, how are you?" He gives me an affectionate two-handed shake.

JP really does fit the description "silver fox". He and Dad have known each other since high school when they both competed in track, like I did. The two men are still lean as they were back then, but where Dad looks all wind-burned and outdoorsy, JP is sleek and well-groomed. Dad subscribes to *Gear Patrol* magazine, and JP to *Esquire*.

Personality-wise, they're pretty similar. But where Dad's hard-driving approach is out there for everyone to see, JP leavens his with an affable charm. People meeting him for the first time can be fooled into thinking he's a pleasant pushover. They wonder how on earth he got the reputation for being a hard-ass. Then they find out. And once the scars have healed, they never make *that* mistake again.

I have never underestimated JP. That's why, right now, I am *chier dans mon froc*, the French equivalent of crapping my pants. But there's too much at stake here to be a pussy. I have to make a case for more investment, and I have to make it watertight.

"Thanks for meeting me at short notice," I say.

JP gestures for me to take a seat, and he sits himself back down in a Wegner Swivel ergonomic chair that I happen to know costs over ten grand. His desk looks Scandi as well, as does the chair I'm in, and no doubt all are mid-century originals. JP's taste is as impeccable as his grooming.

"Obviously, you're here to discuss business," says JP. "But first, how's Mitchell? I got the impression from your mother that he was being a little ... difficult?"

"Dad's not the greatest fan of modern medicine," I understate by a mile.

"And like all unreasonable men, he believes the universe should adapt to him, and not the other way round."

It's not a question.

"Doc Wilson's on the case," I say in the hopes we can end this subject. I don't really want to talk about Dad with

JP. It brings up a whole slew of emotions that aren't conducive to clear thinking.

"Doc Wilson." JP chuckles. He, too, has known Doc for years. "Has he called Mitch a 'durn fool' yet?"

"No," I reply, "but he did call him a 'dang' one."

JP meets my eye, and I know *he* knows exactly what the situation is with Dad. And that it's not in the least bit funny.

"I'll stop by this weekend," he says. "Check in on him."

I have this mental picture of two stags smacking heads together. But JP and Dad go back a long way and have remained friends despite competing in almost every aspect of their lives.

I suspect, but don't have proof, that Mom chose Dad over JP way back in high school. JP went on to marry a supermodel, and amazingly, considering it's highly probable he only married her to one-up Dad, they're still together. Petra and JP are often around for dinner, and when Danny and I were teenagers, the mere trace of Petra's perfume could turn us into stuttering idiots. Max, of course, has always been far too cool for that kind of embarrassing behaviour.

"OK." JP snaps into professional mode. "What do you have for me?"

Crunch time. It occurred to me on the way here, that if it weren't for Shelby, I'd have no problem delivering the bad news. I'd suggest JP cut his losses, carve the business up into saleable portions – land, assets, house, etc. – and flog each to the highest bidder. Plenty of successful vineyard owners who'd jump at the chance to acquire established vines.

OK, so I'd be out of a job, but I've got a pretty attractive resumé. The dismantling of Flora Valley Wines wouldn't be a crisis. For me.

Needless to say, that's not the option I intend to put to JP.

"We need an injection of cash." No point in beating around the bush.

"How much?"

"Thirty grand will tide us over. Until we sell last year's vintage."

"And if you don't sell it?" JP asks the only important question.

To which I can give only one answer. "We will."

JP and I have a poker face-off. Then, when I'm *this* close to yielding, he smiles.

"How are you and Shelby getting along?"

Probably not appropriate to tell him she gave me a key lime blowjob. Or that I've fallen headlong in love for the first real time in my life and will do *any*thing to ensure I can be the man she needs.

"We're a good team," I say.

"I had coffee with her mother, Lee," JP reveals, somewhat startlingly. "She told me Shelby went through a bad patch after Billy died. Pulled through it, but still worries about her. I promised we'd take the weight of running the business off her shoulders, let her focus on what she does best – making great wine."

Jesus, my heart is pounding. What does he mean "a bad patch"? What *happened*?

But JP's out of his ten grand chair. Our business is concluded.

"I'll sign off the cash injection," he says. "Say hello to Shelby for me."

"Thanks," I shake his hand. "I will."

Outside his building, I feel safe enough to breathe out. And then I stand there, car keys in hand, wondering what the hell to do now.

It's four-thirty on a Friday afternoon. Day's almost done. I could drive back to Flora Valley Wines and demand Shelby tells me what happened to her. But then I can one hundred percent guarantee that if she's upset, I will pull her into my arms, and I don't trust my willpower to prevent that contact escalating into something much more intimate.

It was torture enough this morning, trying to keep that hug friendly. The feel of her against me, the *scent* of her, sets every nerve end jangling like the fallout alert at a nuclear power plant. She's established permanent residency in a part of my mind, and I'm *always* aware of her, even when sweating over numbers, like today.

I thought it would be tough taking a break from her. I didn't think it would rank right up there with the twelve tasks of Hercules. In fact, shovelling ten tons of shit from the Augean stables seems pretty attractive right now. Herc, bro, you had it easy.

My phone beeps with a text, and the lovesick part of me

hopes it's Shelby, giving me an excuse to drive back and see her.

It's Danny. Dad's out of hospital. Mom's requested my presence for a family dinner.

Sure. Let's pretend like everything is normal, Mom. Let's talk about sport, and the weather, and force Max to play the piano for us. Why don't we play Go Fish afterwards, just for old times' sake?

Wow, Nate, you're being a serious prick. This is your *family*. Your father's ill, and your mother is worried out of her mind that she's going to lose the man she loves. Your brothers and sisters are putting their lives on hold to be here, and all you can do is think shitty, resentful thoughts. Just because *your* life is a steaming pile of crap doesn't mean you have the right to dump on others. Get a grip. Go have dinner.

I go. I act normal, as does everyone else. We all ignore the constant hum of underlying tension. Max plays the piano while we have coffee. Danny brings out the cards and we start a game of Go Fish. I catch Ava's eye only once but it's enough. She's in the same space as I am, and no doubt the others are, too. We're making an effort for Mom.

Dad goes to bed early. He didn't say two words over dinner, and he still looks weak and worn. After making sure he's settled, Mom comes back down and tells us that he *is* now taking medication, and apparently even considering having an ICD put in. That stands for implantable cardioverter defibrillator. It monitors your heart rhythms and sends an electric pulse if things start to go haywire. The procedure is minimally invasive, performed under a local anesthetic.

Mom's tone is bright, hopeful, like it's a done deal. It's Danny who says what we're all thinking.

"When does he have to make a decision?"

"Oh, I guess, in the next few days," says Mom.

None of us comments, but I guarantee we're all thinking the same thing. Even *one* day is plenty of time for Dad to research a raft of alternative cures, and to talk himself out of the sensible option.

As if sensing our skepticism, Mom hops out of the chair.

"I made a new batch of cookies. I'll fetch them."

When she's out of the room, we all exchange looks of varying levels of despair.

"JP's planning to drop by this weekend," I say. "Never know. He and Dad are so competitive, if JP uses reverse psychology, Dad might do it to spite him."

"Is he bringing Petra?" says Danny, in a casual tone that fools no one.

I meet his gaze. "Didn't say."

Ava rolls her eyes. "She's the same age as Mom."

"Yeah, well, I'm going to let Freud worry about that one," says Danny, with a grin.

"Ee-yew!" says Izzy, as Max chimes in with, "That is *wrong*."

Suddenly, from the kitchen comes a sound of crashing china. As one, the five of us leap up and sprint to the adjacent room.

Mom's leaning on the kitchen counter, face in her hands,

shoulders shaking. A plate is in pieces on the floor, cookies strewn among the shards.

Danny reaches her first, wraps his arms round her. Izzy fetches a brush and pan, as Ava and Max start to pick up the bits of cookie and china.

I approach Mom and touch her gently on the hair. The gesture seems to bring her to herself, and she straightens up and out of Danny's hug.

"I'm so sorry," she says. "I didn't mean to startle you. It was just me being clumsy."

Another exchange of glances pinballs between the five of us.

"Mom." I designate myself spokesperson. "We'll make Dad see sense. We've been relatively polite and patient up till now, but it's time to take the gloves off. We'll rope in Doc Wilson and even JP if we have to. Even *Dad* can't be so bullheaded as to ignore *everyone* who loves him."

I squeeze her shoulder, and she pats my hand, drops a kiss on my knuckles.

"We'll make it happen," I assure her. "I *promise*."

Another promise, to another woman I love.

I used to think I relished a challenge but I realize that, before now, the consequences of failure were limited to my humiliation. Even Anton's winery would have limped on if my marketing ploy had flopped.

Now, if I fail Mom and Shelby, I shatter their hearts, hopes and dreams. I ruin their lives.

Better get it right, Nate. That's all I'm saying.

Chapter Twenty-One

SHELBY

Jordan, Chiara, and I agreed that meeting for drinks two days in a row is warranted, despite the risk that Brendan will kick us out if the bar gets too full, owing to us taking up valuable seating space without spending actual money.

"If you look sad, he might take pity on you again," says Jordan.

"Think that was a one-time offer," I reply. "Brendan's cup of care appears about as often as Halley's comet."

Jordan gazes toward the bar, where Brendan is ignoring two guys who've been waiting there for a good couple of minutes.

"He will notice me *one* day," she says.

"No, he won't," says Chiara. "Brendan has a girlfriend."

"He so does *not*!" protests Jordan. "I've never seen him with *any*one! And I've followed him *several* times!"

"She lives in LA," Chiara informs her, with a certain

relish, I might add. "Actress. She comes up every so often, only for a day or two at a time. Guess we never see her because they're, you know ... busy."

"That sounds like a *stupid* arrangement." Jordan folds her arms in a sulk. "*I'm* right here. All. The. Time."

"And only fifteen years younger," I point out.

"Why didn't you tell me earlier?" Jordan demands of Chiara.

"Just found out," she replies. "I was doing some digging for Shelby here, and I happened upon that juicy little tidbit, too."

"How could those pieces of information possibly be related?" I have to ask.

"One of the nurses on Mitchell Durant's ward is the actress's sister," is the simple answer. "We ended up having a *looong* chat."

The world's intelligence community is seriously missing out on Chiara's talents. You'd think they'd be more onto that.

"And so?" I prompt. "What's the deal with Nate's father?"

"He's got a potentially fatal heart condition brought on by a virus. Happens more often than you'd think. My new nurse friend says it's manageable. If you *want* to manage it, that is..."

She pauses significantly.

I am her faithful stooge. "Why wouldn't you want to?"

"We-ell." Chiara's enjoying this. "Seems Mr Durant senior is a bit of a ... shall we say ... *fringe* dweller when it comes to medical science. He believes the human body has all it needs to heal itself."

"Wrong!" says Jordan. "I knew this super-fit guy once who got bit by some bat in Africa, and he got freaking Ebola!"

"But medical science fixed him, is what you forgot to say," I suggest.

"Nope, he died vomiting blood."

"Cool story, Jords," nods Chiara. "Awesome."

"So back to Nate's dad," I say. "Are you saying he won't take medication for his condition?"

"He refused to take *anything* until he got brought in after a collapse. Now, he's grudgingly on the minimum. But what he needs is some kind of device that regulates his heartbeat. If he refuses that, his chances aren't great. Mortality rate higher than seventy percent, even if he is a damn sight fitter than *my* dad."

Chiara's Italian dad is the cook in the family, and believes cream is a condiment. His cannoli are to *die* for. OK, bad choice of words.

"Why would you be that stubborn when your life's at risk?" I ask.

Then I picture Nate, and answer my own question.

"Have you talked to Nate about this?" says the ever-psychic Chiara.

"Not in detail. I think he was concerned I'd be upset. You know, because *my* dad died."

"Ah, that's really sweet," says Jordan, the romantic. "Nate, I mean. Not your dad dying."

"I think he's worried," I say. "Like *really* worried. I thought all this relationship-on-hold thing was because he was super busy, but now I think it's more like he's super stressed. And to be honest, I'm not sure he's all that good at dealing with it."

"Yeah, he's a pretty solid Type A," says Chiara. "You think he might be heading for a crash like yours?"

"Thanks for reminding me of that dark, terrible time in my life," I say.

"No problemo," Chiara says, with a smile. "Well, do you?"

"How can I tell?" I shrug. "We're supposed to be colleagues now, all business. I can hardly drop something like that into a conversation about cluster thinning."

"You could put one of those signs up, like they have on the Golden Gate Bridge," says Jordan. *"Having suicidal thoughts? Call 1-800-SHELBY."*

"Nice. Subtle."

"Get him drunk?" is her follow-up.

"Not the worst idea," says Chiara, and adds, pointedly, "You recall how he loosened up after a couple of cocktails the other night?"

"Wish you'd invited me," says Jordan, with a pout. The news about Brendan has really put a dampener on her evening.

"You were in the hills roasting coyotes over an open flame," Chiara reminds her. "Making s'mores from squished rattlesnakes."

"I love Ted," Jordan sighs. "But he's not Brendan."

"Speaking of," says Chiara. "I think we may have outstayed our welcome."

I look where she's looking and, sure enough, Brendan is heading our way. Trouble is, he's between us and the door, and he's too big to dodge around. We'll have to bluff it out.

"Get you anything else?" he asks, knowing full well what the answer is.

Jordan and Chiara bought one drink each. I had a sip of theirs. We've been here for well over an hour.

"No, thank you," says Jordan. "We are leaving."

Her cool, haughty tone surprises all of us. Including Brendan. I can tell because his right eye narrows a fraction.

"Come along, girls."

Jordan holds her head high and leads us out the front door. I can't help a quick glance back, and before the door swings shut, I'm pretty sure I see Brendan still standing there, looking after us.

"What now?" says Chiara, when we're out on the street. "Shall I blag us into Bartons?"

"No, I need pizza," says Jordan. "With extra cheese. And then a *lot* of ice cream."

The pizza parlour in Verity is … not great. But Jordan's the one in emotional need tonight, and so that's where we go.

I get home around ten-thirty, to an enthusiastic greeting from Dylan. Dogs are asleep on my bedroom floor and acknowledge me with a brief wagging of tails. The cats are on my bed and couldn't give a fig whether I'm back or not. I brush my teeth and get into what passes for pajamas – a T-shirt even older than the ones I usually wear – and part the cats to either side so I can actually fit onto the bed.

Then I lie there, thinking about Nate. About how he must have felt finding out his dad was critically ill. How frustrating and scary it must be now to witness him refuse treatment.

At least with my dad, he was willing to do whatever it took to fight the cancer, and he kept it up, despite the horrendous toll on him physically and emotionally. Chemo *sucks.* Dad admitted that sometimes he thought he'd be better off giving up. He might die quicker, but at least he'd feel like a whole person and not a retching, feeble, hairless shell of a man.

But he pushed through the chemo, and the cancer went into remission. It felt like such a victory. I really thought – we all did – that he'd beaten it for good. Dad made you believe anything was possible if you put your mind to it. Though he was proved wrong, and cancer got him in the end, I still want to believe that.

How hard must it be for Nate to watch his father put his life at risk, even if the guy doesn't think that's what he's doing…

My phone's on the bedside table. I shouldn't do this. It's late, which isn't professional.

Thing is, I could *pretend* it's a business text, by asking him how his meeting went with JP. Nate told me he was going to see him. Didn't say why, but I assume JP requires a regular check-in.

It's ten forty-five, and all I have is the flimsiest and most transparent reason for contacting Nate. He'll see through it in an instant and, quite rightly, will ignore me until tomorrow morning. Or Monday, which would be the professional time to have this conversation.

Of course, I text him. What did you think? *How did ur meeting go with JP?*

I don't expect a response. I jump out of my skin when the phone rings.

It can't be Nate, surely? "Hi?"

"Hey."

It's Nate.

"I thought you'd ignore me," I say. "Given this is a dumb time to text."

"I'm lying on the bed staring at the ceiling," he replies. "Dumb is the theme of the evening."

My whole being suddenly craves to be there with him. I want to feel his skin against mine, and I want to comfort him with my touch and my kisses. The urge is so strong, for a moment, I can hardly breathe.

"Shit…" I hear him murmur. Maybe he's telepathic?

"Are you OK?" I ask. "I'm worried about you."

"Worried about *me*?" He sounds genuinely surprised.

"I found out about your dad."

May as well come clean. You can waste a lot of energy keeping secrets.

"Did you," he says, flatly. "May I ask how?"

"Chiara."

After a beat, he says, "If she'd been around during World War II, it would have been over by Christmas."

"Preach it," I say, despite being one thousand percent white.

He's silent again for a while. I'm happy to wait. I like listening to his breathing.

"Can I ask you a personal question?" he says.

"Sure," I say, more confidently than I feel.

"I found out something about you, too," he starts off. Then he hesitates.

"I once had a crush on Jon Bon Jovi?"

Not a good time for jokes, but I'm nervous. What's he going to say?

"I had a crush on Penélope Cruz," he tells me. "Still kind of do."

"Fair enough. She's smoking."

More silence. Up to me to fill it, I guess.

"Nate, what did you find out about me?"

He blows out a breath. "That you had ... a bad patch. After your dad died."

"Oh. That."

"Shel, what the fuck *happened*?" He's not hesitant now.

"I got pole-axed by grief," is the best way I can describe it. "Couldn't get out of bed. Cats thought it was great."

"Who looked after you? You're all on your own."

His voice sounds all high and tight with worry.

"Everyone," I assure him. "Mom, Chiara, Jordan, Iris, Cam, my doctor. I had a whole team around me."

Only a slight pause this time. "Cam?"

"You're an idiot," I tell him.

"Granted," he sighs. "So, you had help?"

"I had help, company, medication, chicken soup – everything I needed. Came out of it in a couple of weeks. It's a pretty normal response to losing someone."

I really *am* going all out to reassure him.

"And I'm fine now. Stayed on the happy pills for three months then eased off them. All good."

Possibly might be trying to reassure myself as well.

"Can I ask *you* a question?" I say.

"I can hardly say no," he replies, sounding like he totally wants to.

"How did you find out?"

"JP had coffee with your mother," is the bombshell he drops.

"With *Mom*?"

"It's OK, he's married," Nate says.

"Mom and JP are like polar opposites, anyway. She's *way* too alternative and untidy for a slick dude like him."

Definitely trying to reassure myself.

"We're opposites," says Nate, in a tone I can't quite decipher.

"Not *that* opposite," I counter. "Not in the essentials."

I swear, he groans on the other end, like his leg's gone to sleep, and he's now gritting his teeth through the pins and needles.

"Shel, I've got to go, before I do something I regret," he says.

"No, stay!" I plead, though I've got no valid argument beyond my own desire to stay on the line with him.

"Shel, seriously," he says. "Bed is a *bad* place to be right now. I'm having … inappropriate thoughts. It'd be stupid to act on them. Defeats the whole purpose of putting us on hold."

I can't fault his reasoning. I should respect his wishes, and not try to compromise him. That's unfair, and wrong.

But that's my conscience speaking, and right at this moment, it's being pummelled into submission by my libido, which is dialled up to eleven. My free hand is stealing downwards, and even if Nate insists on hanging up, I know what *I'll* be doing for the next short while.

Oh, boy, I make contact, and a little moan escapes.

"Fucking hell," I hear him mutter. "OK, shit, just … wait a moment. I have to…"

I hear rustling, the thump of shoes being discarded, a creak of bedsprings.

"Ready?" I ask.

"*Shit* no," he breathes. "This is *nuts*."

"Well, you'd better get ready pronto," I say. "Because I've got a two-minute head start."

Chapter Twenty-Two

NATE

I have to confess it's not the first time I've done something like this in this room. *Definitely* the first time there's been a phone and someone else involved.

At least I had the presence of mind to lock the door. Bad enough being in my childhood bedroom. Don't want one of my siblings barging in (as has happened before – thanks Dan, did you forget how to *knock*?). Or, worse, my mother (never happened, thank Christ).

It's not that easy with a phone. Can hardly put it on speaker, though. And too late to ask Max to borrow his hi-tech headphones. Last time he saw me naked, I'd have been ten, and he'd have been four. And certain parts of me would have been more ... modestly displayed.

Fuck, my cock is hard. It sprung to attention the instant Shelby let out that moan, and a lot of blood that should be powering my brain went immediately south.

Hence I'm stroking with one hastily-lotioned hand,

while the other presses my mobile to my ear, listening to sounds that I swear will make me shoot my load in about twenty seconds.

Shit, almighty, what is she *doing*? I suspect my imagination is more vivid than the reality, but still ... holy hell.

"Shel," I whisper. "Speak to me."

"I'm picturing *you*," she says, all breathless.

"So I'd hope," I remark.

She rightly ignores me. "You're fully dressed..."

Wrong.

"...and you're tying my hands to the bedpost, with pieces of soft rope..."

Wait, *what*?

"I can't move," she goes on. "But I'm *desperate* for you, so *wet* and hot. I'm lifting myself up off the bed, *begging* for you to come inside me..."

Damn, she has a talent for this. My breathing is seriously uneven. I try not to speed up. Need to keep a lid on.

"...and now you're taking off your clothes, and you're naked and *so* hard..."

That part's correct.

"I'm begging again, *sobbing* with need. But all you do is get this ... feather..."

A *what*?

"...and you start running it all over my body. You start at my neck, softly, but then you kind of *flick* it across my nipples and I just about *explode* with the sensation..."

Her and me both.

"Then you trace it down my belly, and start to caress the inside of my thighs…"

Shit. Hurry up, Shel.

"I'm begging again. I can't *stand* it. But you're cruel. You trace the feather up and down my thighs, and make me lift my rear, so you can stroke that, too…"

Hurry *up*.

"…and even though you haven't even *touched* me there yet, I can *feel* my orgasm building…"

Ditto. Fuck. Both of us are now breathing fast and rough.

"And then suddenly, you lower yourself over me and *plunge* right into the hilt, and I'm so wet, I take you *all* the way, and … *ohh*…"

Fuckkk. I have to summon all my resources not to yell to the rafters. Shelby, on the other hand, can probably be heard out in the Horsehead Nebula.

Now, I'm seeing stars for real. Nope, it's because my eyes are closed. My breathing is still crazy rough, and I'm not even going to *think* about the mess I've created. I've wiped my hand best I can. Hope I left a towel in my sports bag.

By some miracle, the phone's remained pressed to my ear. I can hear Shelby's breathing start to quiet.

"*Feather?*" I have to ask.

"It was all I could think of on the spot!"

She begins to laugh. "The cats are pissed at me. They've stalked off in a huff."

"I'm thinking I should do some laundry. Sheets have taken a beating. So to speak."

"Didn't you have a sock handy?"

"A *sock*?"

"Mom used to complain about my brothers ruining theirs."

"Didn't that … chafe?"

"I gather they only used them at the last minute. Kind of popped them on top, like a catcher's mitt."

"See, that would *never* be discussed in my family," I tell her. "Because none of us would want to know."

"Mom and Dad used to wander round naked quite often," she tells me. "And no one *ever* shut the bathroom door. Made for interesting times bringing friends back home."

Shit, she's wonderful. I am *this* close to saying "I love you" out loud.

But then rational me finally punches through the layers of lust and delusion.

So what I say instead is, "Shel, we shouldn't have done that."

"Nate," she sighs. "It's done. Don't stress about it."

"This is *me* you're talking to," I reply.

"I know," she says, gently. "Do your best. And sleep tight. I'll see you Monday."

"OK," is my inadequate goodbye.

The phone bleeps its "call over" signal. I place it to one side and, reluctantly, lift the top sheet to assess the damage. Ugh. Funky.

I hop out of bed, carefully, open my sports bag. There's a sweat towel. It's small but it will have to do. One bodily fluid's much like another, right?

Afterwards, I lie back in bed again, in a different spot, and get ready to stare at the ceiling for another few hours, as per pretty much every night up till now, bar the one I got hammered, and the one where Shelby and I...

Amazingly, I fall asleep straight away, and dream of being stroked with feathers. Which feels nowhere near as strange or perverted as I might have expected. Learn something new every day.

I wake up to find I've slept *way* past my usual rising time. I've been trying to get out each day for a run, more for stress relief than fitness, and it helps if the sun's not baking down on me. Plus, early morning's so peaceful around here.

Today, I've missed the dawn slot by a good four hours. I throw my running gear on, anyway. If I go a shorter distance, I should be able to avoid heat stroke.

Halfway down the stairs, I hear voices by the front door. Mom. Shit, JP too. *And* Petra.

I hesitate. My running shorts aren't *that* short, but still, I feel a little underdressed. And no doubt Danny will be looking his sharp preppy best.

Cursing a testosterone-fuelled competitive nature, and Dan for looking like a Ralph Lauren model, I hightail it back upstairs and change.

Mom has taken her guests through to the formal living room. Which means she's still anxious. If she were feeling relaxed, she'd have steered the pair to her happy place, our kitchen. I get the feeling she's working up to petitioning JP, asking him to add his voice to the chorus that Dad has so far tuned out.

Danny's beaten me here. And he's signalled his intent by wearing the pink polo shirt. We all gave him shit for becoming Mr LA but there's no doubt it suits him. The shirt emphasizes his masculine physique while at the same time showing his vulnerable side. And that will be *exactly* Danny's plan, the shameless jerk.

"Oh, Nate, here you are."

Mom puts her hand on my arm, steers me forward to greet the guests. JP and I shake hands. I meet his eye, and he knows I'm grateful that he's here.

"Nathan."

Petra has this husky voice that, I swear, has some quality that bypasses your ears and goes straight to your groin. She's smiling at me, arms outstretched, and she is, without doubt, the most beautiful woman I have ever seen.

I mean, Shelby's gorgeous, and without being weird, my sisters and Mom are all seriously attractive. But when you see Petra, you know *exactly* why the Trojan War started. Even though she's nearly sixty years old, her beauty is mesmerizing.

Petra kisses me on both cheeks. I breathe in her signature perfume and feel my brain turn to mush on the spot. Then she steps back, and eyes me up and down.

"I can't believe it's been so long since I last saw you,"

she says. "How *handsome* you've become. You and Danny both. Though *you*, Nate, you're a *proper* man now."

It takes all my willpower not to direct a shit-eating smirk at Dan. Take *that*, Danny boy. With the emphasis on "boy."

But then in rocks Max, and Petra begins to gush.

"Oh, my God, Ginny. Your children are so *beautiful*."

She kisses Max, who is completely unfazed by her attentions, the little bastard.

"Max, you *must* come round and play for us," Petra insists. "We've heard *amazing* reports of your talent."

"Jealous much?" Dan whispers in my ear.

"Deserves a double dead arm," I mutter back.

Then the cavalry arrives, in the form of Izzy and Ava, who adore Petra, but – obviously – don't have the same pathetic reaction to her presence.

"Dad's just coming," Ava announces. "He's still pretty weak but he wanted to see you."

"Looking forward to seeing him, too," says JP.

"I'll make coffee," says Mom, whose agitation is clear to all.

"I'll help," says Izzy, meaning she'll keep an eye on Mom.

It occurs to me that our whole family is on constant alert, our fight or flight modes engaged practically 24/7. No wonder we're all a little frayed around the edges.

And here comes the cause. My father enters the room, and I observe a flicker of alarm cross JP's face. He's used to hale and hearty Mitch Durant, his not-so-old and seriously fit friend, full of vigour and strong opinions. The guy who walks in looks grey and ill, like the sap has been drained from him.

Guarantee his opinions are still at full strength, though. Proof of which we're no doubt about to witness.

"Mitch."

JP first and then Petra step forward to embrace Dad.

Ava pulls up an armchair for Dad, so he can sit close to his visitors, who take a seat on the sofa. The rest of us arrange ourselves in the background, out of politeness and a wish to monitor the conversation. Max offers Ava the other comfortable chair, but she shakes her head and perches on its arm instead. All the better to leap into the fray. When it comes to fight or flight, Ava only understands the former.

There's a bit of preliminary chat, mostly initiated by Petra. Danny and I exchange a look as she praises Max yet *again*, while the object of her attention remains gallingly indifferent.

Then JP cuts to the chase.

"So what's the deal, Mitch? I hear you've been reluctant to get treatment."

Dad doesn't bother casting an accusatory glance at his loose-lipped family. He's focused on his latest adversary, JP.

"Depends on what you mean by treatment," he says. "Plenty of non-invasive, natural ways to repair the heart."

"Proven to work?" JP's not holding back.

"Not by *your* doctors, perhaps," counters Dad. "But there's sound evidence nonetheless."

He leans forward, holds up his fingers to tick off the points.

"CoQ10 reenergizes every single cell in the heart and can actually *remold* its size and shape. You can supplement that with a regular tonic of cayenne pepper and hawthorn berry, and with B vitamins. Heavy metal chelators, such as cilantro and chlorella, can reduce the risk of a coronary event. Proteolytic enzymes clean out the blood and repair damage to epicardial tissue, and so can *reverse* heart damage."

Ava's head slumps for a second, and I sympathize. We've heard all this before. It still sounds like horseshit.

"What about the arrhythmia?" JP persists.

"A device can regulate the heartbeat," says Dad. "But it doesn't treat the underlying *health* of the heart. You sort *that* out, and the other issues go away."

"Mitch." Petra chimes in with her husky honeyed voice. "Don't you think the risk is too high? Your beautiful family *need* you."

Again, Dad doesn't look our way. I imagine he's aware that his beautiful family's primary wish right now is to beat some sense into him.

"I appreciate their concern," he says tightly. "But this is *my* life and *my* health. I don't interfere with the way they live, and I expect the same courtesy in return."

"Dad, you *ruled* our childhood with a rod of iron!" Ava can't help herself. "It was your way or the freaking *high*way!"

She has Mitch's attention now. And he's not happy.

"You were children, who needed guidance and focus," he says. "As adults, you now have all the freedom in the world."

"Oh, sure," retorts Ava. "Which is why all five of us are here in this house right now. Putting our *adult* lives on hold."

"I never asked you to!"

"No, Dad, you didn't. *Mom* did. Because she couldn't cope with you acting like a dick!"

"Ava." Danny sounds a gentle warning.

"No!" Ava jumps to her feet. "No, I'm *sick* of this *bull*shit!"

She gives JP and Petra an apologetic look. "Sorry, but that's what it is."

JP nods. He places his hand over Petra's, and she twines her fingers in his.

"Dad," says Ava, and there's a pleading note now in her voice. "Even if you down *gallons* of this herbal enzyme whatever, you don't have the luxury of waiting for your heart to heal. It could fail entirely *at any moment*. The hospital said so, Doc Wilson said so – do you *really* know better than they do?"

JP looks as if he's about to speak but changes his mind. He knows his old friend doesn't take kindly to being ganged up on. That's why Danny, Max and I are keeping quiet, too. If it's only Ava going at him, Dad *might* just listen with half an ear.

Or he might not.

Dad gets up out of his chair, and though even that small

effort makes him breathe hard, he stands tall and gazes fiercely around at each one of us in turn, including JP, and Petra, who looks stricken.

"I'm not prepared to have this discussion again," Dad tells us. "If you remain under *my* roof, then you will abide by *my* rules, and I will not tolerate any further disrespect. Are we clear?"

Danny puts a restraining hand on Ava's arm. She shrugs it off, angrily, but stays quiet.

"We're clear, Dad," I say.

Without even a goodbye nod to his guests, Dad walks slowly out of the room. We hear his footsteps heavy on the stairs.

A minute later, Izzy arrives with Mom, who's bearing a tray laden with coffee things and several kinds of cake. Izzy, instantly sussing out the situation, rescues the tray from a bewildered-looking Mom.

"Has Mitch not come down yet?" Mom asks. "I thought—"

We're all on our feet now. Petra puts her arm round Mom's shoulders and guides her gently to the sofa.

"Come and sit, Ginny."

JP blows out a breath.

"Sorry, guys," he says. "That was a bust."

"Not your fault," says Danny. "It'd be easier to convince conspiracy theorists that lizard people aren't a thing."

"What now?" Max asks the room. "Do we just … wait?"

Mom, almost in tears again, catches my eye and I see the

plea. I made a promise to her, but I have to confess I'd pinned my hopes on JP coming through for us.

Can't give up, though. And suddenly, amazingly, I have the germ of an idea.

It's a long shot. Requires me to ask for a favour I'm not sure I'm entitled to. But what other choice do I have?

"I might have a Plan B," I tell them. "No guarantees, though."

"Well, you are the *man*," says Danny, with a smug grin that makes my middle finger twitch. "So, by all means, lead the way."

"Just – you know – get a fucking move on," says Ava.

Mom sucks in a horrified breath. "We have *guests*."

But JP laughs.

"No point in mincing words, Ginny. Ava's right."

He turns his attention to me.

"Whatever you're planning, Nate," he says, "you need to pull out *all* the stops."

Chapter Twenty-Three

SHELBY

I wonder which Nate I'll get this morning. Serious Nate? Or the one who knows how to laugh?

I spent the weekend checking out the vines – everything's looking pretty good. Not too many leaves or extra growth that can interfere with the ripening. Toothless Doug's kept on top of the mowing and the weeds. No rot or fungi. We use only natural pest and weed controls here, and that means extra vigilance. But it also means better wine. In my opinion.

At this time of year, I take a few bunches for sampling, to see if any vines are ripening sooner than others. We don't have a large vineyard, and it's not spread over different terrain, so we don't get too much variation. Helps to check, though, because it can make all the difference when scheduling the harvest.

In the two weeks before our estimated harvest date, I'll

be here every day, testing sugar and acid levels, and what we call flavour ripeness. There's a science to knowing exactly when the grapes are ready to pick. There's also intuition honed by years of experience, which I don't yet have. Dad was a genius at it.

Harvest requires a *lot* of preparation. Every piece of equipment needs to be checked, and I need to order in all the supplies for cleaning, picking, and the making of the wine itself, like the yeasts.

Once those grapes are off the vines, we need to operate like a machine: sorting out any duds, getting the grapes in the cold soak, de-stemming bunches we're not using whole, and then the full-on process of fermentation. That's when I am head down, butt up, because grapes and yeasts are as needy as kids in puppy love. After fermentation, there's maceration, letting them soak in their skins. I'll taste the vats every day during that time.

Then we get to do the fun, physical work of pressing the grapes by foot. I always step up – pardon the pun – and I can usually rope in Jordan, plus volunteers from the picking crew.

Chiara is a big no; she thinks it's gross. Cam, too, has thus far refused to participate. He doesn't like people staring at him, and we can draw *quite* a crowd. Grape stomping at Flora Valley Wines is party time for our community. People bring picnics and watch us go to work. The commentary gets more raucous as the day goes on. We stompers don't get to drink anything but water until we're done, but let's just say, we've been known to make up for it later.

Don't make the mistake of thinking this is some gimmick. Grape stomping might have fallen out of fashion, and been overtaken by more efficient machinery, but it's still *the* most natural way to press wine. Human foot pressure won't break the seeds, which can make the wine taste nastily astringent. And a human has better judgment about when to stop. It's completely sanitary because the alcohol in the wine kills any bugs – and yes, duh, of course you clean your feet first.

Dad always swore that foot crushing intensified the wine, made it bolder. And when you're a little place like Flora Valley Wines, you *need* your wine to stand out.

So, yup, a busy time of year. But wait – there's more! Before all *that* kicks off, we have bottling. It's another reason why our barrel ageing is so short – only eleven months. We have to make room for the next vintage. And don't tell the other vintners, but our secret weapon for the shorter ageing is Cam's magic barrels, the ones he'll only make for us. The flavour they add to the wine is pure alchemy.

We don't have bottling facilities on site, so we use a mobile bottling service. Those guys are all booked in – one job I managed to do before I was demoted. Though I have to admit it's quite a relief to hand over the logistics to Nate. Last year, because Dad was so ill, I had to manage it pretty much all myself. Just about wrecked me.

Cam was my number one practical helper then, and he will be again, along with Javi, my work crew coordinator.

Nate, too, of course. The man with the plan. And the checkbook.

I'm ashamed to say, I still don't have a firm hold on our cash position. I know, what with frantically chasing investors, I let the paperwork pile up. But judging by Nate's desk, and his general personality type, he's got that all under control. And I'm sure that if there was anything wildly amiss – like we're about to file for bankruptcy – he'd have told me by now.

OK, it worries me that the pre-orders are still low. Had a couple more trickle in last week, but nowhere near our usual level. Our ability to keep going has always depended on us selling the whole lot. If we don't ... to be honest, I'm not sure what that means. Guess it depends on how much JP is willing to invest. He's already committed to a tasting room and a proper e-commerce website, but those are longer-term strategies. And they also imply that he believes the business foundations are sound enough to build on. If this vintage is a failure, he may change his mind, and cut his losses.

Nate should know what's up. I'll be brave and talk to him about it this morning. *If* he's in a good mood. Which is where this line of thought began...

I hear the pick-up pull in while I'm feeding Ham and Luke their morning scraps. Only 8am. Nate's early. I toss a cabbage leaf Dylan's way, and hustle back to the house to wash up and put the coffee on.

My plan is to take the coffee over to the office, but just as

I'm pouring it, there's a knock, and the kitchen door is pushed open.

"Hi."

Nate. The serious version, by the look of it. Oh, well, it *is* Monday. No one likes Mondays.

"I was just about to deliver your wake-up call," I say, and hand him a steaming mug.

"Thanks."

He holds the mug in a way that is not relaxed. Hope he's not been angsty all weekend about our little Friday night phone tryst. Though I suspect that if being angsty were an Olympic sport, Nate would have a *large* haul of gold medals.

"Shel, can we talk?"

"Sure."

I sound breezy, but my heart has plummeted. It's either bad news about the winery, or he's ending any possibility of us ever having a relationship. I shouldn't have tempted him on Friday. It was selfish. *Incredible* but selfish. And it might have pushed him away for good. I pull up a chair at the kitchen table and brace myself.

He sits, too, and stares down into his coffee for a bit.

Then he says, "How was your weekend?"

Fig. When Dad was waiting for the results of the second lot of cancer tests, he semi-joked with us that if the specialist started off with small talk, he was doomed. First thing the specialist said was, "So, how about those Raiders?" I've hated that team ever since. Sorry, guys. Not your fault.

"Nate, what's up?" I cut to it, because I'm a bundle of nerves.

There's that left eyebrow twitch again. Which doesn't help.

"If you've got bad news, can you just spit it out?"

Now, he looks embarrassed.

"Shit," he says. "Sorry, Shel. It's not bad news. It's just … I'm not quite sure how to ask what I want to ask."

The winery's safe. He doesn't want to dump me. I can relax about eighty percent of the way. But what the heck kind of question is he working up to?

"Would it be easier if you passed me a note?"

I shouldn't tease, but I'm still a little nervous.

"I appreciate it when you try to build up my self-esteem," he says, dryly.

"My bad," I say. "But I really don't care if you fumble the question. Starting is the thing."

He blows out a breath.

"OK. Here goes…"

And he tells me about what happened on Saturday morning when JP and his wife came to visit. How his dad had stormed out, after forbidding his whole family to talk to him about treatment anymore.

"JP is Dad's oldest friend," Nate says. "I'd kind of pinned my hopes on him getting through to Dad. No dice. The rest of us talked about it later, and apart from being pissed off, we also can't understand *why* Dad's being so insanely pig-headed. If any of *us* were putting our lives at risk, he'd be down on us like a ton of bricks. If it were *Mom* who was sick, he'd be flying her to the world's best hospital, no expense spared!"

He thumps back in the chair and runs a hand angrily over his head.

"It makes no sense," he says. "Dad's always been obsessed with staying healthy, but he's never gotten outright *fanatical* about it until now. He let Mom get us all vaccinated, and take us to Doc Wilson if we were sick. OK, he'd never let us have junk food or cheese in a can, but if we needed medicine, all he'd do was give us a lecture on Big Pharma. Never stopped us from taking it. So *why*, when it's obvious to the *blind* that he needs medical intervention, is he digging his heels in so hard?"

"Fear?" I suggest.

Nate gives me a what-the-fig look.

"If you were afraid of dying," he says, "wouldn't that make you even more willing to get help?"

"Not necessarily."

I'm remembering Dad's initial reaction to his cancer diagnosis. Back then, he saw it as some alien he needed to fight, like he was Arnold Schwarzenegger in *Predator*. By seeing cancer as an enemy, Dad kept the anger high – and the fear at bay.

"Disease, especially when it hits us out of the blue, shakes us to our very foundations," I say. "We'll do anything to get back our sense of control, a sense that we're in charge of our own destiny. The alternative is accepting that a non-thinking entity has a random power over whether we live or die. And that's terrifying."

Nate is listening intently.

"So, in Dad's mind," he says, "if he allows medical intervention, that's tantamount to giving in to the disease? Giving it power over him?"

"Could be," I nod. "I don't know your dad, so I can't say."

"Yeah," he says, slowly. "And, uh, that leads me to the point of this story…'

I widen my eyes expectantly.

"How would you feel about coming to my place to meet him?"

"Meet your dad?"

"I know we've got a lot going on," he says, apologetically. "But maybe one evening this week. For dinner?"

"With your family?"

"Well, yeah…'

"And I'd come as your … *friend*?"

I feel a strong urge to be *very* clear here.

"You can come as Batgirl if you like."

That old trick. Making jokes to deflect from uncomfortable subjects.

"It helps if I know," I say. "So I don't blurt out anything embarrassing. Like—"

"OK, OK," he says, hastily. "Come as a friend – and business partner." He screws up his face. "I'm asking a lot, aren't I?"

"Actually, I'm not sure *what* you're asking," I say. "Why do you want me to meet your dad?"

Nate's gaze travels round until it lights on a photo propped up on the small shelf where I keep all the miscellaneous useful things, like keys, pens and phone chargers, along, of course, with all the completely useless crap I should find a better place for. The photo's of my family, taken about twelve years ago, when we were all living here. At the back, there's Dad, big and blond, and his absolute clone, my oldest brother, Jackson. Middle row is Mom and her long red hair, and Tyler and me, the big and small strawberry blondes. Up front there's the baby, Frankie, another redhead like Mom. We're all smiling. We were happy that day.

"I want you to tell him about *your* dad," Nate says, finally.

His voice is subdued, as if he's asking me against his better judgment.

"I want you to say how hard it was for you to lose him. How much you miss him, now he's gone."

"Right." I get it.

But I'm not sure yet how I feel about it. He wants to use *my* grief to emotionally blackmail his dad. As he admitted, that's a big ask.

What would *I* do, though, in his situation? If Dad had refused treatment right from the start, what lengths would I have gone to, to convince him?

There's also the fact I'm secretly thrilled that Nate thinks so highly of me that he'd trust me with such a big and personal task. Makes me wonder if he kind of … you know … loves me?

And, of course, if I succeed, and his dad gets the treatment he needs, then Nate will be free to re-start our relationship.

"I'm in," I tell him.

He doesn't even try to hide his relief.

"I *will* be wearing the Batgirl outfit," I add.

Nate gives me a crooked grin. "I … owe you."

I smile right back. "You might regret you said that."

Chapter Twenty-Four

NATE

I was *this* close to telling Shelby I love her. But I'm glad I didn't. It might have made her feel even more obligated to say yes to my outrageous request. I could tell she had doubts, and all of them were completely justified.

She might still change her mind, and I wouldn't blame her. It was a pretty shady move to heap all that emotional responsibility on her shoulders. Being desperate isn't much of an excuse. A whole family can't get their own father to listen, so we're going to pass the buck to a complete stranger. Good job, Durants. Stay classy.

I quit the kitchen while I was ahead and went to face the other grim reality of my life – saving Flora Valley Wines.

There's a little voice nagging me to come clean with Shelby about the precarious nature of our financial position. But I can think of so many reasons not to. It'll put her off her winemaking game, and the business needs her in peak form. It's not her job to worry about money; it's mine.

Likewise, it's not her job to find ways to get us out of this financial hole.

Most importantly, I don't want her to have to feel grateful towards me. If – when – Shelby and I get to start our relationship, I want it to be on an even footing. I don't want to think for a *second* that she's with me because she feels indebted to me for rescuing her family's business.

And rescue it I will. Even if it kills me. Because that's how Durant men roll.

I did a lot of hard number crunching over the weekend, and I have some ideas. Trouble is, Shelby will hate them. Which is another fine reason to keep quiet.

First, though, there's the little matter of securing her an invitation to dinner. I didn't want to share the details of my Dad-plan with the family before I knew if Shelby was in or not. I've crossed that hurdle, for the time being, at least. Now for phase two.

I phone Ava, to test my thinking out on her first.

"Wow," she says, but not in a complimentary way. "I thought you *liked* Shelby?"

"I do," I protest. "I like her a lot!"

"A *lot*, hey?" I can hear my sister smirking. "So you guys have—?"

"No! Well, yeah, but … it's complicated."

"Fast work, bro. Only been a week."

I give thanks that we're on the phone, not FaceTime. I rarely blush, but I'm bright red now.

"And only a month since you broke up with Camille." Ava sticks the knife in as only a sister can.

"I'm over Camille," I say, shortly.

"Sure," she replies. "But I bet you're not over being dumped."

This conversation is going downhill fast.

"What exactly are you accusing me of, Ava?"

"Nothing. I'm pointing out the fishhooks. If you really *do* care about this girl, then … just be mindful of your motives. You don't want to lead her down a path you have no real intention of following."

"Thanks for that, Brené Brown."

"You still want to invite her to dinner?"

Jesus, sometimes a simple phone call feels like going ten rounds with Tyson.

"She's said she's happy to come," I half lie. "And do you have a better plan?"

"Nope," she readily admits. "How about Wednesday? I'll rope Max into helping me cook. Mom will hate that, but too bad."

"Ask Mom to contribute cookies."

"Like I could stop her."

There's a beat, then she adds, "I'm looking forward to meeting this Shelby Armstrong. I don't recall you *ever* falling for a girl that quickly before. You took over a month to ask Camille out."

"How do you know *that*?" I demand.

Ava and Camille have met – what – all of twice?

"Camille and I got on pretty well," she tells me now, four years down the freaking track. "Haven't heard from her lately, though. Guess that would be weird."

I take a deep breath. "Can you do me a favour, sis? Can you *never* tell me if she gets back in touch?"

All Ava does is laugh. I fantasize about giving her a dead arm.

"See you and Shelby on Wednesday," she says. "Seven o'clock. Don't be late."

As she ends the call, I have a strong urge to go lie down in a field somewhere and stare at the sky.

Unluckily, there's no rest for the ... whatever it is I am. My to-do list has turned into a mile-long scroll, but I know what my priority is: securing a full sheet of orders for our soon-to-be-bottled vintage.

When I was working for Anton in Bordeaux, the first thing I did before planning any changes was a whole lot of market research. I was on the phone all day, every day, for two weeks, phoning everyone in the wine industry who would talk to me: customers on our mailing list, restaurants, retailers, wine reviewers, sales reps, contacts in international markets. I talked to all our vineyard workers. I even went down to the village and spoke to the old guys playing *boules*, and the women shopping at the market.

Sure, I got a lot of contradictory opinions, but I also got enough intel to know which way the wind was blowing with wine sales.

And intel is what I need now. Why *aren't* our loyal customers putting in repeat orders, like they have year after year? I have a copy of our mailing list – not online, of course; I had to dig it out of the bottom of the filing cabinet. I pick up my phone and dial the first number on the list.

Four hours later and I've contacted around sixty percent. Enough to get a feel for the data. Plus, I'm starting to get hoarse.

The urge to find a field to lie in is even stronger. I had an inkling about what I'd find out, and I'm definitely *not* happy to have my suspicions confirmed.

Billy Armstrong was why they kept buying. They rate the wine highly but being part of Billy's orbit was the main thing that kept them coming back. Shelby told me he contacted them. What she didn't say was that he phoned them all several times a year. He'd get them revved up about the next vintage, but more importantly, he'd ask them about their lives, families, jobs, hobbies, latest trips overseas, etc. He never forgot what he'd last been told, and he made them feel like he was genuinely interested in them. Which he probably was – you can't fake that unless you're a psychopath. And no psychopath would create a daughter like Shelby.

When Billy died, over half of them came to his funeral. Those who could not sent flowers and messages. Simple truth is, they loved him. Now he's gone, they could keep buying, out of loyalty to his memory, but most of them said that having his wine around would make them too sad. Maybe next year, they said.

A year we can't afford to wait.

The only bright spot is that they didn't knock Shelby. Most of them had met her, and liked her, too, but that's not the point. Doesn't matter if her wine blows his out of the water. She's not her father.

So what now? We're bottling in two weeks, and I've got enough money from JP to see us through that and the harvest *if* we keep things lean. But he's not going to keep topping us up. We need to bring in money of our own. Fast.

If I were smart, I'd talk to Javi, the concierge who moonlights as a wine crew coordinator. He impressed me with his industry knowledge and his general can-do attitude. I got the feeling he could meet any of the hotel guests' requests, no matter how out there. You want a bejewelled elephant complete with mahout delivered at dawn? Consider it done.

Trouble is, the plans I have – the ones I can't tell Shelby about – also affect Javi. And I'd feel bad if I pumped him for information and ideas, then turned around and put him out of a long-standing contract. He makes a decent commission from us, and I know he has a young family to support. Not to mention the many friends, relations and acquaintances he pulls in to do the work.

Shit, no, I can't talk to Javi.

However, I *can* talk to his boss, Ted. Not *super* thrilled about the prospect, but this is no time to be a competitive dick. Ted has an address book that must rival the Kardashians' combined. Only I bet Ted's is hand-tooled, gold-embossed calf leather, and he writes in it with a limited edition Mont Blanc.

I need to set up a meeting, and who best to do it than Ted's number one employee, Chiara... Pretty sure even Javi wouldn't waste his time contesting her for that title.

She gave me her cell phone number.

"Nathan Durant," she says, with more than a hint of triumph.

Goddamn, she knows I want something from her. Is she psychic?

Might as well bite the bullet. "Can you get me a meeting with Ted?"

"Why?"

"I'm planning the heist of a major artwork," I say. "Can't tell you more or I'll have to kill you."

"No spill, no meeting."

Jesus. Now, I'm not joking about killing her.

"I need his advice," I say. "On how to get new customers for Flora Valley Wines."

"Oh." Chiara sounds slightly disappointed. "Does Shel know about this?"

"No. And I'd really appreciate it if you didn't tell her."

I wait until I'm graced with a response.

"OK, so he has a window tomorrow between two and two-thirty."

My instinct is to tell her that Ted can jump *out* that window, but beggars can't be choosers. Resentful, yes, but not picky.

"Thanks, I'll be there."

"Have a nice day, sir," she says, knowing full well it will wind me up even further.

A nice day. Filled with women intent on giving me a hard time.

"Knock, knock."

It's Shelby. Shit, I hope she didn't overhear that conversation.

No, she's smiling. Maybe she has good news? I could do with some.

"Hey, um, Cam gave me this."

She hands me a piece of scruffy paper that someone's written on in what looks like builder's pencil.

"And this is?"

"His recommendation for new barrels. I asked him to do an inventory and tell us which ones we should replace. He's included a cost for the replacements."

She points at a number scrawled on the bottom.

"He's already put the wood order in."

"Has he?"

"Yeah, so he wondered if we could part pay him this week. That's what we usually do," she adds.

In my mind, Cam's jumping out the same window as Ted, and with luck, Ted lands on him and breaks Cam's neck. I don't need unexpected, last-minute expenses. I've got barely enough operating capital as it is, and that's only thanks to JP being *mighty* generous. Why the fuck could Cam not have got his act together sooner? And Shelby, too, for that matter, but I'd prefer to save all my anger for Mountain Moron.

"Sorry," Shelby says.

She must have picked up on my shitty vibes.

"Any more bills like this coming in?" I do my best not to sound accusatory.

"I ... don't think so."

There's a field out there with my name on it. With luck, it'll be a poppy field and I'll never wake up.

"Do you want some lunch?"

Shelby sounds worried, like it's her fault I'm pissed off. Which it kind of is, but let's not go there.

"I brought a sandwich," I say.

Not about to confess that Mom made it for me. It's her way of keeping busy and feeling useful, so I'm hardly going to tell her to stop.

"Want to eat it in the kitchen? I've put more coffee on."

That level of caffeine is unlikely to lower my blood pressure. But it would be great to sit with her, joke around, listen to her laugh. Her optimism is infectious and, right now, I could do with catching a dose.

"I'll file this in the shoebox." I wave the barrel bill. "And I'll be right with you."

Chapter Twenty-Five

SHELBY

I convened another emergency meeting of the best friends drinking club. Jordan refused to go to the Silver Saddle, so we're at Bartons. Not centre-stage this time, but at a side table that will allow us to have a private conversation. I've got Nate's sister's dress on again, which I *must* get cleaned, so I can give it back to her on Wednesday. Jordan, who, like me, wears shorts pretty much all year round, is in a pale blue mini, and Chiara is in a figure-hugging one-shoulder green number. Ted hasn't shown himself yet. It's Monday, so he may not. Monday evenings are not peak Ted time.

"So you'll be introduced to Nate's family as – what?"

Chiara gets straight down to essentials.

"I'm guessing his family already knows what the deal is with the winery," I say. "Though Nate does play his cards pretty close."

"But he won't introduce you as his girlfriend, is what I'm getting at."

"I'm *not* his girlfriend," I say. "Yet."

"You're more tolerant than *I* am," Chiara informs me. "No way I'd put up with that kind of covert bs. I mean, the guy's got nasty with you more than once. He should own it!"

"Men are creeps," says Jordan, darkly.

"I'm OK with it!" I insist. "Well, as OK as I can be. And in this circumstance, I'd rather not have the pressure of being the-one-who-came-after-the-fiancée, if you know what I mean? Meeting his whole family will be scary enough."

"He's got a *super* cute brother," says Chiara. "Danny. Looked him up online. Owns a high-end car shop in LA"

"Hey, he's probably the one whose Porsche you totalled," Jordan points out.

"It was a scratch!"

"Is the rest of his family in on the plan?" Chiara asks.

"No idea," I admit. "Knowing Nate, I'd say not. As I said, cards close to chest. Also, I don't think he'd want to get their hopes up, just in case I blow it."

"No pressure, huh?" says Jordan.

"Why does he think *you'll* succeed where his whole family has failed?"

If Chiara doesn't want a career as a spy, she'd make a great interrogator. Wouldn't blink an eye at hooding or waterboarding.

"I'm not sure he *does* think I'll succeed," I say. "But I get the feeling he's run out of options. I may well be his last shot."

"Wow, so you're his only hope to keep his dad alive?" says Jordan. "Kind of sucks to be you right now, doesn't it?"

I lift my glass of water (don't judge me, I'm poor) in a mock toast.

"Thanks for the support, guys. Awesome."

"Well, at least you'll be sincere," says Chiara. "You won't be making anything up when you talk about how much you miss your dad."

"No…"

"Sorry, Shel," Chiara says, gently. "Still raw, huh?"

"Does it ever *stop* being raw?" I ask, though I know neither Jordan nor Chiara have lost anyone close to them. Chiara's Italian *great*-grandmother is still alive and will be ninety-six next birthday.

"Ladies, good evening."

It's Ted. Making an unexpected appearance and looking *particularly* dapper in a slim-fitting suit. Its subtle charcoal-on-black check emphasizes his startling blondness. Ted even has blond *eyelashes*.

"Burberry?" says Chiara, eyeing the suit.

"I'm sure you're right," Ted replies, with a smile. "You so often are."

"Always," Chiara corrects. "I am *always* right."

Ted turns his smile my way. "I gather I'm meeting with your friend, Nathan, tomorrow."

This is news to me. "What about?"

"Oops," I hear Chiara mutter.

"Oh." Ted glances between us. "Have I made a blunder?"

"Might have forgotten to mention he didn't want Shel to know," Chiara says.

"He *told* you that?" I demand.

Chiara raises her hands in the not-my-fault gesture.

"OK, fine," I say, huffily. "So now the cat's out of the bag, what's the meeting about?"

"Er…" Ted looks to Chiara for help.

"Getting more customers for Flora Valley Wines," she says. "That's all I know, so don't come at me."

Fig. That's not good, on several levels. One: it means the lack of orders *is* a problem. Two: it shows Nate's keeping secrets from me. Several: it proves I've been useless at running the winery up till now. It's my fault we're in trouble – and, worse, I should have *known* we were in trouble. But I didn't, because I'm useless.

"He wants to expand." Ted always knows how to put a positive spin on things. "An excellent plan. Your wine deserves a wider audience."

"Does that mean you'll stock it here?" I say, beadily.

"If you charged twice as much, I'd certainly consider it," Ted replies, unabashed. "Now, if you'll excuse me…"

And off he swans.

"That's ironic," says Jordan. "You can't get your wine in the Silver Saddle because it's too expensive, and you can't get it in here because it's too cheap."

"Thought you weren't ever going to mention that place

again?" I say, crossly, though it's not Jordan I'm pissed at.

"Bar's OK," she says. "It's the owner who's dead to me."

"It's not like he led you on." I'm being unfair, because I'm still crabby.

"He *knew* I liked him!" Jordan retorts. "He should have *told* me he was spoken for!"

She has a point. It's important to know where you stand. I wish *I* did. And why don't I? Why is Nate keeping stuff from me?

One of Ted's waitpersons glides up.

"There are three gentlemen at the bar who would like to buy you all a drink."

We glance over. They actually look like nice guys, not sleazes.

Jordan responds on our behalf. "Men are *creeps*."

"I'll tell them you respectfully decline," says the waitperson, and glides off again.

"Tut, tut, should have taken our order first," says Chiara, and raises her hand to attract a different waitperson. "Another water, Shel?"

"Thanks," I say. "This time, make it a double."

I'm home by ten, and I'm never going to sleep in this mood. There's that saying: don't let the sun go down on your anger. Well, the sun's gone down, but the night's not over yet. I do what I absolutely know I should *not* do. I call Nathan.

"You OK?" is how he answers.

I *should* see this as a sign that he worries about me – that he cares. But right now, all I can hear is that's he's being patronizing. He doesn't trust that I can cope with the hard truths.

I launch into it. "You're meeting with Ted tomorrow. And, no, Chiara didn't blab. I heard it from the horse's mouth."

He blows out a breath. "Fuck, you live in a small town."

"Why didn't you tell me?" I demand. "What else are you hiding from me?"

"I'm not hiding stuff from you," he says, with heat. "I'm doing my job! *Your* job's making wine, and I'm making sure you can focus on that!"

"By keeping me in the dark?"

"Why burden you with responsibilities you don't need to own?" He's properly pissed now. "Winemaking needs a clear head and a positive attitude. Don't get on my case for making it easy for you to do your job well!"

"It's *my* winery!" I yell at him, sending cats scurrying.

"It is *not!*" he retorts. "It's JP's winery! When did *that* particular fact pass you by?"

I'm *this* close to hanging up when his tone softens.

"Shel, I'm sorry. You're right. I should have kept you more informed. I just … didn't want you to worry."

"*Should* I worry?"

"I'm working on it," he says.

"You're doing it again!" I accuse. "Brushing me off! What do you think I'm going to do if I hear the truth? Collapse in a heap? I know the realities of this business! Don't be a patronizing jerk!"

"Oh, you *know* them do you?" He's pissed again. "So

that means you knew the winery was in the shit and you just – what? Ignored it? Crossed your fingers and hoped it'd go away? Good strategy."

He's not wrong. And I hate him for it.

"Like *you're* so perfect," I say, the spiteful child in me taking over. "You can't even manage a relationship."

Oh, fig, that's not what I meant. But before I can unplug my foot from my mouth, he starts to speak.

"You know what?" His voice is tight with anger. "You're right. I can't. So how about I don't try? How about we just go about our jobs with the minimum amount of contact, and when my contract's up, I'll be out of your hair forever. Sound good? Thought so. See you, Shelby."

And he's gone.

Guess I won't be going to dinner on Wednesday.

Shit. I can say that word; the situation warrants it. Shit, shit, shit, I blew it. It's all my fault.

Everything is my fault. If I'd been more onto it right from the start, I'd have *made* Dad write a will. I don't believe he didn't want to; he just never got around to it. We had a lot in common, Dad and I.

If I hadn't crashed out after his death, I wouldn't have had to rush so much to find investors. I let so much slide during that time, I know I did. Nate's had double the workload he should have, because of me, and my lack of organization.

No wonder he didn't tell me anything. Why bother, when I've proved myself incompetent? I mean, even this morning, I was handing him Cam's bill far too late.

228

Everything should be budgeted and accounted for by now. I knew that. But I didn't make it happen.

The winery is in the shit, and it's all my fault. And I'm in no position to do anything about it. Nate doesn't trust me an inch now. Why should he? I'm not only incompetent, I'm also a bitch. If I were him, I wouldn't touch me with a barge pole.

People get it wrong about the five stages of grief, my doctor told me. They think they happen sequentially, when in fact they happen in random order, at random times. Denial, bargaining, anger, sadness, and acceptance. Any time, in any order.

People are also wrong when they think grief is only about someone dying. Any kind of loss triggers grief. Losing a job, friends moving away – even feeling like you've been betrayed by someone you trusted.

I've just gone through a bunch of anger, because I felt like Nate had betrayed me by keeping secrets. I've accepted I'm to blame for what just happened between us, and for the sad financial state of the winery.

Now, denial and bargaining are fighting to come to the surface. My thumb's hovering over his number on my phone, and all I want to do is apologize over and over, say I didn't mean it, and beg his forgiveness.

But before denial and bargaining make it halfway, they're beaten to the post by sadness. I've lost him. He's gone. He'll never forgive me, and he'll never come back. I know that for a fact. Nate Durant is a man of his word, and the words he spoke to me were crystal clear.

Trouble is, I've just realized that I love him. I want to be with him forever and ever.

If you don't mind, I'm going to lie down on this bed right now and do a shitload of crying.

Chapter Twenty-Six

NATE

"Where the hell are you going?"

Fuck. Ava's sitting on the front porch. I don't have time for this.

"For a run."

And I start off, down the driveway.

"It's ten-thirty at *night*," she calls after me.

No shit. Guess that's why I'm wearing a headlamp.

I want to run on the trails, really push it up the hills, but I know the ground's too rough to navigate, even with a light. I may be intent on pushing my pain limits, but I don't actually want to go so far as to break a leg. I'll stick to the roads. Run as hard and as far as I can. Forget about everything except the rhythm of my breath, and my feet pounding on the tar. Feel nothing but the burn in my lungs and legs.

I make it back home around midnight. Ava's gone in, thank Christ. My legs are *shot*, and I have to lean on the balustrade as I climb the stairs. I collapse on the side of the bed and fall back onto it. Lie there until the sweat becomes uncomfortably cool.

I get up again, so I can undertake the painful operation of swapping my damp running clothes for a T-shirt and sweatpants. It is then that I observe a cut crystal drinking glass on the antique sewing table filled with amber liquid. Next to it is a note.

In a manner not unlike a newborn foal, I make my way to the table. The note's in Ava's impatient scrawl. 'If you want to talk, I'll be up', it says. 'Bring your glass'.

I don't want to talk. To anyone.

Happy to down the whisky, though. It rushes straight to my already light head, and I have a strong urge to get obliterated again.

No. I need to be fully focused. JP's contract with me is for one year, with a review at six months. If I push this plan through, I'm confident I can get the winery on track in three months, tops. Job done. Contract fulfilled. I'll go back to France. *Not* Bordeaux – another wine region. Plenty of places will hire me. I've got a good reputation.

Have to sit down again. Legs are quitting on me. Like I'll be quitting on JP.

If I get his investment humming, he shouldn't mind so much. And now, I'm free to do it *my* way. No more having to consider the feelings of a certain Shelby Armstrong.

Anger is mighty useful. Blocks all other emotions, so all you feel is pure, white-hot rage. But even with my rage still volcanic, Shelby's name hits me like a fist to the gut.

How *could* she say that? That's the rage talking. But the gut pain feels more like shock. The shock you experience when someone you love betrays you...

Before this evening, Shelby hadn't said one unkind word to me. She'd dealt with my sulk around Commando Cam, and my inadequate communication, with good humour and patience.

She'd agreed with my request to put our relationship on hold, when I couldn't even give her a timeframe. She was prepared to wait. For me.

She was prepared to come to dinner with a house full of strangers for me. Because I needed her help.

And yet, she said what she said.

I've never breathed this to a soul, but when Camille told me she was dumping me for Ass-Bjorn, the first emotion I felt was relief. I didn't love her, and I didn't want to marry her. And yes, that *does* make me an asshole. As does my keeping up the charade of our relationship because I loved working for her father. I'm not sure I had the brains to be aware of that at the time, but it's clear now. I stayed with Camille because I wanted to keep my job at Anton's winery.

Thing is, the *second* emotion I felt, when she said she was leaving, was anger. Ava was right. I hated being dumped. As a man, I pissed all *over* that cross-eyed, bearded drummer. I was smarter, better looking, better educated, more successful. He picked her up in a fucking *Lada*, I shit you not. One of those crappy imitation Jeeps, circa 1970-fucking-8.

Yeah, so I'm still resentful. But I'm not *hurt*. Thinking

about Camille makes me bad-tempered and, yes, ashamed. It doesn't cut me to the bone. It doesn't make me want to cry.

I can't recall the last time I cried. Would have been a kid, I guess. Dad didn't have a lot of tolerance for tears. If we fell, we were expected to get up, get moving again. Tears were a waste of time and energy.

I have to see Shelby tomorrow. I have to work with her for the next three months at least. I've *no* idea how I'm going to get through it.

I love her. That feeling hasn't gone away, but it will have to. If she loved and respected me, she wouldn't have said what she said.

My whole body is trembling now with physical exhaustion – and, I guess, emotion – but I'm very far from sleep.

The empty glass is still in my hand. I set it back on the table and look again at Ava's note. And though I still don't want to talk, I *do* want to be with somebody. I want to feel that at least *one* person in the world cares whether I live or die.

Legs protesting, I make it the short distance down the hallway, lean up against the wall outside Ava's bedroom door, and knock once, quietly.

"Y' cahn't com in," comes the reply in a truly terrible Jamaican accent.

It's a Durant sibling joke. When she was fourteen, pre the Goth phase, Ava discovered British ska band The Specials. That's how one of their songs starts, and we all got in the habit of chanting it, usually when one of us was holding up access to the bathroom.

Ava is sitting up in bed, reading. She's wearing—

"When did you get *glasses*?" I ask, as I sink into the armchair in the corner. *My* room doesn't have an armchair, just saying.

"Two years ago. Just for reading. My distance vision's fine."

Her glasses have tortoiseshell frames, and a kind of fifties slant to them.

"They suit you."

"Do they make me look intelligent?" she says, with a crooked grin.

I have a sudden flashback to Dad giving Ava shit about a school report. He could never find anything to criticize about her sporting achievements, but her grades were always patchy. Even Danny, who refused to go to college, scored solid A-minuses. Ava's grades depended on her level of interest in a subject, and her respect for the teacher. If either of those factors was missing, she refused to do anything but the minimum.

But Dad wasn't interested in asking *why* Ava's grades varied so wildly. All he cared about was the taint of failure.

"Thanks for the whisky." It's my way of apologizing for being a rude dick earlier.

"You didn't bring your glass?"

"No…"

I owe her more than that. "I'll need a clear head for the next few weeks."

Ava appraises me for a moment.

"Max heard you having a pretty heated conversation," she says.

There was no privacy growing up, and there's none now. Sooner I get out of here, the better.

"Don't have a cow," she says, correctly reading my thoughts. "He couldn't make out words, only tone."

As I'm not exactly hurrying to explain, she adds, "Where did you run to? Canada?"

"Felt like it."

Ava closes her book, removes her glasses, and sets both on her bedside table. Her movements are deliberate, as if she's working hard to stay patient. Fair enough. She thinks I've come here to talk, so why don't I get on with it. And now I *am* here, I find I *do* want to offload.

"Dinner's cancelled," I tell her.

"Oh, crap, really?"

Ava looks genuinely crestfallen, which I didn't expect.

"Shit, you told the others the plan, didn't you?" I think I have the right to sound accusatory. "Ava, for fuck's sake."

She purses her mouth in a quick but defiant apology.

"I told Max because I wanted his help with the cooking," she says. "Of course, he told Izzy because the twins have no secrets. And then they felt bad that Danny was the only one who didn't know, so they told him, too. Had all three of them interrogate me about it. They *all* agreed it was worth a shot."

Now, the look she gives me is definitely a little sheepish.

"I had to set them straight about how you felt about Shelby Armstrong."

Do you think it's actually possible for life to go in a single, non-complicated line for more than one fucking day? Seems not.

"*That* has changed," is all I intend to say.

"Everyone has arguments."

Ava has a real knack for the sympathetic response.

"Wasn't just an argument," I tell her. "She said something that I don't think we can come back from."

"That's what happens in arguments." Ava dials up the sympathy another notch. "We can say *terrible* things in the heat of the moment. I once accused a guy of liking the Dave *Matthews* band. It's a wonder he ever spoke to me again."

"Yeah, this is really funny," I say, angrily. "Go ahead. Laugh it up."

"OK, that example wasn't serious," she concedes. "But only because I'm too embarrassed to tell you some of the *truly* awful stuff I've thrown at people I've cared about."

"And did *you* always come back from it?"

"Yeah..." She nods, slowly. "But not without effort. Apologizing is a good start."

"Isn't *me* who has to apologize."

"No?" She appraises me again. "You didn't overreact? Because you were hurt?"

Shit.

"Nate, you're a Durant," she says. "And we've got a long, proud history of immoveable stubbornness. Exhibit A:

our father. So I have to ask, and excuse the choice of words: is this a hill you really want to die on?"

I blow out a long breath.

"I just … I can't trust her anymore."

Sounds pathetic, but it feels like an elemental truth.

"You and Shelby have known each other for a *nano*second," Ava says. "Trust takes time. And OK, I'm not exactly stellar at maintaining long-term relationships, but I *do* know it's how you navigate those early days that makes or breaks you. It's how we respond when we find out that the other is only human, not the incredible perfect being of our dreams."

She smiles at me, with wry affection. "Bro, we all fuck up. Trick is to fully accept that, and not, deep down, keep holding the people we love to impossible standards."

I know she's right. But I'm dead tired, every muscle aches, and I can't get past feeling hurt. I hear Shelby's words in my head, and they still cut me deep. I need time before I even start *thinking* about whether I want to try again with Shelby. Time away from her, or at least at a safe distance.

"Nate." The sudden urgency in Ava's tone sets off alarm bells.

"Izzy, Max and Dan are sick with worry," she says. "About Dad, but even more, about Mom. Dan is convinced Mom's heading for some kind of breakdown. He wanted her to see Doc Wilson, but she refused. They're desperate. *I'm* desperate. We're willing to try *any*thing."

No way. She can*not* be asking me that.

"I know it'll be uncomfortable," she presses on. "But, please – can you do this for us? For Mom?"

"You don't even know it'll work," I protest. "Why would Dad listen to a stranger, when he's ignored his whole family?"

"We're desperate," is her response. And her face reinforces it as the truth.

"I can't ask her, Ava."

I sound pretty desperate myself.

"*I* will," she says, quickly. "I'll go see her tomorrow morning."

When it comes to the family stubbornness, Ava always had me beat. And, frankly, I'm too exhausted to argue. Shelby will never say yes, so I may as well let Ava try and fail.

"Fine," I say. "Go see her, but *don't* involve me. OK?"

"Deal," says Ava, and adds, "Thanks."

"You're welcome."

I haul my carcass out of the chair.

"Now, if you don't mind," I say, "I have to go sleep like the dead."

Chapter Twenty-Seven

SHELBY

Fig. I look like I fell face down in a clump of poison oak. My eyes are all puffed up, and red as a white rat's. Good thing I have no intention of stepping outside today. Any business I need to do can be done via my trusty phone. Folk on the other end needn't know I'm calling from my bed, either.

They *might* detect that I'm not a hundred percent focused. Right now, all my senses are on full alert, waiting for the sound of the pickup, knowing it will instantly bring on the cold sweats.

Anxiety, embarrassment, and regret are already churning around inside me. Soon as Nate arrives, who knows what mad urges will take control? Will I run to him and throw myself at his feet, while lashing my back with some kind of cat o' nine tails?

Wouldn't put it past me. Pretty sure I could dig out a strip of leather from somewhere in this house. If that fails, I could always use an actual cat.

Oh, poop. I'm a mess. Physically and emotionally. But, much as I want to grovel for forgiveness, my instinct tells me it's better if he makes the first move. Until then, I'll have to be patient.

And pray he eventually *does* make a move. Because I don't think I could stand it if he didn't.

One bright side is that only he and I know about this. I couldn't bring myself to text Chiara or Jordan. Maybe later today. Unless I have to spend that time crying again.

Come on, Shelby. You can't change what happened, so you may as well buck up and focus instead on being productive. The winery needs customers. Nate told you that. So go out and get them.

I snuck into the office at dawn and stole the customer mailing list off Nate's desk. He's ruled (with an actual ruler, by the looks) pencil lines through a bunch of names. I may not have been on the ball the last few months, but even I can tell what that means. They won't be placing orders. And I thought I liked those people.

Then again, they haven't heard from *me*. Nate's efficient and capable, but he's not a people person. The first impression he gives is the same one I got, that he's aloof and a little superior. OK, so *I* may come across as needy, and a mite touched in the head, but at least I'm warm and friendly. Our customers adored Dad because his warmth enveloped you like a big bear hug. I'm more of a Beanie Baby-sized bear, but I'll give it my best shot.

Fig! I hear a vehicle! Because my heart's pounding in

my ears, it takes a moment to realize it's not the usual rumble of the pickup. This is the throaty roar of a sports car.

I pull back a curtain, enough to peek outside. Double fig! It's the black Porsche! Nate must have told his brother it was me who dented it, and now he's come to demand payment! Crap, where can I hide—?

Oh. *That's* not a guy. That's—wow—a female Nate. Same hair colour, same cheekbones, same posture. Minus about a foot in height. Plus boobs.

Nate's sister, for who else could it be, is not heading to the office, but to *my* front door. Must be a mistake. Nope, there goes a quick, impatient knock.

Hastily, I rush to the bathroom and splash cold water on my puffy eyes. Then I head downstairs, slowing as I reach the door. What on earth can she want? Do you think she has bad news about Nate?

"Hi," she says, as I peer round the door. "I'm Ava. Nate's sister. Which you probably guessed, owing to us having the same face."

"Is he OK?"

She gives me a crooked smile. "You mean, apart from being a stubborn half-wit?"

I open the door wide, relieved, and, I have to admit, exceedingly curious.

"Want some coffee?" I ask. "Be warned. It kicks like a mule."

"The perfect start to every day," she says, and follows me down to the kitchen.

"Nice place." Taking a chair, Ava glances around the room. "Homey."

It's a slightly odd comment – isn't every home homey? But then, I've no idea how Nate and his family live. Or where, for that matter. I was going to find out tomorrow night, but…

Ava waits until she has a mug of coffee in front of her before speaking again.

"I'm here to ask you to come to dinner still."

Durants obviously don't believe in small talk.

"Um, won't that be … awkward?"

"Absolutely," she replies, without hesitation. "Awkward-plus. But I can guarantee that the atmosphere created by my father will be way worse. He is *not* in a good space right now."

"And this is you persuading me?" I have to ask.

Ava grins. Her eyes are *exactly* Nate's blue. I honestly think I'm going to have heart failure. My urge to see and touch him is *intense*.

"My brother will come round." Seems she's as psychic as Chiara. "But he's a slow burner. Needs time to process."

"I said a horrible thing," I confess. "I didn't *mean* it to be that horrible, but that's how it came out."

"Well, don't hold back when you're speaking to Dad," Ava tells me. "Cut out your heart and lay it bleeding in front of him. And cry. A lot, if possible."

"I think I cried myself dry last night," I admit.

"Do you care about my bone-headed big brother?"

"Yup." No point in lying; she'd see right through me.

"Good. He cares a lot about you. About time, too," she adds.

"What do you mean?"

"We're a family of control freaks," says Ava. "Well, to be scrupulously honest, the control freak gene got partially diluted down the line. My younger siblings tend to be more relaxed – when it comes to emotions, anyway. They're ambitious as all get-out in their chosen careers."

She sips her coffee, and lets out a whoosh, like she's knocked back a shot of tequila.

"Man, I could refuel the car with this."

"It's a secret recipe," I say. "Involves melting down an iron girder."

"I like you," Ava informs me, with a broad smile. "Anyway, as I was saying: control freaks, all of us. But Nate had the extra burden of being the oldest. Given that he was born serious, he took a lot of responsibility on his shoulders that he shouldn't have. And he also decided it was important that he *never* shows weakness. Which meant, the dumb cluck, that he never let himself fully experience any emotions."

That rings true. Nate and emotions are not the easiest of bedfellows. Though now I wish I hadn't started thinking about Nate and bed.

"His relationship with Camille was a disaster," Ava continues. "Should have called it quits after a year. But *she* was equally pig-headed, was convinced she could change him. He hung in there because she did. Never blink first, that was his motto, the dolt. Plus, they probably had a *shitload* of hate sex, which would also have helped."

She gives a small start. "Sorry. My bad."

"Didn't think he'd been a monk."

"Oh, I dunno. Nate was *born* to wear a hairshirt."

On cue, we both hear pickup tires rolling to a stop on gravel.

"He knows I'm here." Ava answers my unspoken, but obvious, question. "I think it'll help," she adds, "you coming to dinner. May not seem like it at the time but trust me."

Weirdly, I do. Nate's sister has a natural authority.

"Oh!" I suddenly remember. "I have your dress! At least, I think it's yours."

I run upstairs to fetch it.

"Sorry, I meant to have it cleaned." I hand it over.

"No problem," she replies. "As you can tell," she indicates her one hundred percent activewear outfit, "I don't get gussied up that often."

"Thanks for coming."

I really mean it. It's been *such* a relief to be told Nate may not hate me forever.

"Don't thank me yet." Ava starts to go. "You've got a Durant family dinner to get through. People abducted by serial killers have been less traumatized."

I see her to the door, and as I open it, we're both startled by a figure standing right in front of us, fist up, ready to knock.

He's equally startled. But, given who he is, all he does is blink a little more rapidly.

"Cam! Hi!" I blurt.

I glance at Ava to find her eyeing him up and down, a look of clinical appraisal on her face, like she's a potential owner checking out horseflesh.

"Cam Hollander, this is Ava Durant," I say. "Nate's sister."

"Hi." Ava sticks out her hand.

Cam blinks a little more and takes her small hand in his giant mitt of a one.

"What do you do here?" she asks.

Cam's eyeballs swivel my way. Translation: help.

"Cam's our handyman, and cooper," I explain.

"What's a cooper?" Ava frowns.

"I make wine barrels," says Cam.

My jaw clunks on the ground. Four words! In a row!

"Cool," says Ava. "Well, nice to meet you, Cam the cooper."

To me, she says, "Seven tomorrow at our place. I'll get your number from Nate, and text you directions."

"Do I need to bring anything?"

"Patience and stamina?" she replies. "Oh, and a safe place to store your sanity."

Ava squeezes past Cam and flashes him a quick smile. We both watch her saunter to the Porsche, hop in athletically, and send gravel flying as she guns it into action. The roar fades into the distance in an impressively short space of time.

I take a good long breath.

"What can I do for you, Cam?"

He's still staring off, down the driveway.

"Hello? Earth to Cam?"

I imagine this is what it's like watching geological structures form. He *is* turning, but it could take a while.

"Pre-check," he says, finally.

Translation: should he start looking over the facilities and equipment, to make sure everything's in working order for harvest?

I'm about to say yes when I remember I've already made this mistake once.

"Sorry, Cam," I tell him. "You'll have to ask Nate. He's the boss now."

Another ice age freezes and thaws, before he says, "K."

Then he heads off in the complete opposite direction to Nate's office. Probably needs a few hours to recover from that much interaction. He can always talk to Nate later.

Wonder if *I'll* talk to Nate anytime tomorrow? We might end up sitting at the same table at dinner and still not speaking a word to each other.

Awkward-plus, as Ava so aptly phrased it. But I'm committed now. And, frankly, Ava intimidates me *way* more than her brother.

I try not to think about him, only a few feet away, sitting behind that preternaturally tidy desk. Nate will be working hard already, because that's what he does. Time for me to do the same.

I decide to be professional about it, and phone sitting at

the kitchen table, instead of on a quilt surrounded by furballs.

The mailing list isn't in alphabetical order, or indeed any order that I can discern. Though, knowing Dad, there'll be some method. My guess is that the people he enjoys talking to most are at the top. That would be a very Dad way to organize.

As it happens, those are the names with the most lines ruled through them. Oh, no, I vow. You won't get away *that* easily.

I pick up my phone and start to dial.

Chapter Twenty-Eight

NATE

I hear Ava drive off. People on the International Space Station hear her drive off. Danny's crazy to lend her his Porsche, though he may not have had much say in the matter. Or, indeed, known anything about it. Ava is very much a student of the seek forgiveness rather than ask permission school.

In the ringing quiet that follows her departure, I catch Shelby's voice through the open office window. No doubt talking to Commando Cam. I saw him walk past the same window a few minutes earlier. I resisted the urge to shoot him with a rubber band.

Every muscle was on fire when I woke up this morning. I chugged the rest of last week's Advil, and made my way painfully down the stairs, only to find Ava had told Mom that Shelby was coming to dinner tomorrow night. So now Mom's convinced Shelby's my girlfriend and can't *wait* to meet her. I smiled, took my sandwich. Only beat my head twice against the pickup steering wheel.

Sleeping on things is supposed to give you a new perspective. Only partly true. I'm still burning about what Shelby said, still stoking those flames of righteous indignation. But in between, I want to see her so bad, I'd be happy to crawl to her on my hands and knees across the gravel.

It's like in cartoons, where a guy has a devil on one shoulder and an angel on the other. My two are currently engaged in a WWE bout, where the devil's got the angel in a vise grip, and the angel's fighting back with a Boston crab. Current status: deadlock.

Good thing I've got plenty to keep me busy. Got to prepare for my meeting with Ted this afternoon. Oh, joy.

And I've got to finalize the lease on the harvester, and the press. Numbers don't lie, and if we lease instead of purchase, we can save a shitload *and* be more efficient.

Of course, a harvester means no picking crew. Or not one of the size Flora Valley usually hires. A pressing machine means no grape stomping. What it *does* mean is Flora Valley lives to fight another day.

As long as we sell this freaking vintage. Despite his floppy hair and fruity accent, Ted strikes me as a man who does exactly what he wants, beholden to no one. There's a core of steel in Ted, and if I don't win him over in this first meeting, there won't be a second. I can't go in there undercooked.

Because my ears are traitorous shits, I hear the front door to the house shut. Shelby will pitch a fit when she finds out I'm doing Javi and his team out of a job. And an even *bigger* fit when she finds out about the end of the grape stomping.

But business is business. Plenty of need for good vineyard crews, so Javi's unlikely to be out of pocket for long.

Shit, that reminds me. If there's no crew, there's no need to feed them. Flora Valley Wines has always put on a big meal at the end of harvest, for the crew and their families. The caterer is Iris, the alligator strangler. I don't think she'd take kindly to an email declining her services, no matter how politely worded. If I'm going to respect Javi by giving him the bad news face to face, I'd better do the same with Iris. If I don't come back, check inside the stuffed alligator.

I remind myself that this effort is now all for JP And for getting me out of this contract as soon as possible. Because that's what I want, right?

The devil on my shoulder is currently having his neck wrenched in a camel clutch. That angel fights *dirty*.

Keep busy, Nate. That's the best way to stay on track.

And don't even *think* about tomorrow night.

I've had awkward moments in my life, but this dinner is shaping up to be even worse than the time I had to break it to Anton that his daughter had left me. *She* didn't bother. Just hopped in the piece-of-shit Lada and drove away with the Dorkwegian.

It probably wouldn't have been so bad if Anton and his wife hadn't felt so sorry for *me*. Didn't care that they'd already forked out a fortune for the wedding, of which they wouldn't get back a dime. No, their priority was seeing how I was holding up. Right then, I *was* feeling pretty fucking sorry for myself, not to mention furious and resentful. So I took their pity and lapped it up. Then burned with shame for days after.

How the hell am I going to sit at the same table as Shelby, and pretend like everything's normal? How will I navigate Mom's expectation that she's meeting a new girlfriend? I tried to put her straight this morning, but I think she was so desperate for good news that all she heard was "blah, blah, blah".

And what will happen if my plan fails? I know it's not just down to me, but it *was* my idea. Now, I've got four siblings counting on it to work. I've let enough people down in my life already. No wish to add to that tally.

Well, Nate, why don't you set tomorrow night to one side, and focus on ensuring you don't let JP down, at least? Good tip, Nate. You're welcome.

I spend the next while securing the leases on the harvester and the wine press. Be cheaper in the long run to buy, but we're not in a position to think that far ahead. In ten years' time, Flora Valley Wines may have been broken up and sold for parts.

The dude working on the website emails me his design, and it's not bad. He and Shelby went to grade school together, and because their moms were friends, they hung out a lot. I am *this* close to asking him what Shelby was like as a kid. Instead, I print out the design and pin it to the wall.

JP's still committed to the tasting room, but I don't believe Commando Cam can handle such a big project. There's an architect in Martinburg who's got a good reputation for jobs like this. I call him, and he's interested. We make a time to meet later in the week. He'll contract construction workers as part of the deal. Shelby's not going to like that, either.

I check the time. Better hit the road. I find Mom's sandwich on the passenger seat of the pick-up. She told me it was chicken salad, and it's been sitting for hours in a sun-baked cab. Sorry, Mom. That bad boy is going in the trash.

As I'm driving down Verity's main street toward Bartons, I see Iris in the doorway of the Cracker Café. She sees me, too, so I nod a greeting. Iris's response is a hard stare, and she's still staring a full minute later, when I take a left into the Bartons parking lot. I know this because I felt an urge to keep checking my rearview mirror.

Bartons used to be a rundown Western-style saloon. But apart from the long, wooden bar, and a few antlers on the walls, you'd be hard-pressed to see any trace of the original building. Now, it could be any luxury hotel, anywhere in the sophisticated world. No idea how much money Ted would have spent on the refit. A fuck-ton ought to cover it.

Chiara, I was relieved to discover, only does the

morning shift. The afternoon receptionist is also drop-dead gorgeous. She tells me Ted is expecting me and shows me to what I've always imagined is called a smoking room. Except that the buttoned-down wingback chairs in here are covered in emerald velvet, and not leather. And instead of portraits of dead ancestors, there's – holy shit, is that a Picasso?

"Nathan, hello."

Ted slips through the door, hand outstretched to shake mine, a smile on his face. He gestures for me to sit, and takes the chair opposite, crossing one leg over the other in a pose only a man who does not give a shit how people judge his sexuality can adopt. He's *Children of the Corn* blond, but his suit is *amazing*. Must have been made for him in London, because there's no way he got that from Neiman Marcus. I'm dressed sharply enough in a dark shirt and pants, but next to Ted, I may as well be in spit-covered baby rompers.

"Well, now," he says. "New customers for Flora Valley Wines, correct?"

"Correct," I reply. "We need to expand the base and reach a new target market. We're going online, but we need influencers to spread the word. Like yourself."

"That's very kind of you to include me in that category," he says.

He's not after flattery; he means it. Ted certainly has an ego, but it doesn't need the outside world to boost it up. Reminds me of Max – and provokes in me the same stab of envy.

"I know that Flora Valley's price point won't suit this hotel," I say.

My time in France taught me a lot about image versus quality. If you want your wine in a high-end hotel or restaurant, you need to price it to match. People's perceptions of quality are entirely linked to how much they have to pay.

"Yes, I'm afraid that's true," Ted acknowledges.

"But if we were to produce a limited edition, exclusive to Bartons, would you consider adding it to your list?"

I'm not personally familiar with the Bartons customer base, but I guarantee they'll be the social hierarchy-attuned wealthy, who like to brag about their latest discoveries. If Flora Valley is the hot, new thing here, it'll be the hot new thing *everywhere*. And if people can't afford the limited edition, they can buy the main range direct from the vineyard. Preferably by the case.

"Of course," says Ted. "It would be my pleasure."

Well, that was easy. Not that we actually *have* a wine to offer him yet. But I have a plan for that, too. We can print new labels – simple. And we can do some blending before bottling – less simple because I have to persuade Shelby to do it. I doubt she'll appreciate being forced to make wine to order, even if it's for her good buddy, Ted.

"It would be marvellous to see Shelby step out of her father's shadow," Ted adds. "I feel the Flora Valley story has so much untapped potential. The natural approach, the hand picking, the grape treading – it feels so *comforting*. So *real*."

The man is in a room that looks like it was beamed over from Buckingham Palace, and he's talking about reality?

"Is that a deal breaker?" I have to ask. "The 'story'?"

"Why?" Ted replies. "Do you have other plans?"

And there it is. The hint of steel behind the smile.

"I'm exploring options." Only half a lie.

"As you must," says Ted, with the kind of generosity that comes from not knowing what a cash flow squeeze even is. "But may I offer this small piece of advice…"

He uncrosses his legs, sits forward, elbows propped on the knife-edge creases of his suited knees. My alarm bells start to jangle.

"There are a myriad of wineries out there," he says, "that produce perfectly adequate pinot noir. There is only *one* Shelby Armstrong."

And in one swift, fluid movement, he's on his feet, smiling, hand outstretched once more.

"Must dash, I'm afraid," he says. "I look forward to our next conversation."

Like a magic trick, the receptionist opens the door, and I'm ushered out in front of Ted, who vanishes behind me so quickly, I half expect to see a puff of smoke.

Only one Shelby Armstrong.

I ponder Ted's words as I walk back to the pick-up. He said it was a piece of advice. It sounded like a threat.

Without Shelby, Flora Valley is just another winery. It's nothing. That's how I interpret it.

I'm without Shelby now, too. So I wonder what that makes me…?

I drive back down the main street. Iris is still in the doorway of the Cracker Café. She stares at me until I'm all the way past the edge of town.

Chapter Twenty-Nine

SHELBY

I'm dying to tell Nate how well I've done today. I got them back! *All* of the customers with ruled lines! Well, except for old Mrs Reynolds in Sacramento, who's on a cruise down the Danube. I'll call her when she gets home.

It was surprisingly easy. So easy, I don't know why I didn't do this before. Oh, I know. I was chasing investors. And having a temporary depressive breakdown.

Also, phoning people who loved Dad any earlier than this would have been wonderful in one way, and unbearable in another. As it was, there were quite a few tears, mine and theirs. But we got through it, and now I have half our soon-to-be-bottled vintage sold. Go *me*.

Nate will be pleased. He *should* be pleased. But even so, he won't want me to tell him in person. Minimal contact, that's what he said.

I suspect he will ignore my texts, and I doubt he'll be in a hurry to read my emails, either.

I know – I'll leave a note on his desk. Quick and to the point, in big writing, so he can't miss it. It *is* about the business, so he can hardly object to that.

He's out meeting with Ted, who I imagine will be super polite, and will smile, even when he's delivering bad news. I already know he won't take Flora Valley's too-cheap wine, but, of course, I didn't *quite* have the opportunity to pass that little nugget of information on to Nate. Bit of a blunder that, as Ted would say.

I wonder, not for the first time, what it would be like being Ted. Or a female version of him, anyway. What would it be like to never have to worry about money? To always be beautifully dressed, and smell delicious, and have your pick of an endless parade of gorgeous partners.

Some people believe having money makes them superior, but Ted's not like that. He has a genuine affection for our community, and his business sense is the only thing that curbs his generosity. Ted knows that Bartons must keep up appearances, as they say in Britain, so he won't do anything to jeopardize its reputation. That's why he said no to stocking our lower-priced wine.

But that attitude protects the community as well as his business. If Bartons continues to attract wealthy people to little ol' Verity, we all benefit from the halo effect. I know Jordan's adventure company has been contracted for *absurd* amounts of money to take groups camping. Locals with nice houses have been able to rent them out when Bartons is full, and Iris has catered for some mega parties. She won't adapt her cooking, of course, and the next rich Brit to call her "quaint" might get a crab claw in the eyeball. But it earns her the kind of money she'd *never* get from just running the Cracker Café. Which, for her, could be the difference between a comfortable retirement, and one where she has to watch every penny.

Ted knows this community is an eco-system, with a bunch of parts that are interdependent on one another to thrive. I'm not sure Nate has fully figured that one out yet. Don't think they teach grass roots economics at Harvard.

Note in hand, I peek outside to make sure he's not back yet. I feel stupid sneaking around, but his final words to me the other night were so cold, that I think I'll burst into tears on the spot if I see that same coldness in his face.

Excellent. No pick-up. I scoot to the office on tippy-toes, like a cartoon spy. It's locked but I have the spare key. I'm about to open the door when—

"Shelby!"

"Mom?"

She's walking my way, with what looks like a cake box in her arms.

"I didn't know you were coming," I say, hastily stuffing the note in my shorts pocket.

"I came in to meet a friend for lunch in Martinburg, so I thought I'd drive over to see you, too."

That's why I didn't hear her. Mom drives an electric car, because of course she does. It's parked by the Dodge, in Nate's spot.

"Is this a bad time?" she asks.

Mom hates negative vibes.

"Not at all," I say.

And then I am immediately proved incorrect, for who should pull up but Nate himself. The pickup halts as he sees Mom's car, and then reverses to park behind the Dodge.

He's getting out. There's nowhere to hide. Well, I could make a *run* for it—

Too late. Mom's walking over to greet him, with a huge smile on her face.

"You must be Nathan," she says. "I've heard so much about you. I'm Lee Armstrong."

She shifts the cake box, so she can offer him her hand.

Nate returns the shake, keeping his eyes firmly not on me, I notice.

"Good to meet you, ma'am."

"Ma'am?" says Mom, with a wry smile. "Either you're very well brought up, or I'm old. *Both* could be a possibility."

"I'm very well brought up," says Nate, proving the point.

Mom laughs. Her red hair cascades down her back. She's only just starting to go grey. It occurs to me that my mother is an extremely attractive woman. If you like the boho hippy look, with loose muslin shirts and floral flares. A look, I have to say, my mother totally rocks.

She smiles at the two of us.

"Have you two hard workers got time for coffee and cake? I picked some up from Iris's."

Good news. Mom makes cakes too, but prefers more *rustic* ingredients. Iris's cakes, on the other hand, are edible.

Trust that to be my first response. *Now,* I realize what she's asking. And I'm praying Nate politely declines.

Which he does, thank you, thank you.

"Sorry, I've got some urgent business to finish," he tells Mom.

"Well, I won't keep you," she replies. "But let me just say that I'm *thrilled* you're here. My daughter is a trooper, but she can't do this on her own. I'm *so* glad you two are now a team."

She smiles at me, and back at Nate. Who's still not glanced at me even once. The man has willpower; I'll give him that. I've been staring at him nonstop since he exited his truck and thinking how much I'd love to run up and throw myself into his arms.

Because I'm staring, I can see Nate struggling with how to phrase his response. He can hardly break Mom's bubble by telling her we're about as cozy a team as early Buffy and Spike.

So, channelling the spirit of Buffy, I decide to save him.

"Mom, let Nate go. He's super busy. Come into the kitchen, and I'll put the coffee on."

Of course, between Mom stepping one way, and me and Nate trying to anticipate each other's moves, we end up sliding by each other. I feel his arm brush mine, and it's like static shock. I catch his Nate-scent, and the longing wrenches me physically. How on *earth* am I going to survive this? I am *this* close to grabbing his arm and pulling him with me into the house.

But he's gone. Office door is firmly shut. I'll have to give him the note later. Lots later.

"Goodness, he's handsome," says Mom, once we're safely in the kitchen. "Is he single?"

"Mom," I say, in a warning tone.

"It's a perfectly innocent question," she replies, blithely, fetching a knife for the cake. "If he is, I know plenty of young women he could meet."

I bet she does. My mom is weirdly obsessed with ensuring everyone on the planet finds his or her soul mate. Trouble is, her idea of compatible can often be like – well, like early Buffy and Spike.

"This is why your other children moved so far away," I remind her, as I put the coffee pot on the stove. "And why you're lucky Cam is still speaking to you, after you tried to set him up with your crazy artist friend, what's-her-name."

"How *is* Cam?" she asks, ignoring the negative, as only Mom can. "He's terrible at answering my emails."

"If you're sending him more than one every six months, then what do you expect?" I say. "You know Cam needs time to process his replies."

"I should stop by and see him, too, while I'm here."

Once again, I speculate on exactly *what* kind of friendship Mom has with Cam. I know she was always faithful to Dad, but now, she's a free agent, and—

Nope, that's icky. Cam's, what, thirty-six? Mom's fifty-seven. OK, so it's not exactly Harold and Maude, but still…

"If you do, remind him he has to talk to Nate about the pre-harvest equipment check," I tell her.

We have coffee in front of us now, and Mom's portioned out two generous slices of Iris's famous strawberry shortcake.

"Yum," I say.

I skipped lunch today because I was too busy phoning people.

"Are you eating?"

The universal Mom question. And redundant, because I have a whole forkful of cake in my mouth.

"I am," I assure her, after swallowing. "I am also sleeping well and getting moderate exercise."

The sleeping part's not *entirely* true, but I'm sure it will improve. Eventually.

"I thought Nathan was looking a little peaky," she adds.

"Mom, you've only just *met* him," I protest. "How do you know that's not how he normally looks?"

"I pick up on people's well-being." She is completely serious about this. "I'd say his iron levels are low."

"Well, bring him a steak next time." I smile.

And then I change the subject, because I really *don't* want to talk about Nate.

"How are you?" I ask her. "How's the studio?"

"Glorious," she says.

Her face is lit with a radiant happiness, and it suddenly occurs to me that I never saw that look much while we were growing up.

"Mom, did you stay with Dad because of us kids?"

Now, she looks stunned. Fair enough. I threw *that* one at her without warning.

"Is that what you all think?" she says.

"Not at all," I reply. "But it worries me that you might not have … enjoyed living here."

"Oh, Shel." Her face softens again. "I *loved* your dad more than any man on Earth. Yes, at times, I found it hard. The lack of money, the hours he put in, the hours he made you *kids* put in…"

She glances up at the photo of us all on the shelf, and her expression is pure affection.

"But he was so special, and we loved each other so much, that there was *no* place I'd have rather been."

She turns to me, with a wry smile.

"Now, that doesn't mean we didn't have our rough moments," she adds. "No relationship is *ever* all sunshine and rainbows, even when one half of the couple is *me*."

Mom has always owned her quirks, bless her.

"Did you ever have any moments when you thought it was over?"

I hope she doesn't want to know why I'm asking.

"Oh, yes," she says, with a brief laugh. "About once a month, as I recall."

"Really?"

They hid it well. I remember a few cross words, but never any major arguments.

"Deep down, we always knew we were both being foolish," she says. "We knew our connection was too strong for us to break."

I feel the sudden prick of tears. The happy-sad kind. I'm happy Mom and Dad loved each other that much, and I'm so sad she's without him now. I'm happy she's OK, though, and making a new, fulfilling life for herself.

But I'm sad that *I'm* not going to be able to do the same. If it were up to me, Nate and I would be back together already, at least in an on-hold way. Nate's so determined though, and he has an absolute right to be angry with me – *he* didn't say terrible things. Our connection is so new that it hasn't had time to get strong yet. So if Nate refuses to yield to the pull *I* feel, then I don't see any hope for us.

Mom had to deal with Dad's death. We all did, of course, but he was her soulmate, and his loss must have been crushing.

If she can get through that kind of loss with grace and humour, then I can handle my own situation.

And I'm sure it will help if I have another slice of shortcake.

Chapter Thirty

NATE

Wow. Shelby's mom. What a stunner.

And what a seriously uncomfortable way to be introduced. With Shelby right there, draining my strength like a piece of Kryptonite.

When we accidentally brushed past each other, I *almost* grabbed her. The desire to inhale her scent, and kiss her neck and mouth and wherever else, practically did me in. I had to lean against the office door after I'd closed it and do a little speed meditating to calm down. The kind I used to do on the start line of a race.

Trouble is, my technique sucks because you still need a bunch of adrenaline pumping through you to race your best. Perhaps I should ask Shelby's mom for tips on how to achieve a total state of calm? She looks like a woman who knows how to align chakras.

She looks like Shelby, goddamn it. Or like Shelby will in thirty years' time.

I could be with Shelby in thirty years' time. We could feasibly have grown kids of our own by then. Now *that's* a freaky thought. It's also incredibly appealing. Fills me with a real longing. I *want* that life. I want Shelby.

So what's stopping me? Why can't I go to her and ask if we can start again? She'll apologize, I know she will, and she'll put any hurt I caused her in the past, forgotten.

So, again, what's stopping me?

Here's the thing. If I hadn't met with Ted, I'd probably still be in the same space I was. Hanging on to the hurt, using it as an excuse to keep my distance.

But when Ted gave me that so-called advice about Shelby, it shook me. Here was a guy who, if he wanted to, could do exactly as he pleased. He's obviously rich as Croesus, so why even bother to *think* about others, let alone give a shit? Yet, give a shit he does. And I bet he'd defend more people than just Shelby.

It takes guts to care about others – to stand with them, and stand up for them. I did some hard thinking on the way back from Bartons. Didn't want to, but I made myself. The discipline I learned for competing comes in handy sometimes. You know how to kick your *own* ass.

I thought about what Shelby said – about Dad resisting treatment because he was afraid. Afraid that if he accepted he needed medical help, then he'd be accepting how sick he really was. Fear makes you irrational. It makes you invent alternative realities, so you don't have to cope with the one you're actually in.

I am afraid of not being good enough for Shelby. I

reacted badly – immaturely – to what she said over the phone. Even though, deep down, I *knew* she didn't mean it.

But those words touched the red button that launched all my insecurities. I was a shit partner to Camille, and I'm afraid I'll be a shit partner to Shelby. I can see now that using Dad to put our relationship on hold was nothing more than an exercise in delusion. I thought I was being rational, doing the right thing, when, in fact, I was a spineless worm. I was too chicken to give it a shot, and instead found a so-called good reason to wimp out.

Trouble is, that's still the case. Soon as I think about approaching Shelby to ask if she'll forgive me, my mind comes up with a million other things I should be doing instead. All excuses, invented so I don't have to risk the one I fear most – rejection. Specifically, being rejected because I'm not good enough.

You realize there's only one course of action here, don't you, Nate? You need to man up. You need to show some guts. Like too-perfect Ted.

Yeah, thanks, Nate. Sometimes you can be a real prick.

Of course, the irony is that I *can't* go charging over to the house to declare my undying love. Her mother's there. And even the most romantic intentions don't tend to survive being witnessed by a person who might end up being your mother-in-law.

I could hang around here a bit longer than usual. Figure her mom won't want to leave the drive back to the coast too late.

Until then, also ironically, I may as well do the work my

craven mind put up as an excuse for me not to go charging in.

I fire up the email. Immediately see an offer for penis enhancement. Ha, ha, universe. Fuck you.

OK, here we go. Lease on the harvester and the wine press are finalized. That means more manning up, in order to go break the bad news to Javi and Iris. I should report to JP as well, and given Ted's hint-slash-warning about the value of Flora Valley's 'story', I now have doubts about how JP will respond. I figure his business sense will override any emotional attachment to old-fashioned winemaking, but my own judgment on matters has been pretty poor lately, so who the fuck knows?

It's four o'clock now, so all that will have to wait until *demain*. Or *mañana*, as Javi would never say, because he's a do-it-right-now kind of guy.

Architect has emailed his terms and conditions for the tasting room project. I spend a stupid amount of time reviewing them and making changes. I waste another twenty minutes googling pictures of tasting rooms in other wineries.

I'm looking at one with vaulted brick ceilings and hand-blown glass chandeliers, when there's a knock on the office door. My heart does a black flip. Shelby?

"Come in."

I get to my feet. Always feel at a disadvantage when I'm sitting down.

Not Shelby. Mountain Man Cam.

"Hey," I say, though I don't try that hard to look welcoming.

All he does is nod. Does the guy have some brain injury, or voice box malfunction? What's so hard about stringing together a few goddamn words?

"What can I do for you, Cam?"

I keep my voice more civil than my thoughts. He is *way* bigger than me. There wasn't that much advantage to be gained by standing up, after all.

"Shelby said to ask you about the harvest pre-check."

OK. So he *can* do it. When he wants to.

"Run me through what it involves," I say.

Granted, it's not *the* most articulate speech I've ever heard. Got the flat tone of a soldier repeating back orders. But he covers all the necessary ground: the equipment that needs to be looked over and serviced, checking the floors and walls in the storage and processing areas for cracks and mould, all the cleaning and sanitizing that needs doing, plus a whole lot of miscellaneous stuff, right down to re-stocking first aid kits.

"And you do all this on your own?"

"Pretty much," he says.

"Fee?" I ask. Brevity is catching.

He shrugs. "Usual."

It's been a *looong* day.

"Here's the thing," I explain. "The accounting in this place has been … haphazard, at best. As an example, every payment to you has just been labelled 'Cam.' So you can see my problem, can't you?"

There's a substantial pause, where, I *guess*, he's mulling over his response. Who knows? Could be chewing cud, like a cow. He's got those big, brown cow eyes.

Finally, he names a figure. It's actually slightly below what I'd budgeted. But I'm tired and in a bad mood, and just looking at him makes me feel inadequate. He's got arms like freaking John Cena, with a hint of Stallone-style knuckle-drag. I'm in good shape, but he could twist my head off without even breaking a sweat.

"OK, let me get back to you on that," I tell him.

I don't say by when. If he wants to know badly enough, he can ask.

This whole conversation has been carried out with minimal eye contact, as seems to be Cam's normal MO. But he looks right at me now, eyebrows raised ever so slightly.

"Do something to offend you?" he says.

Got to admit, I'm taken aback by his unexpected forthrightness. Caught on the hop, too, because, yeah, I *do* find him offensive. He offends my ego. My stupid, childish ego.

But what I lack in maturity, I make up for in mastery of the poker face.

"As I said, the accounting here has been a mess. I can't commit until I've run all the numbers."

We lock stares, but I have *no* intention of blinking first.

Sure enough.

"K."

"Thanks for coming," I say, as he heads back out the door.

He flicks me a glance over his shoulder but keeps moving.

Just before the door shuts, I hear Shelby's mom call out "Cam!"

Trying not to be seen, I peer out the tiny slit of a side window, which looks toward the house.

Shelby's mother is walking across the gravel toward Mountain Moron, huge smile on her face. Can't see his response to this, but it doesn't matter because I'm distracted by Shelby appearing in the house doorway. She leans up against the jamb, arms folded, also smiling.

I want her to look my way, and I also *don't* want that because it would be humiliating to be caught staring at her.

Shelby's mom and Cam are talking by the corner of the office. I can't see them, but I can slide the window open a fraction, and eavesdrop. Guess this must be the International Day of Immaturity.

There's the usual, "How are you?" small talk. Small as to be pretty much non-existent on Cam's part.

But then from Shelby's mom comes, "What are you doing right now? Want to have dinner with me and Shelby in Verity?"

Cam makes noises of prevarication.

"Oh, come *on*," says Shelby's mom. "My treat?"

And then, shit, Shelby's right there with them. I was so busy listening, I forgot to keep watching. Don't sign *me* up to be the next James Bond.

"Come on, Cam," Shelby says, and I can hear the smile in her voice. "You can choose. Burger at the Silver Saddle, with a side order of surly Brendan. Or terrible pizza, with extra cheese that contains one hundred percent no dairy. What's it to be?"

And I am overtaken by a jealousy so powerful, I'm glad there's nothing breakable within easy reach. Fucking Mountain *Meathead* gets to go to dinner with Shelby and her mother. Gets to laugh and talk with them and have a good time. And sit close to Shelby all evening.

Yeah, OK, so that could be me if I hadn't been such a jerk. Or if I'd figured out sooner what was stopping me from patching it up with Shelby.

Or if Mountain Mutant was bound and gagged in his shed, unable to move an inch.

My jealous rage is indiscriminate, and it's making the blood pound so loud in my ears that I only catch the tail end of what Shelby's mom says.

"… Nathan, too," is all I hear.

Before I can process the words, the office door is pushed open and there's the woman herself. I shift hastily from the window, pretend to be heading toward the calendar pinned on the wall.

"Nathan, will you join us at the Silver Saddle?" says Shelby's mom. "I'll pick up the check. My way to welcome you to Flora Valley Wines."

My eye is drawn past her shoulder and out the door, to where Shelby is now standing. Mountain Moron is out of frame, for which I am thankful. Don't want to see what he thinks of the invitation.

Shelby's response is pretty obvious. She's embarrassed.

That could be for a lot of reasons. One, moms are always embarrassing. Two, she doesn't want me to say yes. Three, she knows Cam doesn't want me to say yes. Four, she *does* want me to say yes, but isn't ready to admit it.

Last option is the best. It's not the one I hold out much hope for being true.

"Thanks," I say. "But I've got a few hours' work left."

Not entirely a lie. Though I'd planned on those few hours taking place tomorrow.

"Are you sure I can't tempt you?" She smiles, and reminds me of Shelby so much, my guts hurt. "The Saddle does a pretty fair T-bone."

I shake my head, and say, "Next time, ma'am," using my well-brought-up manners.

"That's a promise," she replies. "Don't work *too* hard now, will you? You're young. You need to enjoy life."

To my relief, the door is shut again, and I don't get to see Shelby's reaction to the news that I won't be joining them.

Five minutes later, the Dodge rattles into life. If that electric car makes any sound, the Flora Valley Wines truck drowns it out. And then, there's silence.

They're off to have a fun, relaxed meal, in a casual environment. A total contrast to tomorrow night's occasion, which is looming like the shadow of a guillotine. The Durant family dinner.

Shelby will be there, too. But she'll be there for Ava. Not for me. She might not even speak to me all evening. We certainly won't laugh and joke.

If I were to follow my own man-up advice, I'd talk to her

tomorrow morning, apologize for being a jerk, and tell her how I really feel. Then the dinner might even become enjoyable. Or, at least, bearable.

OK, I will. I'll talk to her first thing.

There, I said it. Now that, in the word of Shelby's mom, is a promise.

Chapter Thirty-One

SHELBY

I'm up at crack of dawn, because my mother has emotionally blackmailed me into visiting her in her studio. To be fair, she's had it a while now, and I've only seen it in the photos she's sent. And, as she pointed out, I have Nate now to share the load, so I should be able to take *one* day off without everything falling apart.

Of course, I feel guilty about leaving Nate on his own. But she's my mother, and mother-guilt trumps anyone else's. My only condition for the visit is that I have to leave at five sharp, in order to get back to Nate's house in time for dinner. I've packed a change of clothes in the Dodge. Won't be Bartons dress code level, but I hope it'll do.

I feed the animals, who are all annoyed at being woken early, even for food. Dylan greeted me and Cam when we came back last night. I offered to drop Cam at his shed, but I think, after that hectic round of socializing, he needed a walk in the calm summer night air. It's about twenty-five minutes from my place to his, and I'm pretty sure any mugger would think twice about tackling him.

Mom asked Cam to visit, too. But, unlike me, he remained impervious to her blandishments. He was happy to see her, though. Mom's always been the person Cam's most comfortable being around.

Even Brendan succumbed to Mom's charms. If *I'd* said I couldn't have more than one drink because I was driving, he would have been grumpy. But it was totally OK coming from Mom. He even gave her a doggy bag, which *never* happens. In Brendan's view, if you don't eat everything on your plate, you didn't deserve that meal in the first place.

It might be because Mom's older and wiser than I am. Cam and Brendan not only like Mom, they respect her. Or, they have the hots for her, but let's not go there.

Cam was a little – odd – when Mom mentioned Nate last night. As she did *several* times, causing me to eat more than I should have, owing to desperately needing a distraction.

Cam didn't exactly *say* anything, but he gave off a very un-Cam-like vibe. I remember my brother, Tyler, aged about five, taking against some kid he'd only seen across a room, and pretending to laser zap him Buzz Lightyear-style. My father laughed out loud at the determined scowl on Tyler's face. Cam's vibe reminded me of that scowl. But asking questions about Nate was the last thing I wanted to do, so I stuffed my face with curly fries, instead.

I should let Nate know where I'm heading. The note from yesterday is now in the trash because it got all screwed up in my pocket. I don't have time to write that out again in full, so I scribble, *At Mom's for the day. Call if urgent. Will see you at 7*, and tape it to the office door.

And then I hit the road, off to the coast. Hoping the Dodge will go the distance, and that Mom hasn't had time to bake a cake.

———————

Five o'clock on the dot, and I'm heading back. When Mom found out where I was going to dinner, she practically set an alarm.

"Are you and Nate—?" she did manage to ask before I left.

"Nope," I said, truthfully, while wishing with every ounce of my being that it was a lie.

I should talk to him. That would be the brave thing to do. I mean, sure, he could reject me again, but at least I would have *tried*. And the worst another night of crying will do is give me puffy eyes, right?

Doubt we'll get a chance to talk this evening. I really do not know what to expect, and I'm feeling nervous about what's expected of me. Ava, and Nate, too, if he's still in on this plan, want me to lay the emotion on thick for their dad. My feelings of sadness and loss are never too far from the surface, so odds are high I'll be able to come through. But how will Mr Durant react? What if this all goes horribly wrong, and I make things worse?

My phone is directing me to the house. I'm about fifteen

minutes out of Martinburg, in a semi-rural area, where the wealthier folk live. Phone says turn right down a gravel driveway lined with big trees. It winds through a green corridor for about a minute, and then—

Lordy. I've come home to Tara.

OK, so the style is more country than neo-classical, but it's *huge*. Two-storey, cream and white weatherboard, a covered porch, gables and stuff. The driveway ends in a big circle of gravel, and I pull in next to the black Porsche, keeping company with a couple of other less flashy vehicles. I *don't* spot Nate's pickup. But then, checking the time, I see I'm ten minutes early. That's OK. I'll just sit here for a bit.

Or not. The front door opens, and there's Ava, waving at me. Right. Deep breath. Show time.

"Welcome," she says, as I step inside. "I'm Ava, and I'll be your security detail for this evening."

"Don't listen to her."

A tall, sun-bleached blond guy in a polo shirt appears beside her. This must be the brother who owns the Porsche. He doesn't look irate, so I guess he had insurance.

"I'm Danny," he says, and shakes my hand. "The middle Durant."

He has a killer smile, and though his hair is light and his eyes are a softer blue than Nate's, I can see the likeness. The gene that controlled the cheekbones was clearly determined to crush all other competitors.

"And we're the youngest equal."

Golly. Twins. A boy – Max – and a girl – Izzy.

Dark red-brown hair, hazel eyes, and those figging cheekbones again make these two the best-looking of an extraordinarily handsome family. My own family, though I do say so myself, are pretty darn cute. But *this* lot are next-level gorgeous.

"Ava and I are cooking," says Max, who, now I've got over being dazzled, I see is indeed wearing a striped apron. "Mom's trying not to interfere."

Izzy links her arm in mine. "Come and meet her."

I take surreptitious glances around the interior of the house, as we walk from the spacious entranceway into a truly enormous kitchen. It's nicely decorated, in soft hues, giving an overall feel of tasteful, low-key opulence. A contrast to Mom's studio, which is messy, sparkly, and ablaze with every colour of the rainbow.

Weirdly, though, Nate's mom reminds me a *lot* of my own mom. Similar age, beautiful, long hair, except that Mrs Durant's is the same blond as Danny's. But unlike Mom, she does not seem relaxed at *all*. There are worry lines around her mouth, and circles under her eyes. She looks thin, too, as if she hasn't been eating properly.

"Oh, Shelby." She clasps my hand with both of hers. "I am *so* pleased to meet you."

I glance at Ava, who gives a quick shake of her head. No, Nate's mom isn't in on the plan. Makes sense. She looks stressed enough as it is.

"Drink?" says Danny. "I can fix you a margarita, or there's wine."

Every part of me *craves* to knock back a jug of margarita, but I'd better keep a clear head.

"Wine would be lovely," I say.

"Cheese puff?" Izzy holds out a tray.

Being the centre of attention might be nice, except that I'm also carrying the weight of everyone's expectations. Anxiety dries my mouth, making the cheese puff tough going.

This is *not* eased when Ava says, impatiently, "Where the hell is Nate?"

"I'll phone him," says Danny, and steps out of the kitchen to do so.

Max is busy by the stove, stirring and checking. He looks up.

"We're ready to go," he says to Ava. "Shall we wait?"

"No, it took me freaking ages to persuade Dad to eat with us," she replies, frowning. "We'll start without."

Oh. That's right. I still have to meet Mr Durant. Ignoring my own advice, I take a decent slug of wine.

Escorted by Izzy and Mrs Durant, I find myself seated at a large dining table, set in a way that would make Martha Stewart cry tears of envious joy.

Immediately, I bob up again, as a man who can only be Nate's father enters the room. Dark hair salted with grey, lean and handsome, the dead spit of his two eldest children.

"You must be Shelby," he says. "I'm Mitchell Durant."

He, too, looks thin and worn, his jaw clenched as if he's battling pain. But his blue eyes are cold as an alpine lake. I start to understand a little more about what Nate's childhood might have been like.

"Good to meet you, sir," I reply, hoping he can't see that I'm quaking in my boots.

He turns his gaze to his wife and youngest daughter.

"It's well past seven," he says, pointedly.

"Sorry, Dad."

Max bustles in with a big casserole dish in oven-gloved hands. Ava's on his heels, with bowls of potatoes and green beans.

Danny enters.

"Nate's on his way," he announces. "He says to start without him."

I spy Ava shoot him a hard look, but Danny is busy pouring wine for everyone at the table. Except, I notice, his dad. Guess that makes sense. Though, personally, I think wine's good for what ails you.

Max finishes arranging the dishes on the table, counts serving spoons, checks the condiments.

"It's chicken, with braised leek and fennel," he informs us all. "Good for you in every way. Dad, you're head of the family. Dig in."

Might be my imagination, but I get the feeling Max doesn't have the same wariness as the others seem to, when it comes to their father. He's not disrespectful, exactly, but he certainly doesn't choose his words as carefully.

"Guests first, Max," says his dad.

"Oops, sorry Shelby," says Max, with a smile. "Here. Pass your plate."

My ears must be trained for the sound of the pickup, because I seem to be the only one who hears it. The others raise their heads only when the front door is opened and shut.

"About time," mutters Ava.

I don't realize I'm holding my breath until Nate appears. He looks alarmingly pale and pinched. I hope he hasn't had to deal with a bunch of problems at work, while I swanned off to drink matcha tea by the coast.

"Hands?" says Max, in that tone everyone with a little brother will recognize.

"Still got two," says Nate, with a back-off edge to his own voice.

He takes his seat, nods around the table, but doesn't *quite* look at me. "Sorry I'm late."

And then dinner is served, and we begin to eat. Danny is the one who keeps the conversation going. He tells funny stories about rich people in LA, and prompts Max and Izzy to fill me in on what they're studying. I am equal parts impressed and intimidated. This is a *high*-performance family.

Mr Durant speaks very little, other than to ask his wife to pass him things. Nate, too, is pretty much silent, giving only terse answers to a couple of questions from his mother. He doesn't look at me at all. Ava, I think, at one point, kicks him under the table, because they have a short glaring match, until Ava gives a quick, impatient shake of her head, and chips into Danny's story about a guy who spray-painted his car to colour coordinate with his dog.

I'm holding my end up in the conversation perfectly fine. They're easy to talk to, funny, and nice. Like Nate on a good day.

But then, I hear Mr Durant say my name. And, suddenly, I get the cold sweats.

"Shelby, how long has your winery been operating?"

"Um, just over twenty-six years," I reply.

"And yet it's stayed small," he says. "Was that a deliberate decision?"

I *could* take offence at that – his implication that we were never good enough to get big.

"My father wanted us to remain exclusive," I say. "He didn't want just *anybody* to be his customers."

Take *that*, rude man.

"And your father has retired now, I assume?"

Oh, *fig*. Has *no* one told him?

I'm frozen to the chair, can't even look at Ava for help. I *have* to answer.

"I'm sorry," I stammer. "My father died."

He goes completely still. There's no air in the room, as if all of us have sucked it into our lungs. The silence is horrendous, like waiting for a jury verdict in a murder trial.

Then he says, with *icy* fury, "Get out."

"Dad—" begins Danny.

Mitchell Durant rises slowly to his feet, and says *"Out. All* of you. I don't want to see your faces for another *second."*

"Mitchell, please." Nate's mom gives it a go.

But her husband is aglow with anger.

"How *dare* you." His voice rises. "Do you think I am an *imbecile*?"

"OK, that's it." Ava pushes back her chair. She beckons to me, and her siblings. "Come on, let's go. Let's leave this asshole alone."

As we hesitate, she grabs her closest siblings, Izzy and Max, by the shoulders.

"Come *on*."

Danny takes my arm way more gently, and leads me out, with Izzy, Max and Ava close behind.

"What about Mom?" I hear Izzy say.

But Ava is intent on marching us into what looks like a TV room.

"Fuck, I'm sorry," she says to me, breathing hard with anger. "You should never have taken that crap."

"We might have guessed," said Danny, glumly. "Dad being Dad and all."

Izzy looks like she's near tears. I suspect they're *her* response to being furious.

She opens her mouth to say something, but suddenly, there's shouting. Nate and his dad have started going at it. Full volume. No holds barred, by the sound.

"Fuck," says Ava. "Dan, let's go. Better intervene before—"

"*Nate!*" we hear his mother exclaim, her voice high and terrified.

Danny and Ava exchange one alarmed glance, and then start to run. Izzy, Max and I are hard on their heels.

Rounding the dining room door, we see Mr Durant,

arms propped on the table, breathing hard. His wife is on her knees, and her hands are cradling the head of her oldest son, who is sprawled on the floor, unconscious.

Danny slides to his own knees beside his brother.

"Nate! Shit," he says. "What *happened*?"

"He just … collapsed," says his stricken mother.

Danny checks Nate's pulse, taps him lightly on the cheek.

"Come on, buddy, wake up."

"I'm calling Doc Wilson." Ava has her phone. "He's closer than an ambulance."

"Nate, come on."

Danny taps him on the cheek again. Nate's skin is like wax, and he's covered in a sheen of sweat.

Izzy and Max are on either side of me, and as if on some telepathic cue, they each slip a hand into mine.

And we stand there, watching, helpless.

Chapter Thirty-Two

NATE

I'm trying to wake up, but it's like crawling out of a black tunnel. I can hear someone calling my name, far away at first, then closer.

Finally, I can open my eyes, and when everything comes into focus, I find I'm staring up at Dan. I can feel polished wood under my hands, which would suggest I'm lying on the floor. What the almighty fuck is going on?

"Steady."

Danny's hands are on the back of my shoulders, supporting me as I sit up. My vision blurs a little, and I pull up my knees, so I can hang my head between them.

"Nate, you OK?"

Danny hasn't sounded this concerned about me since he accidentally hit a baseball smack into my eye when we were kids. Then, he was more worried about getting into trouble. This time, it seems genuine.

There's a cool dampness on my skin. Seems I'm sweating.

"What happened?" I ask Dan.

"You fainted," is his reply.

I give him a look. *"Fainted?"*

He grins. "A threat to your masculinity is your top concern right now?"

"Damn straight."

"OK, then, Butch, you passed out. Went down like a felled tree, according to Mom."

I have no recollection of that. Last thing I remember was Dad being a prick to—

Shit, Shelby. Is she here?

Looking around makes me dizzy, but I see her, standing between the twins, her face twisted with worry. I catch her eye, and see a plea. If I had any confidence in my ability to stand, I'd go to her, and pull her into my arms.

But I don't get a chance to even try.

"Howdy all."

And now it's Doc Wilson sticking his face in mine.

"Jesus, Ava, how fast did you drive?" I hear Danny say.

Doc Wilson is pointing one of those mini torch things into my eyes, so I don't catch her response.

Now, he's wrapping a cuff round my arm. "Let's check your blood pressure."

"I'm fine, Doc," I say.

And I am. I'm feeling much better.

"Well, here's the thing, son," he says. "Young fit men

don't normally hit the floor like a sack of potaters. So we need to find out what's up."

He makes me go through a bunch of "follow my finger with your eyes" exercises, listens to my heart, pokes and prods a bit more, and then packs up his bag, and parks his butt in one of the dining chairs. Smiles down at me, still sitting on the floor, now feeling more stupid than dizzy.

"You been eating regular meals, son?"

"Mostly," I reply, cautiously.

"How much exercise you doing?"

"He runs *miles*," says Ava, the snitch. "Up at dawn each day. Runs at night, too."

"I ran *once* at night." I hold up my middle finger to her. "*Once*."

"Been under any stress lately? No, scratch that," says Doc immediately. "You're a Durant. If there's a type above Type A, you're all it. When I diagnose any one of you, I have to account for what I call the Durant premium: everything's ratcheted up about ten notches."

"Ray, what's your opinion?"

Dad. Being his usual impatient self.

"I'll want to take some blood tests," says Doc. "But my guess is his iron levels are through the floor."

"*Iron?*" I say, meaning all this drama for *that*?

The rest of the room has much the same reaction. I can feel the air current, as they all breathe out.

"I'll want to run an ECG, too," adds Doc.

And the air is sucked back in again.

"Could it be his heart?" says Mom, almost frantic.

"Ginny, his heart sounds fine to me," replies Doc in his steady way. "But in my field, we err on the side of caution. Boy's not going to be worse off for having a thorough check-up. Do him good to take a bit of time out, even if he has to spend it in a clinic."

He pushes on his knees, rises from the chair.

"Come see me in the morning, Nate, and I'll set you up. But listen to me ..." He waits till he has my full attention. "Take it easy for the next few days. Lie around on the couch. Watch bad TV. Get to bed early. Eat good food, and plenty of it."

"We'll look after him," says Ava.

I don't like the way she's smiling.

"Run you home, Doc?"

She jangles the Porsche keys in her hand. Danny snatches them from her.

"*I'll* run him home," he says.

"Spoilsport," Ava mutters.

Once Danny's left with Doc, I decide I may as well try getting to my feet. I'm OK during the standing process, but sway a little when I'm fully upright. Suddenly, I have Izzy and Max on either side. They grab an arm each.

"Where to?" says Max. "Bed or couch?"

"You're *not* putting me to bed," I tell him. That's enough humiliation for one day.

"Yessir. Couch it is."

"Nate?"

Mom comes up, cups my face with one hand. She looks

upset, and exhausted. Possibly, I don't look that snappy, either.

"You lie down, and I'll bring you some food," she says.

"We've got that covered, Mom," says Izzy. "Don't you worry."

"But—"

"Mom." Ava has her arm around our mother's shoulders. "Chill. He'll be fine."

Mom bursts into tears, and Ava pulls her into an embrace, stroking her hair and gently shushing her.

Dad, who's been glowering this whole time, stalks off without a word to any of us. I see Ava raise her middle finger at his departing back.

And then I spot the other silent witness to this little drama. Shelby. Standing back, hands clasped so tight, her knuckles are white.

Her big blue-green eyes lock onto mine, and, as I'm trapped between the twins, I make the best apology face I can. I hope she knows it's not just for right now, but for the last few days as well.

Shelby's hands fly to cover her mouth, but then, like a miracle, she blows me a kiss. I feel light-headed again, but this time it's from sheer relief. I'm about to draw the twins' attention to her, but Izzy's already on the case.

"Shelby," she says. "Follow us. We'll get Nate settled, and then ... don't know ... break out the bourbon?"

"Is bourbon medicinal?" asks Max, as we head towards the TV room.

"It is now," I say. "Although I should probably have a sandwich or something."

The twins lead me to the couch and make as if I should be lying down.

"Nope," I resist. "Sitting is just fine."

"I'll fetch supplies," says Izzy. "Back in a sec."

Shelby's hovering near the doorway. Max looks like he's about to get comfortable in an armchair, until he twigs that, you know, maybe, we could do with a moment alone.

"I'll go see if Mom and Ava are OK," he says, and leaves, taking with him my eternal gratitude.

I lock eyes with Shelby again. A lot of words come into my brain, but none seem right. Luckily, Shelby decides not to overthink matters. She hurries from the door, slides onto my lap and kisses me hard.

I kiss her back with every ounce of energy I have. Which isn't that much, to tell the truth, but it'll do for now. She feels so *good* in my arms, the smell of her, the warmth and softness of her skin. If I died right now, I'd be the happiest dead guy on the planet.

"I'm so sorry," I murmur, when we take a break to breathe, and at exactly the same moment, she says, "I love you."

I'm not sure I've heard correctly. But then she says it again, and kisses me again, and I think I *have* died, and this is a weirdly domestic kind of heaven, complete with armchairs and occasional tables.

She stops kissing me, and punches me on the arm. This is definitely real. Her fist is *strong*.

"Ow," I say.

"Why haven't you been *eating*?" she demands. "You need to look *after* yourself!"

"I'm fine," I assure her. "I got low iron all the time when I was doing track. Doc Wilson used to inject me in the butt with a big dose, and next day I'd feel like a million bucks."

"In the *butt*?"

"Cheek," I clarify. "Gluteus maximus muscle, if you want to get technical."

I'm so happy to be holding her, I can't stop smiling. Shelby's not quite done being cross with me, though.

"You scared the crap out of me," she says, accusingly. "And you've also proved my mother is a witch."

"Your mother?"

"She called it," says Shelby. "When she saw you yesterday, she *knew* your iron was low."

"Huh," I say.

Then I remember, I have something much more important still to tell her.

"I love you, too." I punctuate it with a kiss. "And I'm sorry for being such a dick."

"*I'm* sorry," she says. "I didn't mean what I said at all."

"I know. You'd never be intentionally unkind." I smile wryly. "Doesn't mean it wasn't true, though."

"No, *don't* say that!" She looks equal parts ashamed and irritated. "You're the *best*. And don't argue—"

She forestalls any rejoinder by kissing me. I have *no* desire to argue with that.

"Ahem."

Someone's fake-coughing in the doorway. Shelby makes to hop off my lap, so I grab her by both gluteus maximi, and prevent her from going anywhere.

"Uh, sorry to interrupt," says Max, waving a bottle. "But we have bourbon and cookies. And a beef sandwich for Nate."

Well, it's not like I can shut my whole family out of this room so Shelby and I can have sex on the couch. I'd *like* to do that, but it's not totally practical.

"Bourbon and cookies?" I say to her.

"I should get home," she says, apologetically.

"No!" Izzy's arrived, with a tray. "Stay! We've got room."

Shelby manages to elude my grip, and get up off my lap.

"I've got animals to feed," she says.

"Can't someone else do that?"

Ava's here now. The room's getting crowded.

Shelby glances at me, hesitant. "I suppose I could call Cam…?"

Right now, even mention of the Commando can't kill my buzz.

"Stay," I tell her. "Ask Cam to critter-sit. Come with me to see the Doc tomorrow morning. We can talk business on the way."

Shelby looks for final confirmation from Ava. "Are you sure your parents won't mind?"

"Mom would love it," Ava replies. "And, frankly, who gives a fuck what Dad thinks? His behaviour this evening was unforgivable, and we owe you an apology."

"Oh, no…" says Shelby. "No, I understand why he might have been upset."

"The apology is for *our* behaviour, too."

Danny's back. All my siblings in the one small room. I'm glad they're here. Might even love them, the cretins.

"Our plan was stupid," Danny continues. "We should never have made you party to it."

"It was *my* plan," I remind them. "And, yeah—" I reach out for Shelby's hand "—I'm sorry. Dumb idea. Backfired spectacularly."

She squeezes my hand in return.

"Worth a shot." She smiles.

"OK, that's settled." Max flops down in an armchair and picks up the TV remote. "Any requests?"

Izzy puts down her tray, hands me a sandwich, filled with what looks like half a cow. Then she hands me a glass, which contains a *tiny* drop of bourbon.

"Alcohol lowers your blood sugar," she informs me. "You need to be careful."

"I *also* need to be slightly drunk," I reply. "So if you don't mind…?"

"You're a worse patient than Dad," she mock grumps. But she fills the glass to a more acceptable level.

Shelby has stepped outside to phone Mountain Man. I'm guessing he rarely has social plans, so chances are high he'll say yes.

Sure enough, Shelby comes in smiling. "Dylan will be thrilled," she says.

"Who's Dylan?" asks Ava, the nosy parker.

"My goose."

Shelby accepts the invitation of my outstretched arm, and snuggles next to me on the couch.

"My nemesis," I add. "That goose fucking hates me."

"Nate, your *language*."

Now, *Mom's* here, with what looks like a cake. Did she bake one just now? I wouldn't put it past her.

Max has been channel surfing. "*Die Hard!*" he says. "Awesome!"

"No fucking way," says Ava. "We get that *every* Christmas."

Mom, conceding defeat, shakes her head. She's taken the other comfortable chair, Izzy's perched on the arm of Max's, and Danny and Ava have pulled up the beanbags. The Durant clan hasn't crammed into the TV room like this since ... well, the last Christmas we were all together, probably watching *Die Hard*. I don't want to count how many years ago that was. Too many will do.

All that's missing is Dad. But I'm with Ava about his behaviour tonight. If he insists on pushing us away, then let him. He can stew in his own bitterness upstairs, alone.

Ava has the remote now. Max never stood a chance.

"If you pick *Seabiscuit*, I'll hold a cushion over your face," Danny threatens her.

"If it were up to you, bro," Ava retorts, "we'd be watching *The Fast and the Furious*, one through however many of those shit films they made."

She lands on *Ghostbusters*. Family favourite. Good choice.

"I *love* this movie," says Shelby.

She has a cookie in one hand and a glass of bourbon in the other. She is the most beautiful thing I've ever seen.

I put my mouth up to her ear, and whisper, "I love you."

Then I add, "My room's first on the right up the stairs."

She turns and gives me an *Are you kidding?* look. But then I nuzzle her neck, and hear her quiet sighs of desire, until she gets embarrassed, and pulls away.

I grin, and return to eating my longhorn wedged between two slices of rye. Tonight has been seriously weird and uncomfortable. But I'm pretty sure, it's about to get a *whole* lot better.

Chapter Thirty-Three

SHELBY

Ava and Izzy kit me out with spare girly pajamas dug out of a drawer, plus a towel, toothbrush – "Unused, we swear" – and toothpaste. They show me to a guest bedroom, which, I'm very glad to see, has an ensuite bathroom. In my family, we never shut the bathroom door, but we knew each other very well, and didn't mind nudity. I don't know this family well at all. Except Nate, of course. I have seen *him* naked.

Speaking of, he wants me to come to his room later. But should I? He needs rest, not potentially strenuous physical activity. And his whole family, whom, did I mention, I hardly know, will be sleeping nearby. What if I get caught tiptoeing down the hallway? What if I get lost and knock on the wrong door? Who the *heck* has affairs, when sneaking around is so stressful?

I toss the world's surplus of pillows onto the floor, lie on top of the bed, and stare at a painting of a greyhound. It's very lean, which makes me think of Nate, naked, and that fantastic muscle definition he has. I recall how it felt running my hands over his chest and down his washboard abs and—

OK, looks like I'll be sneaking down the hallway. Good thing I hadn't quite got into my jim-jams yet. They're blue with horses on them. Three guesses whose they used to be.

I listen for signs of life in the hallway. It's quiet. Holding my breath, I open the door and peer quickly out. No one. Nate's room is that-a way. Everyone cross your fingers. I'm on the move.

First on the right. My heart is pounding and it's been all of twenty seconds. I don't want to knock ... too *loud*. So I try the door. It opens. If this is the wrong room, I'm going to be *seriously* embarrassed.

In the soft light of a bedside lamp, I see Nate sitting on the edge of the bed. He opens his arms, and for the second time in a few hours, I straddle his lap, and plant my mouth on his. Oh, my. The man really *does* know how to kiss.

"You're not to overdo it," I manage to say, in between.

"Sure."

He answers but he's not listening. His eyes are black with desire, and his hands are lifting up my shirt. I give up trying to sound a note of caution and help him remove my shirt and bra. He whips his T-shirt off over his head, and there are those muscles. Bet he knows the technical names for all of those, too. We might have a lesson later.

Right now, though, I need to be in the moment. Nate's

mouth is on my breasts, paying close attention to each nipple, until I think I'm going to have to make some noise.

He lifts his head and kisses me, but the tactic is only partially successful. I'm insane with lust right now, and not exactly in my right, cautious mind.

"Shh," he murmurs. "Seriously, Shel, this house is old and the walls are *thin*."

"Who's next door?" I whisper.

"Max. Young and impressionable. Also raging with hormones. Probably has a glass against the wall, and his ear pressed to it."

That *does* have an effect. I might have to see Max at breakfast. I don't want his imagination working overtime when I'm pouring milk on Captain Crunch.

"OK, I promise to be quiet," I say. "Can you go back to doing what you were doing?"

"No." He smiles. "I want to do *this* now…"

He unbuckles my belt, unbuttons my jeans. I wore my good pair that only have a couple of small holes. I lift up to let him slide them partway down my thighs, and then he hooks two fingers inside my panties, and applies himself to another sensitive part of my anatomy.

I do my utmost to stay silent. It's pretty much impossible, but I bite my lip and focus on trying to breathe. Every nerve is crying out for him, and even though he's doing very fine work here, I'm desperate to have all of him, right here, right now.

"Goddamn," he mutters. "You're so wet. I am *so* fucking hard for you…"

That does it. I hop off, and shed the rest of my clothes in half a second. Then I stand over him and begin to unbuckle *his* belt, while watching his glorious ab muscles flex as he breathes rapidly in and out.

"Wait," he says, as I start to pull off his jeans. Better condition than mine, just saying.

He stands up, shifting me gently backwards.

"A man *has* to take off his own pants," he informs me.

And with one swift move, he drops pants and boxer briefs to the floor and steps out of them. Nate naked. Again. Also, he wasn't lying about being hard.

I'm about to drop to my knees, but he catches me.

"I want to feel your skin on mine," he says.

He maneuvers me onto the bed, so that we're both kneeling, facing each other, and then pulls me tight against him, one hand cupping my rear, one on my back, and kisses me so deeply I feel like we're fused together.

His erection is pressed into me, and I push myself against it, striving for connection to the part of me that's crying out to be touched again. Nate's warm hand strokes my rear, my thigh, and then slips between us. Connection is made, and I am *this* close to coming. I arch back, and I *can't* keep quiet.

Gently, he kisses me, first my bottom lip, and then my top one, and then his tongue explores mine, and the rhythm of his kisses matches the touch of his hand, and I'm *gone*. The orgasm builds slowly, but then it rushes through me like magma, lighting up every particle in my body until it erupts through the top of my head. Pretty sure Max won't need a glass against the wall to hear *that* one.

I come back to the world to find I'm gripping Nate's shoulders like an eagle does a rock. And to find he's laughing quietly.

"Hope Max knows the sock trick," he says.

"That's *not* romantic," I protest. "I do *not* want to think about your little brother doing … that."

"Better make you forget him, then," Nate says, and kisses me hard this time.

I reach for his erection, only to find he's made productive use of my time on cloud nine and rolled on a condom. It's so great being with a guy who's organized.

"You OK with this?"

He lies back, so I can be on top. I am *very* much OK with this.

"You need to conserve energy," I say with a smile.

"Happy to oblige."

I lower myself onto him, slowly, and revel in the sound he makes. I start to move, and now it's *his* turn to find out how difficult it is to stay quiet. Poor Max. With luck, he has earplugs.

This is a great position. I can run my hands up his abs and chest, and he can fondle my breasts, and I like that considerably. I can also set the pace, which I like most of all.

His breathing becomes ragged, and his hands clamp onto my hips—I suspect we'll both have finger bruises tomorrow—as he tries to thrust into me harder and deeper.

But he's weaker than usual, so I toy with him in a cruel but enjoyable fashion by keeping the pace slow and steady.

"Shit, Shel," he groans. "Have mercy."

If I were taller and could walk in stilettos heels without twisting an ankle, I could be a pretty good dominatrix.

Being a sore loser, of course, Nate decides to fight back. He shifts one hand off my hip and slides it between us, and now I'm at *his* mercy. Now, *I* want the pace to accelerate, but he won't do it, the monster. If I could open my eyes, I'm sure I'd see him laughing at me.

He takes me to the edge, synchronizing his touch with every glorious, controlled thrust, and to be honest, I no longer give a fig about Max eavesdropping.

And then, right when I'm about to see stars, he grabs both my hips again, lifts his fantastic rear off the bed and fills me harder, deeper, faster until I feel his heat as well as mine, and we explode together in a million points of light.

I surface first, to find I'm half lying on top of him. He has one arm flung over his face, which, sensing me stir, he raises. He blinks at me, his blue eyes cloudy, dazed.

"Second time tonight I've had to crawl back to consciousness," he murmurs. "This episode was a *lot* more pleasurable."

Now, I feel guilty. He needed rest, and I have not rested him one bit. I prop myself up so I can get a good look at his face.

"Are you OK?"

He gives me a quizzical smile. "We've just had mind-blowing sex, and you're asking me if I'm OK?"

I see his point, but—

"The doctor said you had to take it easy. We were a little … energetic."

"Shel, he also told me to reduce stress," he says. "And judging by the fact every muscle of mine is now as relaxed as a wrung-out dishcloth, I'd say goal achieved."

That may be true, but he needs more than temporary relief. All right, so it's somewhat late in the play, but I resolve to be a more diligent caregiver.

I drop a quick kiss onto his forehead. "I'm going to let you sleep now."

And I start to slide out of bed.

"Wait, no." He catches my arm. "Sleep here."

I elude his grip. He really *is* weak. "No can do, buddy. You need *proper* sleep. No booty calls in the small hours."

I can see by his expression that I've judged it correctly. I retrieve my scattered clothes and re-clad my nakedness. Nate watches, half amused, half regretful.

"I love you," he says. "Also, I can't believe we just had sex in my childhood bedroom."

Only now am I taking in the décor of the room. "You had an antique sewing table in your childhood bedroom?"

"Mom made a few changes," he says, with a wry grin.

I also now spy a mountain of discarded pillows on the floor. Nate follows my gaze.

"Yeah, I don't understand that, either," he says. "But I'd say some country's economy is now reliant on my mother's pillow habit."

Now decently attired again, I bend over him. The

musky, sexy smell of him almost undoes my resolve, and so instead of the deep, long farewell kiss I had planned, I peck his cheek.

"Coward," he accuses, accurately.

"Love you, too," I say. "I'll see you in the morning."

I skip quickly out the door before lust hormones change my mind.

The hallway is dimly lit, and I begin to creep back to the guest bedroom, feeling a little like whoever that Greek guy was who laid a trail of string in the Minotaur's labyrinth. I just have to go past the stairs and around the corner, and then I'm almost th—

Figgety-fig! It's Nate's figging *father*! What the fig is he doing up at this time of night?

"Are you lost?" He sounds remarkably mild, considering his rage of earlier.

"No, I was just … checking on Nate."

Lame, I know, but all my brainpower has been sapped by orgasms.

Nate's father nods. It's too dark to read his expression.

"Good night, then, Miss Armstrong," he says, and my knees go a little weak with relief.

"Good night, sir." Nate's manners are catching.

We pass each other, but when I'm only inches from safety, he speaks again.

"Miss Armstrong?"

Dreading what's coming, I turn around.

"When did your father die?"

Come back, brainpower. I *need* you.

306

"Last year," I reply.

"Was he ill?"

"Cancer."

My short answers sound rude to my ears, but Nate's dad isn't taking offence, far as I can tell.

There's a worrying pause, though, but then he says, "I'm sorry."

"Oh, God," I blurt, without thinking. "So am I. Every day."

And now I've started talking, I can't stop. Grief is like that. It takes hold and then you're spilling your heart out in front of anyone who'll listen. Even if they've made it clear that listening is the last thing they want to do.

"Sometimes, I forget he's not around," I say. "I'll find myself picking up the phone to tell him something, before it hits me that I can't. And I think I *see* him, too, all the time. Catch sight of the back of a head, or hear a laugh like his, and I expect he'll appear, like it's all been a huge mistake. It's so cruel, that, because the grief when you realize you're wrong just *socks* it to you. Sometimes, I have to go curl up in a ball until it passes. It's awful, and it never seems to end. You think it's lessened, but then it comes screaming back at full force and takes all the wind out of you like—"

Nate's dad makes a movement, maybe impatient, maybe not, but it's enough to halt me mid-ramble.

"Sorry," I say.

"Don't be," is his surprising reply. He raises his hand, gives the wall a single pat. "Sleep well, Miss Armstrong."

"You too, sir," I babble, and then I make a break for the guest bedroom door and shut it quickly behind me.

The horsey pajamas are where I left them on the bed. I change into them, and slip between crisp and *ironed* (who does that?) cotton sheets. High thread count. Nice.

I expect to dwell on that weird encounter with Nate's dad, but my body has other plans and sends me into a sleep so deep, I lose even the power to dream.

Chapter Thirty-Four

NATE

I wake with a sense that I have something important to remember.

Oh, yeah. I've got to visit the doc this morning, on account of my womanly fainting.

Oh, *yeah*. Shelby and I! We're back together, and absolutely scorching it in bed. God, I love her. I am *so* goddamn lucky.

Oh. Yeah. Max…

Sorry, little bro, but it couldn't be helped. When you grow up, you'll understand.

Amazingly for this time of the morning, the bathroom is empty. I may have sung a little in the shower. My head's still slightly woolly, but an iron jab will sort that out. And the ECG is just Doc being cautious. No biggie at all.

Look, I could be facing a hangman's noose and I'd still be chipper. The girl of my dreams loves me. The sun is shining, and if a cartoon bluebird landed on my windowsill right now, that would be totally natural.

I jog downstairs to find the kitchen full, and Izzy making pancakes. Max has his hi-tech headphones on but pushes them off one ear when he sees me enter. Uh-oh. Here it comes...

"How are you feeling?" he says. No trace of accusation, or, as would be me if I were in his shoes, disgust.

Mom chimes in. "Did you sleep well, sweetheart?"

I glance at Max, but his expression is suspiciously innocent. I feel a potential blackmail threat brewing.

"Like a log," I say. Which is true for the last hours, at least.

"Doc Wilson phoned," Ava informs me. "Says nine sharp at his clinic. Make sure you eat beforehand."

"That's why I'm cooking bacon, too," says Izzy, unnecessarily, as I smelled it halfway up the stairs. "It's not *red* meat, more pink, but..."

"You get first helpings," Danny tells me, with a hint of resentment.

I take a chair round the big wooden table. There are two people missing, I note. Dad, no surprise. And Shelby. I wonder if she's still in—?

"Hey, Shelby," says Max.

I turn to smile a greeting, in time to see her blush. Max's face is *still* entirely innocent. Man, he's got that Durant poker face *nailed*.

"Hi, everyone," she says, slipping quickly into the chair

next to me. I feel her hand reach for mine, and I take it and squeeze tight.

"Hope you like pancakes," Izzy says to her.

"What kind of weirdo doesn't like pancakes?" Shelby replies.

"Our father," says Ava immediately. "But he's not here, so he gets no vote."

Shelby blushes again. Not sure why – because she accidentally implied Dad was a weirdo? She should know by now that nobody at this table would disagree with *that*.

Izzy places a plate in front of me, on which is a tower of pancakes surrounded by a wall of bacon.

"Do you have plans for my liver?" I ask her. "Stuffing me solid, so you can have Nate *foie gras*?"

"I hope you *never* ate that in France," Izzy shudders. "It's sadistic. The poor geese."

I reach for the syrup, instead of answering. My sister need never learn that I consider pan-seared *foie gras* one of the greatest delicacies on earth.

Shelby nudges me with her elbow. "That's why Dylan doesn't like you. Geese *know*."

How did *she* know, is more to the point. I must be losing my own poker face. Maybe Max has stolen it from me?

"You really going to eat all those?" Danny scowls at my pancake tower.

"Yup." I'm starving. No points for guessing why.

"Don't have a cow," Ava says to Dan. "Izzy's a pancake-making machine."

To Shelby, she says, "Did your brothers compete over

food? Dan and Nate used to *measure* each other's portions with a *ruler*."

Mom laughs, and we all turn to look at her. It's been a long time since she even *smiled*.

"It's why I bought cookie cutters," she explains. "To prevent arguments."

"Dan *still* counted the chocolate chips per cookie," I remark. "I think he's even kept the score sheet."

Dan has his own tower of pancakes now, so he's OK with being ribbed.

"This from the guy who'd snivel if I got given more Halloween candy," he says.

"You *always* got the most Halloween candy," complains Izzy. "You were a slimy salesman even back then."

"*Slimy?*" says Dan. "I'll have you know my clients would trust me with their children. Which, to be fair, they usually value less highly than their classic cars."

"One Halloween," Max tells Shelby, "Danny dressed Izzy and me like Ewoks, and he took half *our* candy as commission for making us look cute."

"In case you're wondering," I tell Shelby. "Halloween was the *only* time Dad wouldn't monitor our sugar intake."

"Yeah, because he knew we'd go all *Lord of the Flies* on him if he did," says Ava. "Dad has *some* survival instincts. Least he did back then."

"You children need to stop that." Mom's tone is quiet but severe. "You were brought up to show respect to everyone, *particularly* people whose opinions differ from your own. Your father is not an exception to that rule."

Ava's expression is mutinous, but she swallows the smart comeback because she knows Mom is right. We all do. We diss Dad partly because he frustrates us, but mostly because we're terrified of what might happen to him. He may be a hard son-of-a-bitch, but he does love us, and we love him. We *don't* want to lose him.

"Sorry, Mom," I say on behalf of us all.

Izzy hands out the last plate of pancakes and slumps into her chair. "Phew."

"Thanks, Iz, you're the best," says Dan, in a shameless play for seconds.

My plate is cleared in record time. Shelby, I observe, is hardly eating. But I can't ask her why, not in front of everyone.

"I'm seeing the doc at nine," I tell her, instead. "Do you still want to come?"

"Of course," she replies, with only the briefest smile.

She's definitely not herself. My bubble of happiness begins to wobble. Was it something I did? I'll ask her after we've been to Doc's. Won't have a chance before; we have to take separate cars.

After breakfast, I head up to my room to grab my stuff. And bump into Max coming the other way.

"Hey," I have to ask. "You sleep OK?"

"Like a baby," is his reply.

Then the little bastard raises an eyebrow at me.

"You didn't think I'd be stupid enough to sleep in *my* room last night, did you? No, *I* crashed in the other guest bed. I've already got a ton of material for therapy," he adds, as he starts to stroll on down again. "Didn't need your porn movie soundtrack burned into my brain, too."

What can I say? That young man will go far.

Back downstairs, I find Shelby at the front door, saying goodbye to the whole crew. They really like her, I can tell. I'm glad, but to be honest, if they didn't accept her, I'd ditch the lot of them in a heartbeat. I love her. I want to be hers forever.

Mom hugs me like I'm going off to war.

"Let me know what Ray says." She squeezes my hands, as a plea.

"Text *all* of us," insists Izzy.

All this attention is kind of embarrassing. Nice, but embarrassing. It's not like there's anything *major* wrong with me. I'm not Dad.

Then, as if I've telepathically summoned him, he appears. He looks … OK. Not angry. At least, I don't think so…

The group parts to let him through, expecting, I guess, that he wants to talk to me.

But it's Shelby to whom he offers an outstretched hand.

"Goodbye, Miss Armstrong," says Dad. "I appreciated your candour."

A "WTF?" vibe zings around the bystanders. We are, to a Durant, astonished.

"Oh…!"

So is Shelby, by the sound of it. But she rallies and returns his handshake. I see my Dad's eyes widen briefly in surprise. If he and I were on speaking terms, I'd have warned him about the strength of her grip.

"It was a pleasure to meet you, sir," she says. "You take care, now."

I think Ava's about to have an *actual* coronary.

Now Dad does approach me, and, holy fuck, gives me a *hug*. It's robot-stiff, but it's a bonafide, genuine hug.

"You're in good hands with Ray," he says.

"Thanks, Dad."

"OK, Nate, we'd better go."

Shelby's taking charge. The rest of us have had our faculties impaired by shock.

At the vehicles, she veers toward the Dodge, but I waylay her.

"Everything all right?" I ask.

She hesitates, glances down at her boots. Then she takes a deep breath in and looks me in the eye.

"I talked to your dad last night."

"So I gather."

"And it brought back how terrible it was to lose *my* dad. How it's still terrible. And…"

Her head dips again. I place my hand gently under her chin and coax it up. Her big blue-green eyes are brimming with tears.

"I couldn't bear it if something happened to you," she says in a rush. "I *couldn't*."

I pull her into my arms, kiss her hair. "It won't. I'm fine."

"But he wants to run an ECG," she almost wails.

"Because he's a good doctor," I reassure her. "If he had *any* real concern about my heart last night, he'd have had me in Martinburg hospital before you could say 'dang'."

Shelby has the trace of a smile. "Doc Wilson says 'dang'?"

"Has been known to employ the word 'varmint' too, on occasion."

She wraps her arms around my neck and kisses me.

"Thanks for humouring me," she says, when we're done.

"Anytime," I reply. "And now we need to skedaddle. Doc doesn't take kindly to folks being tardy."

She smiles. "You do that well."

I smile back. "Years of practice."

Doc Wilson's practice is on the edge of Martinburg. His clinic manager is called Priscilla and she's ornery. But she's spared the pleasure of tar and feathering me because Shelby and I arrive *precisely* on time.

"Doctor will see you now," says Priscilla, begrudging my existence.

Shelby gives me a quick kiss. "I'll wait here."

To be absolutely honest, I *have* been a little anxious about seeing Doc. People worrying about you tend to make *you* worried.

But it's fine. I'm fine. Doc runs a mini-ECG and I have the heart of an ox. Doc takes blood and tells me the results will be ready that afternoon. I guess, depending on how low I am, it'll be iron tablets or a needle in the ass. Fun times.

"Cut the stress, son," Doc tells me. "Eat three square meals. Exercise like a sane person."

I make multiple promises, thank him, and exit into the waiting room.

Shelby isn't there.

"Outside." Priscilla hooks a thumb toward the parking lot. "She took a call. Got a little … upset."

If they ever bring back stoning as a punishment, Priscilla will be first in line at the quarry, stocking up on supplies.

On the way out, it occurs to me I haven't checked *my* phone since I got home last night. Before the dinner catastrophe, and the swooning.

I slip it from my pocket, fire it up. Seven missed calls: four from Javi, one from Ted, and two from Chiara. There are messages, too, but I've spotted Shelby by the Dodge. She's still on the phone, but as soon as she sees me, she says a few quick words to whoever's on the end and ends the call.

She strides towards me, and because I'm not expecting it, I don't at first notice that her expression is both appalled and furious.

"What have you *done*, Nate?" she accuses, and her voice, her whole body is trembling. "Javi called me," she goes on. "You've leased a *harvester*? And a *wine press*?"

I've never seen her so angry. I didn't think she was capable of it.

"Shel—"

I reach out to her. But she throws up her hands to ward me off.

"I can't talk to you right now," she says. "I don't even want to *see* you."

And she runs back to the Dodge, hops in, and guns it out of the lot.

Jesus. How am I going to come back from *this*?

Chapter Thirty-Five

SHELBY

I have to pull over, because I'm a danger to other road users. The Dodge's steering wheel gets alternately beaten with fists and soaked with angry tears. It's tough. It can handle it.

How *could* he? I yell this in my mind and out loud. I *scream* it.

And I complete it in so many ways. How could he do that to Javi? Put him and all his team, who depend on that work, out of a job? How could he go against everything Flora Valley Wines stands for? What Dad dedicated his life to? We'd *never* replace good people with soulless machinery. We'd *never* tell our community that they don't matter, that we'd cut them out just so we can make more profit.

How could he not *tell* me? This was not a decision he should have made without consulting me – this was *huge*. He knew how I'd feel about it. He knew I'd see it as a betrayal of everything, and everyone, that's important to me.

How could he tell me he loved me? How could he sleep with me, knowing what he'd done?

Javi was so distraught when he rang me just now. He'd only found out about the machinery lease by accident because he bumped into someone at the leasing firm. He was furious, too, that Nate hadn't bothered to let him know, *and* that he wouldn't even do Javi the courtesy of taking his calls.

Javi was furious with *me*, too, until I managed to convince him I knew nothing. Pleading ignorance didn't really make me look much better, but at least I was on his side. I made a hasty promise that I'd deal with it, because I was determined that no machinery would be used on my watch. But, from what Javi had said, the lease contracts are signed and watertight. We can't get out of them.

I don't know what to do. I don't know how to fix this.

My phone beeps. Chiara: *U OK? WTF up with ur man?*

My man? Not anymore. Not after this.

I text back: *U busy? Need help.*

She comes back right away: *Break at 10. C U at hotel.*

I rummage around the Dodge in the hope of finding tissues. There's a scarf, batik cotton, probably Mom's. It'll do. My reflection in the rearview mirror is some leagues short of Bartons-acceptable, but I think Ted will understand. Guaranteed *he* knows everything now, too.

Not wanting to sully the Bartons parking lot, I leave the Dodge on the main street. Shutting its door, I'm overtaken again by a wave of distress. Dad was so proud when he got the truck painted up with the Flora Valley Wines logo. He did laps of Verity, so everyone could see. I don't even want to *imagine* how he'd take this latest news. Or what he'd think of me for letting it happen.

Chiara's waiting for me in the Bartons lobby. She takes my arm and swoops me into the hallowed space that is Ted's office, which is exactly how I'd imagined it, green velvet and all.

"Shelby, darling."

I expect Ted to double-kiss me, but instead, he embraces me. And, to my absolute humiliation, I start to sob against his chest. His beautifully tailored, expensively shirted chest.

"There, there."

Ted holds me, and I don't know whether his cologne contains some calming therapeutic oils, or if it's just his naturally unruffled demeanour, but I manage to pull myself together before his shirt is soaked right through.

"Sorry," I say.

But all he does is smile and whip out a pristine white cotton handkerchief. Which I take gratefully, knowing I can make it as soggy as I like because he will never expect it back. My guess is he has a team of women in some remote English village, who hand-sew them especially for him.

"Come along."

Ted steers me to a beautiful green velvet chair, into which I slump. Chiara arranges herself much more elegantly on another, while Ted stays standing.

"Tea, coffee, or a shot of the hard stuff?" he offers.

"Tempting," I reply. "But it'd better be coffee."

A quick word out the door, and Ted pulls up a wooden chair that looks antique. Not small-town junk shop antique, the itemized on the insurance policy, heirloom kind.

He cuts right to it. "I've given Javi the day off. He's normally a model of self-restraint, but this morning, I feared he'd put a fist through a hotel wall."

"What the hell, Shelby?" Chiara steps in. "Did Nate have some kind of *brain* bleed?"

I can only shake my head. His actions are beyond my comprehension, too.

"Did you really know nothing about it?" she adds.

I glare at her. "Of *course*, I didn't!"

She raises her hands in the surrender pose. "OK, OK. So he ... what? Just didn't tell you?"

Chiara has a real knack for digging her thumb into those pressure points.

But she's right. There's no way I come out of this looking good. Either I've been stupidly ignorant, or I've allowed myself to be deliberately ignored. Given I'm supposed to be a senior person in my business, both are unforgiveable.

A small tap, and Ted jumps up to open the door. Mei-fen, who's usually on in the afternoons, enters with a tray. Coffee in a silver pot. See-through porcelain cups and saucers.

"Thank you, Mei-fen," says Ted.

She sets down the tray, and arches one perfect eyebrow at Chiara.

"Break ends in eight minutes," she says.

Ouch. Steely.

Chiara, of course, gives her the steel-eye right back. This could turn into a scene from *Faster Pussycat, Kill, Kill.*

"I'll remind Chiara," says Ted, with his own brand of velvet-clad iron.

Mei-fen departs in an elegant stalk. Chiara watches her, with a small, satisfied smile.

"Really, you two," says Ted, mildly, before turning back to more pressing matters – me.

"Shelby, I have to confess, I feel a little to blame."

"You do?"

"When Nate met with me the other day, he broadly hinted that he was investigating different management options. I *did* give him a gentle caution, but perhaps I should have been more forceful."

"It's not your responsibility," I tell him.

"But you could have mentioned it," Chiara accuses him. "Weren't you an army officer? Did you not think a preemptive strike was called for?"

I've never had a boss, but I am *very* sure I'd never talk to them like that.

Ted, however, displays his ability to remain calm under direct fire.

"I was unaware his plans were so far down the track," he says. "But, yes, you're quite right. Discretion is not *always* the better part of valour."

"So what do we do?" Chiara is an action woman.

"Now, I realize that emotions are running high," says

Ted. "But if I were in Nathan's shoes, I would want a chance to present my side of the story."

"How can he possibly have anything to say that would make me forgive him?" I assert. "There's no explanation that could make what he's done look better!"

"So he's guilty without trial."

Ted's tone is neutral, but his message is clear.

"I don't want to talk to him," I say, and then cringe at how childish it sounds.

It's *your* wine business, Shelby, and the buck stops with *you*. Grow up, and step up to your responsibilities. People are depending on you.

"OK, I'll talk to him," I sigh. "I'll head back to the winery. I guess that's where he'll be. Making space for the figging wine press."

"I don't know," says Chiara, with a shudder. "The harvester I am *dead* against. But that foot stomping thing is disgusting."

Ted gets swiftly to his feet.

"Time's up, my dear. Duty calls."

He could be speaking to both of us. No doubt he is.

While Mei-fen gives her the evils behind the reception desk, Chiara extends her break by another thirty seconds in order to hug me.

"Drinks tonight," she says. "Silver Saddle. I'll force Jords to come."

"Thanks," I tell her.

Up till then I'd envisaged spending the evening curled up in bed, driving the cats away with my constant snivelling. But drinks and company would be good. I can always curl up and snivel later.

Soon as I make the turn into the Flora Valley Wines driveway, my stomach starts flipping. The adrenaline that pumped through me, fuelled by anger and outrage, has subsided, and now all that's left is a clammy dread, and a churning conflict of emotions.

I'm desperate to see Nate, and I don't want to see him ever again. I want to hear his side of things – Ted's right – and I will never forgive him as long as I live. I love him, and I hate what he did. I don't want this to be the end of us, but I can't see how we can *ever* bridge this gap.

The pickup isn't here. I shut my eyes and open them again, just in case, but the gravel is bare. No Nate.

Damn it! I've worked myself up into a lather! The *least* he could do is be here so I can find out if the doctor said he's okay. And if he's okay, then I can yell at him some more.

It's awfully quiet. Usually, if anyone pulls up, the dogs will make a noise, and Dylan will make an even louder noise. Maybe they're shirty with me because I haven't fed them this morning. Better do that right now before they decide to eat *me*.

My phone beeps in my pocket, and I jump. Nate?

No, but close. Ava. She texts like Chiara, short and to the point: *WTF did U say 2 dad?*

I don't have time for this now. If she really wants to know, she can ask him herself. He's *her* father.

I head round the house to the back door, where the food supplies are. And bump into Cam.

"Fed them," he says, correctly interpreting my purpose.

Suddenly, I'm finding it hard to speak. "Thanks."

He peers at my tear-puffed face.

"You OK?"

And I burst into tears AGAIN!

Cam, who isn't a touching kind of person, makes like Ted and folds me into his arms. Unlike Ted, his T-shirt has holes, and he smells like sawdust, with a hint of pig. Has the same calming effect, though. Cam has natural solidity, like a muscular redwood. My head barely reaches his chest.

I relieve Cam from hugging duty, and fish Ted's handkerchief (no longer crisp) out of my pocket.

"Sorry."

Apology seems to be my theme of the day. That, and dampness.

"Heard about Javi," Cam tells me.

He doesn't need to elaborate. Not that he was going to, anyway.

"I'll have to call him," I say. "Don't know how I can make it better, but…"

"Iris, too."

"Oh, *fig*," I groan. "I completely forgot about Iris!"

I have to lean my forehead against Cam's sternum again, just to steady myself. He pats me tentatively on the back.

Deep breath, Shelby. You've been through worse. You can handle this.

Cam tenses, just a little, and an instant later, I know why.

Tires are rolling over gravel. Could be anyone. But I know it's not.

"Boss man." Cam knows it, too.

"I have to face him." Wish it weren't so. Wish this whole *nightmare* would just go away.

"Can you come with me?" I shamelessly beg.

Cam looks like I've asked him to run naked down Verity's main street for charity. It's the last thing he wants to do, but it's for a good cause, so he can't refuse.

"K," he sighs.

Nate's just got out of his truck. Seeing us, he freezes for an instant. Then, he shuts the pick-up door and walks purposefully toward us.

"Can you just hear me out?" he says to me.

"I'll, uh…" Cam hooks his thumb in the direction of away.

"I'd appreciate it if you stayed," Nate says to him. "I owe you an apology, too."

His tone is businesslike, his face composed. But I know this must be costing him.

"Want to come in the house?" I suggest. Don't think the office will fit the two of us plus a full-size Cam.

"Thanks." Now, I see the plea in his eyes.

"I'll make coffee," I say. "I think we could *all* do with some super-charged caffeine."

Chapter Thirty-Six

NATE

I guess, when I'm older, I might look back on all this, and realize that what I thought was the worst time in my life was a breeze compared to what came later. Not that I want to wish on myself a shitty future or anything, but I once thought that Camille dumping me was the worst thing ever, and fate has certainly proved *that* to be a lie.

Seeing Shelby angry at me, seeing her look at me like she *hated* me, was positively the worst moment of my life so far. I'm off-the-charts determined, but the shock of *that* galvanized me like nothing before, not even the starting pistol of a track final.

OK, I had to take a minute to regulate my heart rate, but then I acted. First, I called Javi, and had to wait a while until he stopped cursing me in Spanish. I thought the French had a lot of inventive swear words, but even though I understood only a handful of them, I can now confirm that the Spanish oath collection is world beating.

When I finally got a chance, I told him I'd made a mistake. I was cancelling the lease on the harvester, and unless he never wanted to set foot in Flora Valley Wines again, he and his team would be welcome to pick for us.

"It will cost you to get out of your lease contract," he said, suspiciously. "Thought the whole point was to *save* money?"

"Yeah, well, sometimes what you think is the right thing to do, isn't," I replied. "Lesson learned on my part."

There was a long pause on the other end. Then he said, "You want grape stompers, too?"

"Yup," I said, trying not to sigh.

"You're doing the right thing now," Javi told me, as we ended the call. "This is how it *should* be."

That's all very well, I thought. But to get it done, I have to put Flora Valley in the red. I have to put us in debt. And I now have to explain to JP why.

Needless to say, my second call was to the man himself. It was long, and it was tough. JP may have a sentimental streak in him when it comes to Flora Valley and the Armstrongs. But his killer instinct comes to the fore when there's any threat to his investments.

"I thought you were smarter than this, Nate," he said, not unreasonably.

"I believe it will pay off," I told him. "The market craves authenticity now, brands that have the human touch, that do good in the world. I made the decision to cut costs because it was a short-term solution. But I risked ruining our long-term reputation, our unique story. I risked destroying the whole future of Flora Valley Wines."

"What does Shelby think?" he asked.

"She wants to protect the Flora Valley ethos," I said. "She didn't support my original decision."

"But you're still a team?" he pushed.

"We are," I lied, while crossing my fingers, and saying a little prayer that I *might* be able to make it true.

Again, a long pause. Guess if you act without due consideration, then your special punishment is to wait, so you really feel that sword of fate hanging over you.

"OK, let me know what you need," said JP, and ended the call.

I had one foot out of jail. But the rest of me wouldn't be free until I'd made my case to Shelby. The sword was still hanging above me, its sharp blade swinging away.

So now, I'm driving to Flora Valley Wines, and I don't *really* have a plan.

The Dodge is there, which means so is she. I park, get out, and have to re-start my heart when I see Shelby and Cam come round the side of the house.

Shelby watches me warily, as I approach. She probably still hates me, but it's too late to back off now.

"Can you just hear me out?" I say and kick myself for how blunt it sounds.

Cam wants to leave, but I ask him to stay. I'd planned to apologize to him for my shitty manner, so I may as well get that over with, too. Two birds with one grovelling stone.

Shelby meets my eye, and it just *kills* me, her coolness.

But like a miracle, she invites us to the house for coffee. I feel like I've had a last-minute stay of execution. Don't blow this next part, Nate. Seriously. Don't.

Shelby is up at the kitchen counter, wrangling coffee, while Cam and I sit at the table, several chairs apart, in uncomfortable silence.

Damn it, I've done enough nervous waiting today.

"I've cancelled the equipment," I announce. "Picking and stomping will happen as usual."

Shelby turns around slowly, and leans against the counter. She doesn't look thrilled by the news, I have to say.

"But why did you do it in the first place?" she asks me. "Why would you *do* that?"

Yep, still angry at me.

"Because the winery is flat broke," I explain. "I got a short-term cash injection from JP, but that depended on me promising we'd sell out of this next vintage. When I followed up on our regular customers, I got a big, fat zero number of orders."

I lift my hands in the air. "So I had to figure out how to keep the winery afloat. JP thinks you're Christmas, but if it all goes ass-ways, he won't hesitate to carve this place up and sell it for parts. I knew you wouldn't like my decision, but it bought us time. Time for me to focus on how the *fuck* to sell this wine we're about to bottle."

My voice has got loud, I know, but goddamn it, I'm *not* a villain. I made a wrong call, but that doesn't make me Gozer the freaking Gozerian!

The coffee pot hisses on the stove. It doesn't approve of me, either.

Shelby lifts it off the heat, and stands there, holding it.

"Why did you promise JP sales when you weren't sure you could get them?" she asks.

"Because I wanted to protect the winery. Prevent JP from selling it off." I take a deep breath. "I wanted to protect it for you."

She's biting her lip, which she does when she's thinking. I can hear the sword blade swishing as it descends.

"You should have talked to me," she says.

"Yeah," I agree. "I should have."

"Trusted me."

"That, too."

It takes a moment to register that Cam is speaking to me. "Must have been tough working through it."

"Yeah, it was," I reply. "Trouble is, when you want something very badly, you don't always make the best decisions."

"Got enough to tide you over?" he asks.

"Hope so. I managed to beg another top-up from JP. He still thinks this vintage will pay off, though."

Shelby sets down three coffee mugs, and slides one each to me and Cam. She takes a chair across from me. Still keeping her distance.

"So you asked JP for more money knowing our orders were still low?" she says.

"Yep." I screw up my face. "I've had *one* idea, but you probably won't like that, either."

"Is it a done deal?" she asks.

"Not entirely…"

Shelby sits back in her chair, contemplates me for a good half-minute. The sword blade is skimming the top of my head, now.

All of a sudden, she hops up. "Wait here." And scoots out the door.

I'm alone with Cam.

"I owe you an apology," I tell him. "For being a jerk."

"Had things on your mind," is, I guess, his way of accepting it.

Shelby's back. She stands by my chair and slides a few stapled sheets of paper in front of me. I recognize this. It's the customer list. Or, more accurately, the not-customers-any-more list.

"I wanted to help," she says. "So I snitched this off your desk, and called them again."

"You … what?" My brain is fried.

She taps her finger on the list. "I called them. All the ones you ruled a line through. They've placed orders!"

I need a moment to process, because I'm experiencing both confusion and conflict. Shelby called the customers I'd called, but somehow they said yes to her and not to me? I can't help feeling like chopped liver. What does *she* have that I don't?

Jesus, Nate, chill with the competitiveness. This is *great* news.

"You're sure?" I have to ask.

"No, I'm a delusional idiot," she replies. "Yes. I'm sure. I even noted the orders in the book."

"What book?"

"The – oh…" Her gleeful look turns into guilt. "I may have forgotten to give it to you. Dad always kept it in the house, on the shelf with the photo albums, because he said our customers were like family."

Cam's running his thumb up the bridge of his nose, but I can see his mouth twitching.

"And then I didn't get a chance to tell you because we weren't on speaking terms," Shelby adds.

I nod. Makes perfect sense. Apart from the photo albums, but I'll let that go.

"Are we on speaking terms now?" I ask her.

She stares at me, solemn faced. I think the sword just sliced into my scalp.

"I should have let you explain this morning," she says. "I shouldn't have flown off the handle. I'm sorry."

And like that, the last of my already iron-depleted energy deserts me, and I slump forward onto the table, so I can rest my head on my folded arms.

"Nate?"

Shelby sounds alarmed, so I inhale deeply and sit up again.

"I'm great," I say. "Truly. It's just been a *very* long day."

Of course, my phone chooses that moment to ring. It's Ava. Has to be important; she'd text if it was day-to-day communication.

"Yup?" I haven't the strength for anything more.

"Dad's in the hospital—"

I'm on my feet immediately. "Shit. OK, I'm—"

"No, no, shut up! Listen!" Ava orders. "He's having the procedure! To put the IC-thingy in!"

My head is swimming, and it's not all due to lack of a key mineral. I sink back down in my chair again.

"He's ... did he have another attack?"

"No, he went in voluntarily!" Ava is as astonished as I am. "Apparently Doc had booked in a surgery date ages ago, hoping to have convinced him by then. When he rang Dad to remind him, assuming he would cancel, Dad did the opposite!"

"But *why*? Why the sudden change of heart? Excuse the choice of words."

"I think you should ask your girlfriend," says Ava. "Anyway, gotta go. Dad's just gone in, and we're going to wait at the hospital till it's over, which is in about three hours, if you want to hang with us."

Seriously, I don't know which way is up anymore. I blink at my phone screen until I realize that both Cam and Shelby are staring at me, one looking a lot more anxious than the other.

"What did you say to Dad last night?" I have to ask her. "He's getting treatment."

Her face lights up. "That's fantastic! And, I didn't say anything, really. Just told him how much I missed my own dad..."

My plan. It actually worked. Well, that's *one* gamble that paid off, at least.

Now, if only—

"What a pair we are." Shelby's smiling at me. "Do you think it'll be easier from now on?"

"We forgot to use the codeword," I remind her. "The one to stop us being dicks."

"That's right! We forgot to use 'cookie'!"

"Cookie?" Cam glances between us.

"I could do with a cookie right now," says Shelby. "More than one, in fact."

"We could pick some up on the way," I suggest. "I want to be at the hospital with my family until Dad's procedure's over. Do you want to come with me?"

Shelby hesitates.

"I'll feed the animals," offers Cam.

Can't imagine why I resented him before. Now, I love him like a brother.

The love dies a little when Shelby runs around to hug him.

"I owe you *big* time," she says. "I'll bring you back a cookie."

I'm still in the chair, thinking about getting up, when Shelby takes my hand.

"Come on." She pulls me out of the chair with her mighty grip. "I'll drive."

"Thanks," I say to Cam, as we head out the door.

"Anytime." He gets to his feet, starts to clear away the coffee mugs.

Man is a prince. I won't hear a bad word said against him.

Chapter Thirty-Seven

SHELBY

I don't like hospitals. But I'd forgotten how much, until I stepped inside this one.

Nate's holding my hand, and so he notices when I slow down.

Turning in enquiry, he sees my face, and because he's amazing, realizes immediately what's up.

"Sorry, Shel, I should have thought," he says, and pulls me to him. "It's fine. You don't have to stay."

I drove us here in the Dodge, because he was half dead on his feet and we'd had enough drama for one day without ending up in a ditch.

"Go to a movie," he suggests, and kisses me. "I'll call you when Dad's out of the operating room."

"Are you sure? I don't like to leave you on your own."

"You may have noticed that I have a million siblings," he says. "I can count the times I've been on my own on one finger."

The smell of the place is getting to me. The sight of people in scrubs and white coats. My chest is tightening. It's hard to breathe.

"Go," Nate orders gently.

Don't need to be told twice. I hurry out, and gulp down air that doesn't carry a tang of disinfectant and boiled meat.

There's a little garden here, with neat strips of lawn and flowerbeds, and wooden benches, for those who don't need to be wheeled around on a gurney. I sit down and turn my face up to the sun.

And then I realize I'm being a total coward. For goodness' sake, Shelby, you just abandoned the man you love to two hours' nervous waiting, while his father has a device implanted in his chest. Would he abandon *you*? Of course, he wouldn't. He'd do *anything* for you, and you know it.

I bend and inhale the sweet fragrance of the roses next to me, then walk reluctantly back through the main doors.

Oh, boy. Breathe, Shelby. It's only a hospital, and not even *the* hospital. That was a big one, with a cancer ward. This is only a small one, where people get warts burned off, and broken arms put in plaster.

The foyer is empty of Nate, and I don't know what ward his dad's in. I ask the receptionist.

She looks me over. "Are you a relative?"

"I'm his daughter-in-law," I lie.

Might be true. One day.

"OK, you want the family lounge in ward five."

She points me in the right direction, which is, of course,

farther into the bowels of the hospital. I spy a water cooler, and zip across to fill a paper cup. Not for drinking. For splashing on my face if I feel faint.

I'll try not to pass out. Nate's family are probably over people collapsing around them.

Nate and I didn't talk much on the way here. Didn't have to. Did a lot of smiling at each other, though, and occasionally held hands, because we were too wrung out emotionally for any sexy fondling.

We *did* say "I love you," when we got out of the Dodge at the hospital. I love him so much, I feel like I'm being pulled toward him right now. When I enter the family lounge, even if it's packed, he'll be the only one I see.

Or not.

"Shelby!"

A chorus of Durants, who rise from their seats en masse to greet me. All the Durants are here. Except the guy in surgery. And Nate.

"We thought you were meeting us later." Izzy takes my arm, and leads me to a chair between her and Max.

"Nate's with Doc Wilson." Ava picks up on my unspoken question. "Apparently, his iron levels were so low, he might have to be re-classified as a different species."

"Doc's infusing him," says Danny. "He'll be back soon."

"Infusing?"

"Apparently, medical science has moved on since the ass injection," Danny says, with a grin. "Now, they stick you on a drip."

Oh, poop. The mere mention of it, and I have to drop my

head between my knees. Of course, this brings every Durant to my side. I have hands on my back and worried murmurs in my ear.

"I'm OK." I raise my head slowly and try to look reassured. "It's just – hospitals."

"Good thing you missed the description of Dad's procedure," says Max. "We were all a bit green by the end of that."

"Max, *how* does that help?" Izzy smacks his arm.

Her brother clutches his arm over-dramatically. "Nurse!"

"Children, please," says Mrs Durant. "Let's make this a *peaceful* time."

Danny is rummaging on a shelf where a lot of old board games are stacked.

"No Monopoly," warns Ava. "Peaceful, remember?"

"Ah ha!" Her brother pulls out a deck of cards. "Go Fish, anyone?"

"Oh, *we* used to play that!" I say.

"Then gather round," says Danny. "And let the great Go Fish battle commence."

Two games in, and Nate returns, a Band-Aid on the back of his left hand, which I try not to look at.

"Your girlfriend's cleaning up," Danny tells him.

Nate makes Izzy shift, so he can pull his chair next to mine. He wraps his arm around me and drops a kiss on my temple.

"You OK?" I ask.

"I'm now permanently aligned to the magnetic North," he replies. "But, yeah, feeling better already."

"Want me to deal you in?" Danny asks.

"No, thanks." Nate smiles. "I'll just sit here and enjoy watching you get creamed."

We play three more games. I win every one. I can feel Nate silently laughing beside me. His family are less amused. Competitive bunch, they are.

"How about we play Texas Hold 'em." Danny tosses his losing hand on the table. "I'm actually half decent at that."

But no one gets a chance to answer, because right then, a doctor steps through the door.

"Mrs Durant?" she says.

Nate's mom hastens forward, anxiety all over her face. The rest of us get up, and stand behind her, like bodyguards. I slip my hand into Nate's and he squeezes it tightly. He's worried, too.

"Your husband's procedure went very smoothly," says the doctor. "He's back in the ward now, recovering. We'll keep him overnight for observation, but I don't anticipate any issues."

"Can we see him?" asks Nate's mom.

"He's sore and dizzy, and he needs rest," the doctor replies. "I suggest you come back tomorrow morning. If all's well, you can take him home in the afternoon."

"We want to see him," says Ava.

The doctor eyes her for a moment, and then nods.

"Two minutes," she says. "Follow me."

"Want to stay here?" Nate murmurs in my ear.

"Nope," I reply, and keep a firm grip on his hand.

I do linger at the back, however, while the family gathers round the bedside. Mr Durant looks pretty grey and tired, but he manages a smile for his family, and submits to having his cheek kissed multiple times.

He sees me, and nods. I smile back, even though I am *this* close to losing the cookies we bought and ate on the way here.

And then, thank you, thank you, we are leaving. Fresh air and freedom await.

As we gather outside the main entrance, my phone beeps. I check the text.

"Oh, fig. I forgot I was supposed to have drinks at the Silver Saddle with Jordan and Chiara."

"Friends of yours, Shelby?" enquires Danny, casually.

"You could all come, if you like," I say, rashly. The fresh air has gone to my head.

"Bar's in Verity." Nate goes into damage control. "*Long* way away."

"It's thirty minutes, max," says Danny. "Ten if Ava drives."

"You kids go," says Nate's mom. "Have fun."

"No, we can't leave *you*." Izzy hooks her arm in her mother's.

The main hospital doors open, and the old doctor who came to Nate's house emerges.

"What do you suppose is the collective noun for a group of Durants?" he says, as he reaches us. "A determination?"

"Ray, what are you doing for dinner tonight?" says

Nate's mom. "Would you care to join me at home? These young people have somewhere to be"—she smiles, mischievously—"and I could do with some *grown-up* company."

"Mom, harsh!" protests Max.

"It would be my pleasure, Ginny," says Doc Wilson. "Allow me to escort you in my trusty jalopy."

I hear Nate blow out a breath. "OK, Silver Saddle it is."

He gives me a look. "Better warn your friends."

I'm already texting Chiara: *Hot guys on way!* But Nate doesn't need to see that.

Danny has his Porsche keys in his hand. "I'm outta here."

He nods to Izzy and Max. "Ava can drive *you* two in Mom's car."

"He wants to be first to check out the girls," says Max, darkly.

"That so?" Ava has an evil glint in her eye. "Well, buckle up, kiddos. You're about to find out *just* how fast an old Toyota Landcruiser can go."

Chapter Thirty-Eight

NATE

I zzy votes to ride with Shelby and me in the Dodge. Says Ava's driving makes her want to hurl.

Five minutes out of Verity, we happen upon evidence that Ava's tactics did not only include pushing Mom's Landcruiser to its limits. Danny's Porsche is on the side of the road, and a few feet away, my brother is having what looks like a *very* uncomfortable chat with a highway patrol officer.

"Oops," says Shelby. "Bad luck."

"Doubt luck had anything to do with it," I tell her. "I see the evil hand of my sister written all *over* that."

"You mean she ratted him out to the *cops*?"

When Shelby gets better acquainted with Ava, she won't ask such questions.

"Ava hates losing," says Izzy, unnecessarily. "Plus, she'll be punishing him for being a sexist dick who's only interested in showing off to women. Ditto Max."

344

"What will she do to poor Max?" Shelby asks.

"No 'poor Max' about it," I remark. "That boy is as cunning as a sewer rat. And I say that with no small amount of admiration."

"I think Ava and Chiara will get on like a house on fire," says Shelby. "Or a nuclear explosion, whatever."

The Landcruiser is outside the Silver Saddle. I can almost see it sweating and puffing, like a Pony Express horse after a cross-country gallop.

It's the first time I've been in here. It's a typical Western-style bar, with a jukebox, pool tables, and a bunch of general redneck-themed memorabilia. Not that I'll say that out loud because the guy behind the bar is a beefy biker-looking dude, with tattoos and bulging biceps. Probably does double duty as bouncer as well as barman.

He's serving drinks to Ava, and laughing at something she's said.

"Wow," says Shelby beside me. "Brendan hardly ever *smiles*, let alone laughs."

My jealous side rabbit punches me in the kidney.

"You're on first name terms with Hulk Hogan there?"

Shelby wraps her arms around my waist and hugs me, when, in fact, what I deserve is a punch in my *other* kidney.

"I've known Brendan since I was a kid," she says. "He used to be a truck driver and bought the bar about twelve years ago."

She lowers her voice. "Jordan has had a crush on Brendan for at *least* that long. But, unhappily, she's just found out he has a secret girlfriend."

"In his basement?"

"Ha, ha. No, in LA. She's an actress."

We walk over to a big table, where Max, the little bastard, has installed himself opposite Chiara, who seems only marginally interested, and right next to Jordan, who's all over him.

Thing is, *I* now know that's probably because she's trying to make Biker Barman jealous. But I'll store that piece of info for later, when I need to take Max down a peg.

"What happened to your hand?" Chiara's eyes miss nothing.

"Iron infusion," I reply.

"Ugh, please." Shelby shudders. "No more medical talk."

"And *you* must be Max's twin," Chiara says to Izzy. "I'm Chiara, Shelby's best friend of all time forever and ever. And this is Jordan, her *second*-best friend, after me."

"Huh?" Jordan pulls her attention away from Max. Her face lights up as she spots Izzy. "Oh, wow, *two* of you! God, you guys are so *cute*."

Ava arrives, and hands out drinks. Bourbons all round, which is very Ava; too impatient to take individual orders. She shoves the tray on the neighbouring table, sits down, and lifts her shot of Jack.

"Here's to at least *one* day without any more major dramas," she says, and we all clink glasses.

"Where's your other brother?" says Chiara.

"Yeah, Ava," I say, pointedly. "What *do* you suppose has happened to Danny?"

"Here he is!" says Izzy, who's facing the door. "Hmm, he looks ... annoyed."

We all turn. Danny strides over, face like thunder, yanks out a chair, drops into it. Then he leans across the table and sticks his middle finger right in Ava's face.

Ava is unmoved.

"It's your own fault," she tells him. "You've had twenty-five years to get used to me. Can't help it if you're a slow learner."

Chiara smiles the smile of one who approves of Ava's tough-love approach. Shelby was right; they're cut from similar cloth. But the world will be a safer place if they *don't* team up.

Fortunately, Chiara has turned her attention to Dan. Who, now that the rage mist has subsided, is able to pull himself together and switch on the charm.

"Can I buy you a drink, other brother?" Chiara says.

"Allow me," he replies, and gets to his feet. "What will you have?"

"Surprise me," she says, with a look guaranteed to instantly double Dan's quota of testosterone.

"I'd better help." Shelby hops up. "Otherwise he could be waiting at the bar for half an hour. Brendan's kind of allergic to preppy guys."

"Brendan." Jordan mutters his name like she's using it as a hex.

Max gives her a curious look, and I smile on the inside.

In Dan's absence, I become Chiara's focus.

"So you were forced to back down?" is her conversation opener.

"I made a mistake." No point in getting defensive. "And then I fixed it."

"I'm so glad." Jordan beams at me. "I *love* stomping grapes. It's so ... *physical.*"

The emphasis she gives the last word makes Max cough on his bourbon.

"You should *all* come grape stomping," she says to us. "Mid-September. Not far away now."

"We'll be back at college," says Izzy, glumly. "Otherwise, I'd love to."

"I'll be here," says Ava. She gives me a look. "I've decided to stay."

"How come?" I'm genuinely surprised.

"Don't you want me around?"

She has her usual smile on, but I've known her long enough to catch the vibration of vulnerability.

"Couldn't think of anything I'd like more," I say, with absolute sincerity.

I've been apart from my family for too long. Now, I'll have at least *some* of them close by. Maybe Ava will want to get an apartment with me? OK, no, that's probably a step too far.

Danny and Shelby are back. Dan hands Chiara what looks like a Manhattan.

"Weren't a whole lot of options," he says, apologetically.

"Good thing this is my favourite, then," she replies, with another of those looks.

Dan has the Durant ability to not give much away, but there's a watchfulness about him. My guess is he's realized even the worldliest LA women have *nothing* on Chiara, and that he'd be advised to proceed with caution. Time to wind my brother up.

"Ava's told us she's staying here," I say. "You thinking of doing the same?"

"Oh, are you staying, Ava?"

Shelby, bless her, is also obviously delighted. I enjoy watching my sister come as close to blushing as she ever does.

"Yeah," she says, quickly. "I just – you know – Mom and Dad…"

"Same," says Dan. "You think you'll have years with them, and then…" He shrugs. "I can't leave my business yet, but I can make plans."

"Does that mean Max and I will be the only ones who are miles away?" Izzy's bottom lip is a little trembly.

"Only for two more years, Iz," says Max. "Oh, right, no, you're doing a PhD. Nate'll be a grandfather by the time *you* finish."

The biker bar guy appears by Shelby's shoulder.

"Get you anything?"

He's speaking to the table, but looking at Jordan. Who draws herself up and lifts her head away nose first, like a well-to-do Victorian lady being accosted by a hobo.

"Another round would be great," says Ava.

Barman Brendan gives Jordan one last stare. She continues to ignore him.

"Sure," he says, brusquely, and turns on his heel.

Jordan, we all observe, watches him out of the corner of her eye.

"What's going on with those two?" Max murmurs to Shelby, on his other side.

"Nothing," she whispers back. "That's the problem."

"Ah…" Max's shoulders slump, along with his hopes.

"Cheer up, little buddy," I tell him. "Just think. You'll be back with those violinists in no time."

"It's the cello players you've got to watch out for," he says, with a grin.

That's Max. Can't keep him down for long.

"Is anyone else starving?" says Shelby. "Those cookies wore off *hours* back."

"My turn to order," says Izzy. "Nate, are you paying?"

"Me?" I protest. "Dan's the one rolling in it."

"Not after tonight's little contribution to the state coffers, I'm not," he says, with a sour glance at Ava.

"Halves?" I suggest.

"Why not," Dan sighs. "No more drinks for me, though. I may be a slow learner, but I know full well when you shouldn't push your luck."

I wrap my arm around Shelby's shoulders. I pushed my own luck to the breaking point, and I give thanks to whatever force decided I deserved a second chance.

"How's your energy?" Shelby murmurs in my ear.

Oh, I'll have enough gas in the tank for later on. That's a promise.

I know lust diminishes in intensity over time, but

honestly, I can't see myself ever not loving being in bed with Shelby. Every moment with her, every kiss, every touch, is a sheer joy. She is a joyous person, and sexy as hell. If love is madness, then consider me certifiably insane.

We were the first to say our goodbyes this evening. Despite Danny's vow not to drink, the rest looked like they were settling in for a good old session. Guess Brendan would throw them out, possibly literally, when he wanted to close up.

Dylan greeted us rowdily as usual, but I squared my shoulders and confronted that bird like a man. As it happened, he shoved his head in my hand, and for the first time in my life, I petted a goose. I decided then to swear off *foie gras* forever. No need to tempt fate any further.

It occurred to me, as I stroked a feathery neck, that I hardly ever thought in French these days. And that my shame and regret about my time there had lessened, so all I felt now was a faint pang.

I won't stop owning my part in that break-up – if you don't remember history, you're condemned to repeat it. But I won't beat myself up over it anymore. I've got a whole life in front of me, and dwelling on mistakes uses up valuable energy and makes you cranky. Makes you risk averse, too, and you win way bigger prizes when you're brave. When you put your heart fully on the line.

"Where'd you go?"

Shelby is smiling down at me. After kicking the cats off the bed, we made love slowly and intently, savouring the feel and taste of each other. Her orgasm brought on mine, and it *did* transport me to another plane. An astral post-orgasm plane. Great place to visit. I recommend it.

"Not sure," I reply. "There were pink clouds. Might have seen a unicorn, too."

"Oh, *that* place," she smiles. "I always want to buy fairy lights when I come back from there. And candles that smell like vanilla."

"Could I love you any more?" I say.

It's a rhetorical question.

"I love you, too. *So* much."

She kisses the hollow in my collarbone, then my jawline, then my mouth. Parts south start to stir again. Lust can hang around a while longer. I'm totally OK with that.

"Mmm…"

Shelby's hand has tracked south, and she's making that sex-bee sound again. I've been harbouring this desire to kiss every one of her freckles, from top to toe, but that will take a very long time, and things are suddenly feeling a whole lot more urgent. Good thing I stocked up again at the hospital pharmacy.

"Anything in particular you want me to do?" I murmur.

I have such good manners, I should get a prize.

Woah!

OK, right, we're doing *that*—

It's always the innocent-looking ones with big blue eyes, isn't it?

All I can say is … lucky me.

Chapter Thirty-Nine

SHELBY

We've got no shortage of volunteers for the stomping, but we'll need every one of them, because it's hard work, plus your feet *freeze*. The grapes are only around forty degrees, and after a while, you can't feel your toes. Good to have someone ready to take your place, so you can thaw out.

No shortage of spectators, either. This is the biggest crowd the Flora Valley Wines stomping has drawn since I can remember. Iris has set up a food stall, and every spare bit of flattish ground is covered with people on blankets, eating, drinking, and laughing. The weather has that cool hint of fall, but it's sunny and there's no wind. Most people are still in summer clothes, making the most of it.

The stomping bins are all in a row, and there's a big wooden pole that runs across the front of the whole lot, so we've got something to hang on to. Cam built it for Dad a few years back. He's here somewhere, because he promised me he'd come, but I haven't spotted him yet.

It's not my turn to stomp, though I *do* want to have a go. I've been running around like a headless chicken since harvest ten days ago. The grapes have been cold soaking and fermenting, and now it's time to separate out the skins, so we can get the juice in barrels and kick off the ageing.

My first vintage was bottled three weeks ago, and all of it was shipped off to our customers. I made a special blend for Ted – Nate's brilliant idea – and, judging by the increased traffic to our website and number of new sign-ups for our mailing list, it's gone down well with the Bartons clientele. Higher demand means we *could* push our prices up, but I refuse to take advantage of our loyal customer base, and Nate agrees. If we buy in grapes, however, we can make more of my exclusive blend for Ted's posh clients, who are also now *our* posh clients. Hoorah, as they probably don't say in England.

Ted is here, too, looking like something out of *Brideshead Revisited*, with linen pants and shirt, and a straw hat. Ted never stomps, mainly because he wouldn't be caught dead in shorts. He has one of his shiny women with him, whose name I forgot the instant after he introduced us.

Chiara is here with her parents. Her dad brought enough cannoli to feed the entire state and has been dispensing them right and left with his usual Italian verve.

Jordan is in the bins, stomping. Being an outdoorsy girl, she can do longer stints than any of us. She may actually be impervious to cold. Her shorts are very short, and her tank top has drawn quite a crowd of young men, of whom she remains oblivious. Brendan never attends the stomping, as he has a bar to run. It's possibly why Jordan is so enthusiastic. She's gonna stomp that man right out of her hair.

Nate's brother Danny is back in LA, and Izzy and Max are out East, at their respective colleges, but threatening to come home for Christmas.

Ava is here, though, and so are Nate's parents. His dad looks like a new man and has taken to hugging people in a way that those who know him are constantly surprised, and mildly alarmed, by. Nate's mom has shed ten years' worth of worry and is positively radiant. She's chatting with my mom, and the pair look set to become good friends.

Next to them are JP and his *incredible* wife, Petra. Nate tried to explain how beautiful she was, but words didn't do her justice. I had to suppress a laugh when she greeted Nate, because, honestly, he went all pink and tongue-tied. He told me she's had that effect on him since he hit puberty, but that Danny was *way* more uncool around her.

"Do you sanitize your feet at *all*?"

Ava's next to me, holding a paper cup of wine. She's wearing running shorts and a cross-backed top. In black, as is Ava's wont.

"You wash them, and you *can* spray them with ethanol," I say. "But we prefer to keep it chemical-free. Human pathogens can't survive in wine, anyway, so why bother?"

I nudge her arm. "Will you give it a go?"

"Might do." She's surveying the crowd. "Where's the big guy?"

"Big guy?"

"The barrel maker."

"Oh." I peer around. "Somewhere. Cam doesn't like crowds."

I point in the direction of a clump of trees. "Try over there."

"Thanks," she says, and heads off.

I don't have time to wonder about it because Javi is calling my name.

"Shelby!" He beckons me over. "You're on!"

Stomping time.

Up by the bins, I take off my sneakers and wash and dry my feet.

"Bin number three," says Javi.

I get in and feel the familiar cold squish. Chiara's right, it *is* kind of gross, but fun gross, like making mud pies when we were kids. Jordan is in the bin next to me, still going. She beams at me. Her feet are purple, but it's not from the cold, just grape mess. Jordan's a hardy one.

"Right." I hear Javi clap his hands. "Who hasn't done their turn? OK ... *you*. Yeah, you. Get over here."

I turn to see who he's singled out. It's Nate. Because of course.

"I'm not wearing shorts," he protests to Javi, laughing.

"Ooh!" Jordan is watching, too. Before I can stop her, she cups her hands round her mouth and yells, "Strip!"

And suddenly, there's a chorus. "Strip! Strip! Strip!"

Nate's expression says, "Oh, crap, no", but the chorus is relentless. I can see Chiara chanting with glee. So he throws up his hands in the surrender gesture, and with one hand, pulls off his T-shirt.

Wolf whistles and cheers. Fair enough. My man has an incredible bod – all lean, gorgeous, well-defined muscle. My feet don't feel so cold now, because I think my core temperature just rose about twenty degrees.

Nate's shaking his head, for he knows that now must come the shedding of the jeans.

And they're off! The crowd goes wild! Nate makes a slow turn, hands out, acknowledging the applause with a wry grin.

I see him glance over at the bins and confer with Javi. Who nods and smiles.

"Sure, man," Javi says. "Go for it."

And my gorgeous Nate, clad in nothing but his Calvins, walks toward me, cheered on by the crowd.

"Room for one more?" he says.

"Unconventional," I reply. "But I'll allow it. Feet clean?"

I'm sorry, but hygiene trumps romance when this is your living.

"Now?" he says on his return.

I take his hand. "Hop on in."

"Oh, man." He makes a face. "This feels *funky*."

"Don't be tentative," I order. "You gotta be fast and firm."

"I'd rather you were saying that in a different context,"

he mutters, but takes hold of the bar, and we stomp together.

"I think I've died from the shins down," he says, after a pretty good long while. "Everything has gone numb."

"OK, we can quit," I say, and he blows out a breath of relief.

Javi, ever vigilant, is over like a shot.

"You cats finished?" he asks.

"Almost," says Nate. "Just one more thing."

I look up at him puzzled, and I'm not any less puzzled when he pulls me into his arms.

"We're going to fool around in front of a million people?" I say.

"Nope." He's not smiling. Looks almost *nervous*, in fact.

"OK, so—"

"Shush for a second," he says. "I'm working up to it."

I shush.

"Shelby," he says. "Will you marry me?"

"Holy SHIT!"

Jordan is beside herself. She yells into the crowd, "Hey, *everyone*! Nate just asked Shelby to *marry* him!"

Crowd goes wild a second time.

"Jesus, you'd better say yes." Nate has to raise his voice to be heard. "Or we'll be eaten alive."

"Yes," is exactly what I say, and I repeat it over and over. "Yes, yes, *yes*."

"Thank fuck for that," says Nate, and kisses me hard.

I'm going to be Mrs Armstrong-Durant. I am the luckiest girl in the *world*.

Acknowledgments

Thanks to the team at One More Chapter for taking me on and being so much fun to work with, and to my super-agent, Gaia Banks, who made the connection. Thanks to Romance Writers of NZ for being an endless source of inspiration since 2008. I finally got around to writing an actual romance series!

ONE MORE CHAPTER

YOUR NUMBER ONE STOP
FOR PAGETURNING BOOKS

The author and One More Chapter would like to thank everyone
who contributed to the publication of this story...

Analytics
Abigail Fryer
Maria Osa

Audio
Fionnuala Barrett
Ciara Briggs

Contracts
Sasha Duszynska
Lewis

Design
Lucy Bennett
Fiona Greenway
Liane Payne
Dean Russell

Digital Sales
Hannah Lismore
Emily Scorer

Editorial
Kate Elton
Arsalan Isa
Sarah Khan
Charlotte Ledger
Bonnie Macleod
Jennie Rothwell
Caroline Scott-
Bowden

Harper360
Emily Gerbner
Jean Marie Kelly
Emma Sullivan
Sophia Walker

International Sales
Bethan Moore

Marketing & Publicity
Chloe Cummings
Emma Petfield

Operations
Melissa Okusanya
Hannah Stamp

Production
Emily Chan
Denis Manson
Simon Moore
Francesca Tuzzeo

Rights
Rachel McCarron
Hany Sheikh
Mohamed
Zoe Shine

**The HarperCollins
Distribution Team**

**The HarperCollins
Finance & Royalties
Team**

**The HarperCollins
Legal Team**

**The HarperCollins
Technology Team**

Trade Marketing
Ben Hurd

UK Sales
Laura Carpenter
Isabel Coburn
Jay Cochrane
Sabina Lewis
Holly Martin
Erin White
Harriet Williams
Leah Woods

**And every other
essential link in the
chain from delivery
drivers to booksellers
to librarians and
beyond!**

Whoever invented love at first sight should have left instructions for what to do when it only strikes one of you...

...is all Ava Durant can think as she watches the man of her dreams from across the room at her brother's wedding. Handyman Cam Hollander takes the 'strong, silent type' label to new extremes and getting more than four words at a time out of him is Ava's primary life goal. But when Ava's health takes a hit it's Cam who unexpectedly steps in to nurse her.

Read on for an exclusive extract!

Extract: You're So Vine

Weddings give me hives. For a start, it's bad form to wear black and black is all I wear. Okay, I had a purple phase in my teens, by which I mean I still wore black, but I dyed my hair purple and cut it mohawk style. My dad said I should have gone the whole hog and shaved it off—better airflow for track. Then I won all my race meets and he stopped complaining.

At fourteen, I painted my bedroom black. Thirteen years later, it's primrose yellow because Mom finds black depressing. Can't see that myself. Black is smart, simple, and efficient. Every item comes pre-coordinated: no fuss, just grab and go.

Except when you're at a wedding. Your big brother's wedding at that. In the vineyard he now partially owns with his new bride. The ceremony was under an arbor built for the occasion from old, woven vines, the backdrop red-gold—the last of the fall leaves hanging in there so as to be as picturesque as possible for the happy couple. There's a chill in the air but the sky is blue and there's not a breath of wind. It's beautiful. Perfect. I want to take a flamethrower to the whole scene.

Okay, no … no I don't. I'm super happy for my big bro, Nate. His last attempt at getting married ended with him being jilted the week before, so us Durants breathed a sigh of relief that this time he got to say "I do"—and to a girl who we all love almost as much as Nate does.

Shelby's cute and funny and *way* more relaxed than Nate. Which isn't hard. When God was handing out the sweet treats of inner calm, Nate was loading up on a double helping of gristly determination with a side order of dried duty. As our family doctor says, "If there's a type above Type A, Nate's it." Actually, he says that about our whole family, but this is Nate's big day, so he gets singled out.

Yep, it's Nate and Shelby's big ol' wedding day and I'm wearing a dress that I bought in a hurry because—I may have mentioned this—everything I own is black. The dress is dark green and makes me look like I've been poisoned. I also did not follow Mom's advice to take a shawl and now I'm blue with cold as well as poisoned-looking.

We're being ushered toward the barn for the reception, which means this wedding is not even halfway through. Shelby and Nate own pigs that Nate swears would eat a human if you let them. Has anyone ever committed suicide by pig? Asking for a friend.

"You're looking a little peaky, sis. One too many caramel apple martinis?"

Danny. Durant sibling number three. Up from LA for the weekend. Makes the perfect usher because he comes across as charming. Don't be deceived.

"If you tell me we're sitting together, I'll brain you with an ornamental pumpkin."

"Nope," says Danny, way too cheerfully. "Durant clan's being split up. Tables are all a random mix and match. Idea being that we get to mingle, meet the other guests, make new friends."

Where did Nate say the pigsty was again?

Danny runs his finger along the seating plan.

"You're on table three. Straight down, hang a left."

A brief lurch in my gut. What if *he's* on the same table—?

"You're with Chiara," says Dan, "Shelby's brother Jackson, Ted, Ted's girlfriend du jour, and a guy named Doug."

"The famous Toothless Doug?"

"I didn't ask him to open his mouth."

"Oh, Doug has a full set of teeth. Shelby told me."

"Huh," says Danny. "Shelby and Nate's kids are going to be pretty weird, aren't they?"

I don't stay to answer because a queue is forming behind me. Everyone is eager to get into the warmth and start drinking in earnest. Or maybe that's just me: the only person at this whole wedding who's cold and morose.

Ava, snap out of it. It's the happiest day of your brother's life. Just because your life is in the crapper doesn't mean you can skulk about all green and pinch-faced like a vengeful enchantress. Do better.

I make an effort to admire the barn. It's cute. If you're into décor based on an advertisement for pumpkin spice lattes. Loads of fairy lights strung from the rafters. Trestle tables covered in simple white cloths, tea lights, and flowers in jelly jars. Wine barrels with more jelly jars, surrounded by pinecones and the aforementioned ornamental pumpkins, a vegetable I don't mind looking at as long as I don't have to eat it.

Shelby's mom, Lee, did the décor. She's an artist and moved up the coast when Shelby's dad died from cancer, leaving Shelby to run Flora Valley Wines on her own. That's how Shelby met Nate. He was brought in to manage the place when McRae Capital took a stake in it. That's J.P. McRae, who's two tables away, sitting with his wife. J.P.'s an old friend and former business partner of my dad's.

Yes, it's a small world. But not small enough, apparently, for me to spot the one guy whose presence *somewhere* in this barn is partly responsible for my antsy mood. Last time he and I were in proximity, I asked him on a date. He turned me down—in a kindly manner, but as you know, a refusal no matter how polite often humiliates. I took the hint and backed off, kept my distance. That was two months ago, and I haven't stopped thinking about him since.

Damn it, I *wish* we were seated together so I could get that uncomfortable first-meeting-after-a-knock-back over with. I don't know how I'll feel about seeing him, and not knowing is one of the things I hate most in the world. After being rejected, of course.

"Ava, how lovely to see you."

I know two people at table three, and this is one of them. Ted. Blond, foppishly handsome in that upper-class British way. Current owner of Bartons, a boutique hotel that would fit perfectly in cosmopolitan London but because it's in the main street of small-town Verity, looks like it's been beamed down from an alien planet. Its patrons are like aliens, too: rich, shiny, and mostly English with hee-haw accents. Ted doesn't hee-haw. He's much too smooth.

Ted gestures to the woman sitting next to him.

"Ava, may I introduce"—there's an infinitesimal pause —"Imogen."

Imogen (because surely she would have protested if that hadn't been her name, no?) twiddles her fingers in a wave. She's anywhere between twenty-three and a Botoxed thirty-five. Glossy blonde hair. Slender, polished, extremely beautiful: an exact clone of every other woman Ted's dated. We call them the Ted-ford Wives. Not that Ted's about to marry any of them. I'm amazed he didn't skip this wedding for fear of catching marital cooties.

I see Chiara give me an eyeroll. She works for Ted at Bartons hotel and knows his ways. Chiara is one of Shelby's two best girlfriends. She was born and brought up in Verity but isn't destined to spend her life here. Chiara has ambitions, and the brains and looks to achieve them.

"Ava, this is Jackson," she says, "Shelby's oldest brother. Jackson, this is Ava—"

"Nate's sister." He reaches out a hand, smiling. "Yeah, I can spot the resemblance."

It's true. Nate and I have basically the same face, plus

Dad's dark hair and cool blue eyes. Jackson Armstrong is big and burly, with pale blond hair and a beard. Looks nothing like his petite, strawberry blonde sister.

"Whereas I'm the spitting image of my dad," he says, then looks rueful. "He'd have loved today. He always thought this barn would make a great wedding venue. Isn't that right, Doug?"

"Sure," says Doug.

Doug's a lean weather-beaten guy in his late fifties with a mustache that gives him a Sam Elliot vibe. All I know about him is that he does the mowing at the vineyard and occasionally helps out Flora Valley Wines' cooper (that's a barrel maker) and main handyman, otherwise known as the guy whose apparent invisibility is currently frying my brain.

To distract myself, I say, "Okay, seriously, why do they call you Toothless Doug? You look like you've got a pretty good set of choppers there."

Doug grins, proving my point.

"When I was a kid, I started a tooth collection—"

"Not at all creepy," remarks Chiara.

"Animal teeth," he explains, "from animals we hunted or found dead in the woods. Other kids used to bring 'em to me, too. Cleaned 'em up, made a box to put 'em all in. Thought I might make a necklace—"

"Ugh." Chiara shudders delicately.

"We got a new dog, a Labrador called Maisie. She found my box of teeth and ate the lot."

been looking around for h
conflicted over how you
stop wasting time and em

She makes a valid poin

"Have you ever seen C

"Never," says Chiara.
the first hurdle. If he does
at the mulled wine station

"What if he says no? A

I've no doubt that Ch
It happened at the Crush
the Flora Valley grapes
convinced Cam and I we
wouldn't be surprised if
video recording.

"He might," says Ch
You'll never know unless

Another valid-yet-ha
myself as brave, but late
little "no" and I retreate
blame my physical state
back. It's fear that his
deficiency in me than s
What if my life has peak
on the downhill slide?

I wanted to know hot
be honest, I don't knov
mother. Lee's laughing ar
I don't know what emot

"How can a dog eat teeth, Doug?" is Ted's question. "They're much harder than bones."

"Maisie kind of swallowed them whole, like kibble. I guess I hadn't cleaned them all *that* well."

"Trip to the vet?" I ask.

"Nope, she just—"

"Don't say it, Doug," Chiara insists. "Ted's very sensitive."

"My dear," Ted protests. "I have done my fair share of mucking out."

"Is that what you call it in England?" says Chiara, with a lift of an eyebrow.

"You still a hunter, Doug?" says Jackson. "I remember you taking me on a…"

I tune out. Ted's mention of mucking out reminded me too much of the *other* reason I'm not in a party mood. You see, until a couple of months ago, I used to work for a racing stable in Kentucky. I've been a horse lover since I was a kid— nothing but running and riding when I was growing up. Given I'm small, I thought I might be a jockey, but I found that world too cut-throat, so I became an exercise rider. My job was taking the racehorses for their morning workouts and teaching them the skills they'd need to win. I quit because my dad, Mitchell, developed a life-threatening heart condition, and all five of us Durant siblings rushed home to be with him and Mom. At least, that's the reason I gave. In reality, it was a useful cover story. I didn't choose to quit; I *had* to. I'd been finding the job more and more exhausting—crawling into

bed at the end of every
the morning. I quit be
bosses knew it. They kn

Another reason wh
I'm unemployed, I'm
still exhausted. The ti
can't tell anyone becau
and defeat. A Durant
an iron maiden before
And I am a Durant thr

Shit. Of course. No
is the moment I finally
Right. Shelby's mom,
headed artist who's in
very beautiful red-he
super close to his …
made her laugh, and..

"There'll be danci
then."

It seems Chiara is
discussing hunting.
Chiara's name doesn'
she's got skills that
Goonies.

Thing is, being a I
life honing your pok
you'll always have th
"My move?" I ask
"Don't even *try* t

to simultaneously feel red-hot attraction *and* white-hot rage?

"He looks pretty busy right now." My poker face is set to rigid, but unfortunately so is my jaw, and the words come out with full giveaway grit.

"Shelby says Cam and her mom have a special kind of friendship," Chiara tells me.

"*How* special?" I'm not even trying now.

Chiara shrugs. "Well, if Cam used more words a day, we might have found out by now." She gives me a small and only partially evil smile. "Guess we'll have to rely on *you* to solve that little puzzle for us."

She picks up her empty champagne glass and emits some kind of telepathic signal because in an instant, a young server is at her elbow. It's also possible no signal was required because Chiara is the most striking woman in the place by some margin. She's wearing a pale gold camisole top and matching wide pants under a cream silk blazer. On her feet are stiletto pumps. If you broke off the heels, you could use them as knitting needles. Beside her, I feel small, green, and crumpled. Like a leprechaun who's had a hard night.

I look over at Cam again because I'm a glutton for punishment. He's dressed in a shirt and tie, which he never is. His normal look is what my brother Nate calls "Survivalist Ken", but that's only because he's jealous. Nate is six-feet easy, fit, and lean, but Cam Hollander is six-five and muscled like guys who do physical labor all day, every day. He has shaggy blond-brown hair and brown eyes.

"How can a dog eat teeth, Doug?" is Ted's question. "They're much harder than bones."

"Maisie kind of swallowed them whole, like kibble. I guess I hadn't cleaned them all *that* well."

"Trip to the vet?" I ask.

"Nope, she just—"

"Don't say it, Doug," Chiara insists. "Ted's very sensitive."

"My dear," Ted protests. "I have done my fair share of mucking out."

"Is that what you call it in England?" says Chiara, with a lift of an eyebrow.

"You still a hunter, Doug?" says Jackson. "I remember you taking me on a…"

I tune out. Ted's mention of mucking out reminded me too much of the *other* reason I'm not in a party mood. You see, until a couple of months ago, I used to work for a racing stable in Kentucky. I've been a horse lover since I was a kid— nothing but running and riding when I was growing up. Given I'm small, I thought I might be a jockey, but I found that world too cut-throat, so I became an exercise rider. My job was taking the racehorses for their morning workouts and teaching them the skills they'd need to win. I quit because my dad, Mitchell, developed a life-threatening heart condition, and all five of us Durant siblings rushed home to be with him and Mom. At least, that's the reason I gave. In reality, it was a useful cover story. I didn't choose to quit; I *had* to. I'd been finding the job more and more exhausting—crawling into bed at the end of every day and dragging myself out again in the morning. I quit because I couldn't do the job and my bosses knew it. They knew I was worn out, like an old nag.

Another reason why the last two months have sucked. I'm unemployed, I'm living back at my parents', and I'm still exhausted. The tiredness just won't go away. And I can't tell anyone because that would be admitting weakness and defeat. A Durant would be voluntarily impaled inside an iron maiden before they let slip an iota of vulnerability. And I am a Durant through and through.

Shit. Of course. Now that I'm at my absolute lowest ebb is the moment I finally spot him. Who's he talking to? Oh. Right. Shelby's mom, Lee. The artist. The very beautiful red-headed artist who's in her late fifties but doesn't look it. The very beautiful red-headed artist whose head is bending super close to his … and now he's said something that's made her laugh, and…

"There'll be dancing later. You can make your move then."

It seems Chiara is more interested in spying on me than discussing hunting. But then, as Nate's pointed out, Chiara's name doesn't include the letters CIA for no reason: she's got skills that make their top agents look like the Goonies.

Thing is, being a Durant means you've spent your whole life honing your poker face. Don't let anything show and you'll always have the advantage.

"My move?" I ask.

"Don't even *try* to out-bluff me," says Chiara. "You've

been looking around for him all evening because you're still conflicted over how you feel about him. My advice is to stop wasting time and emotional energy and find out."

She makes a valid point. I hate her for it.

"Have you ever seen Cam Hollander dance?" I ask.

"Never," says Chiara. "But you're hardly one to fall at the first hurdle. If he doesn't want to, invite him to join you at the mulled wine station."

"What if he says no? Again."

I've no doubt that Chiara knows about the knock-back. It happened at the Crush, the big community event when the Flora Valley grapes are pressed. And though I was convinced Cam and I were alone when I asked him out, I wouldn't be surprised if Chiara somehow made a secret video recording.

"He might," says Chiara. "Then again, he might not. You'll never know unless you try."

Another valid-yet-hateful point. I used to think of myself as brave, but lately, I've been a giant weenie. One little "no" and I retreated into my shell like a snail. I can blame my physical state but that's not what's holding me back. It's fear that his rejection signals some greater deficiency in me than simply being tired and worn out. What if my life has peaked, and at only twenty-seven, I'm on the downhill slide?

I wanted to know how I'd feel seeing him again, but to be honest, I don't know. He's over there with Shelby's mother. Lee's laughing and Cam looks like he's won a prize. I don't know what emotion I'm experiencing. Is it possible to simultaneously feel red-hot attraction *and* white-hot rage?

"He looks pretty busy right now." My poker face is set to rigid, but unfortunately so is my jaw, and the words come out with full giveaway grit.

"Shelby says Cam and her mom have a special kind of friendship," Chiara tells me.

"*How* special?" I'm not even trying now.

Chiara shrugs. "Well, if Cam used more words a day, we might have found out by now." She gives me a small and only partially evil smile. "Guess we'll have to rely on *you* to solve that little puzzle for us."

She picks up her empty champagne glass and emits some kind of telepathic signal because in an instant, a young server is at her elbow. It's also possible no signal was required because Chiara is the most striking woman in the place by some margin. She's wearing a pale gold camisole top and matching wide pants under a cream silk blazer. On her feet are stiletto pumps. If you broke off the heels, you could use them as knitting needles. Beside her, I feel small, green, and crumpled. Like a leprechaun who's had a hard night.

I look over at Cam again because I'm a glutton for punishment. He's dressed in a shirt and tie, which he never is. His normal look is what my brother Nate calls "Survivalist Ken", but that's only because he's jealous. Nate is six-feet easy, fit, and lean, but Cam Hollander is six-five and muscled like guys who do physical labor all day, every day. He has shaggy blond-brown hair and brown eyes.

Shelby told me he'd been a soldier but said he doesn't talk about that part of his life. Or any part of his life. He might have grown up in Wyoming, might not have, and I should really stop staring at him because he's going to notice...

He's noticed. Shit.

Okay, the *worst* thing that could happen now is that he nudges Shelby's mom and they both have a good old chuckle at the cross, crumpled green chick.

He doesn't. He nods, once, and the corner of his mouth lifts ever so slightly. So slightly, I could be imagining it.

"Move slowly," says Chiara. "Softly-softly catchy big guy."

I hate her for knowing me better than I know myself. But the only outlet for my irritation is a stack of breadsticks, so I reach for one and give it a good hard snap.

"Ladies and gentlemen."

Best man Danny is dinging a wine glass with a spoon.

"The moment you've all been waiting for... The speeches!"

I need another drink, but only Chiara seems to have the mindpower to summon servers.

"Traditionally," says Danny, "the father of the bride would give the first speech. At this time, we'd like you all to raise your glasses and toast the memory of Shelby's dad and founder of Flora Valley Wines, the late Billy Armstrong."

"To Billy," we all say.

"And seeing as Billy couldn't be with us today, we're going to throw tradition to the wind and open instead with the mother of the bride," says Danny. "Will you welcome to the mic, Lee Armstrong!"

Applause and a few wolf whistles. The very beautiful red-haired artist who does not look her age gets up from the table and because I'm watching like a hawk, I see her rest her hand on Cam's shoulder as she passes by him. Could be nothing. She could have been caught a little off balance and needed to steady herself. To me, though, the gesture looked affectionate, purposeful. *Don't worry,* it said. *I'll be back soon.*

Without a word, Chiara hands me another breadstick.

Available in paperback and ebook!

YOUR NUMBER ONE STOP

ONE MORE CHAPTER

FOR PAGETURNING BOOKS

One More Chapter is an
award-winning global
division of HarperCollins.

Sign up to our newsletter to get our
latest eBook deals and stay up to date
with our weekly Book Club!
<u>Subscribe here.</u>

Meet the team at
<u>www.onemorechapter.com</u>

Follow us!
@OneMoreChapter_
@OneMoreChapter
@onemorechapterhc

Do you write unputdownable fiction?
We love to hear from new voices.
Find out how to submit your novel at
<u>www.onemorechapter.com/submissions</u>